Social Engagement

Social Engagement

A Novel

Avery Carpenter Forrey

MARINER BOOKS
New York   Boston

FIRST EDITION

Designed by Renata DiBiase

Library of Congress Cataloging-in-Publication Data has been applied for.

ISBN 978-0-06-329490-5

23 24 25 26 27 LBC 5 4 3 2 1

For my parents, for everything

He had built up within himself a kind of sanctuary
in which she throned among his secret thoughts and
longings. Little by little it became the scene of his
real life.

—**Edith Wharton,** *The Age of Innocence*

"She would've made such a lovely bride
What a shame she's fucked in the head," they said.

—**Taylor Swift,** "champagne problems"

Social Engagement

Prologue Now—February

Red sauce splatters my wedding dress. The white crepe train serves as a picnic blanket for a large pizza, which I ordered to the Ocean House honeymoon suite after my marriage blew up. We lasted six hours, seven if you count the first look.

I try to remember the best remedy for stains—seltzer and letting it sit, something involving baking soda and a no-rub policy—but this is probably too far gone. My mud-smeared blue satin heels lean against the warm, greasy cardboard box, tableau vivant of a hot mess. *Portrait of the Divorcée as a Young Woman.*

I flick the sauce off my dress and climb into the marble bathtub, which is deeper and probably more expensive than a casket. I hike up the skirt to my waist. "When you're stressed, do something with your hands," my mom always told me growing up. She meant paint or bake or exercise, not masturbate and binge eat, but every piece of advice is subject to creative license. I picture his face—not my groom's—during the wedding ceremony. The stained glass above his pew cast a dusty light onto those long curls, the ends I used to touch in the gray liminal hours before sunrise.

The pizza crust is a hardened sponge in my mouth. My groom snores in the king-sized bed, unaware that his almost ex-wife is housing the pizza he told me not to order, because how could I care about food at a time like this, on the best-turned-worst day of our lives?

In a plot twist fit for an Alanis lyric, the wedding day was perfect before we broke up. Watch Hill, Rhode Island, in February was an odd choice, but I liked the idea of a winter wedding. It was unexpected, cheaper, and easier to schedule; sweatproof, fur friendly, and nostalgia resistant. I grew up going to Watch Hill every year and feared a summer wedding would be a palimpsest over too many memories, moments surfacing with forceful clarity: bike rides to town and walks on the beach where I once swam with Virginia, Ollie, and Gray, the years stretching from floaties on to suits off altogether. A winter wedding would be too cold for skinny-dipping, even in unseasonably warm, sunny weather like we had been handed today.

I pick up my phone. Time flattens and folds, origami-like, on this screen—I can access an image from decades ago as easily as one from today, this morning's breakfast (poached eggs) next to a new picture of an old picture (my parents in their thirties on the same beach where we held tonight's reception). The feed has already tried to immortalize my wedding: more than a dozen pictures were uploaded earlier tonight, none of our guests yet aware that forever lasted only six hours.

Aunt Linda with a close-up of her place setting, floating candles in decorative basins etching light onto the calligraphy.

My mother with a picture of us during the first look, the New England winter sun as bright as an operating room.

Bex with an overly filtered image of herself and her husband, Greg, and a variation of the caption I've seen so many times before: **My best friend married her best friend.**

My father-in-law with the first dance—a frozen sway to Van Morrison in the Ocean House's ballroom, buttons curving up the back of my dress like an external spine.

My best friend, Virginia, with nothing because we weren't speaking. After what happened at the wedding, I wasn't sure when we'd talk again. I almost texted her an hour ago, when I walked into the honeymoon suite, but then I remembered. The spontaneous amnesia is similar to waking up in a new place disoriented, the contours of the unfamiliar room swimming to remind me I'm no longer home.

I scroll and zoom and squint until my eyes hurt, then go to my own page. Over the last year, I attended so many weddings and wedding-adjacent events that the nights began to congeal. But thumbing back, images unknot themselves, become singular and inevitable. I avoided posting too many posed pictures of us as a couple, thinking it would make me look cliché. Or was my reluctance a clairvoyant guard against the future, subconscious breakup insurance?

Everyone talks about how their phone is a rabbit hole, but tonight, I imagine it as a magnifying glass. I want to trace my relationship's demise like a forensic scientist vultured over a bloated corpse. I'm being dramatic and deflective, sure, but these are dramatic and deflective times. I'm in a bridal suite, no longer a bride, my failure white and pallid against the bathtub. At least the ghost is attractive and well made.

My phone is full of proof, images that betray my complicity in tonight's disaster. My social feed stretches back years, each picture leaving filtered bread crumbs. Then there's my camera roll, the private trail that tells a different story. I often click on these two squares—the drab gray camera, the bright pink-and-orange peephole—when I'm bored enough to flip through the past in my pocket. We all carry this weight: the constantly refreshing feed and the photo memories feature remind us of our rearview even when we want to look forward.

I click on a post I put up a year ago, on the day I moved into the apartment with Virginia. A sunset over Park Avenue, the citrus sky saturating with fiery streaks. Despite the image, that day marked the rising, not the setting, of the strangest year of my life—the bright start of an arc that could only end in darkness. I lean back toward the brass faucets and scroll.

1 January—thirteen months earlier

calliememaybe uptown girls 🏙️

I moved into 1100 Park Avenue on a rainy Thursday, yellow cabs sluicing curves of water onto the sidewalk like a screen grab from a film set in the Big City, still gleaming through a spew of liquid shit. On this stretch of the Upper East Side, even the sewers looked like they'd require a guarantor.

Virginia was on her phone. Mimi, who had finally convinced me to stop calling her Mrs. Murphy, was holding a box of croissants from what she claimed was the best bakery in Manhattan, expertise earned from her "glory days" in her twenties when she rented a place a few blocks from this three-bedroom apartment she now owned, both of which were only an hour from her primary residence in Connecticut where the taxes were lower, square footage was higher, and you didn't have to launch a political campaign to get your kid into pre-school. She'd explained this to me so many times that I almost said, *The lady doth protest.* I refrained, not because she would've been offended, but because it would've prompted a long anecdote I'd already heard about the time she visited Shakespeare's grave as a study abroad student and fell into a three-month affair with the funerary site tour guide. In her move-day state, Virginia might have snapped at her mom for talking too much, which would've embarrassed us all.

"'Ello, Marcus," Mimi said to the doorman, inexplicably in a British accent.

He laughed. Money made you laugh.

"Mrs. Murphy, good morning!" He tipped his hat, the kind of rigid popover found on the heads of men standing in lobbies up and down the island of Manhattan. "I'll take good care of the girls, Mrs. Murphy."

One of my literature professors once pointed out that good dialogue eschews personal address, because name callouts rarely happen in conversation, most of us acknowledging people through eye contact, head movements, or generic *hey*s. This did not apply to the doorman-owner dynamic. Marcus and Mimi were caught in a perpetual volley of each other's names, she brandishing his like an advertisement for thoughtfulness, he using hers as a bid for a fat end-of-year envelope.

"Marcus, did I show you the pictures from St. Barts? Oh my *god*, it was *divine*." Emphasis as if she hadn't abandoned church before Virginia turned ten, when the hot forty-something pastor was replaced by a Dumbledore look-alike who induced sleep within minutes of starting his sermons.

Mimi flipped through her camera roll, narrating an international trip to someone who probably hadn't left a thirty-block square of the world in years, if ever. This was Mimi—intent always magnanimous, outcome often tone-deaf.

"The movers are here," Virginia said. She hadn't looked up from her phone in minutes; one of them must have texted her.

Mimi asked Marcus if he wanted a croissant ("No thank you, ma'am") and skipped outside to stand under the awning, waving at the movers with gleeful abandon like they were a long-gone ship pulling in to shore. She'd been in this sunny mood ever since Virginia moved home from L.A. After we graduated, Virginia had gotten a job at a small art gallery out there, a decision that confounded her parents, East Coast stalwarts hoping for grandchildren nearby and as soon as possible. Virginia, their oldest daughter, hadn't introduced them to a significant other since high school.

Virginia twisted her long brown hair into a pink clip, one of those plastic crab claws that I normally associated with tweens or old ladies. She consistently made ugly crap look cool, which, to me, was the clearest measure of attractiveness.

They waited for the elevator. I opted to take the stairs, thanks to a compulsive and embarrassing need to monitor my step count. The stairwell was white, gold, and immaculate—a far cry from the rubber steps and dirt-swirled walls of the Bushwick building I'd left behind.

Moving into the Murphys' pied-à-terre rent-free had been pure, unimpeachable logic, but I'd still resisted. I liked my Brooklyn neighborhood. The apartment itself was bleak and the landlord was a creep and it took me almost an hour to get to work, but I was *doing it*! Supporting myself in a city that made you bend to its terms. Mimi's offer to move in had been a loophole in the abstract contract we all signed—*we* being people under thirty without family money or a job in finance—to live here. *You will sleep in a closet and complain about your bank account like it's a problematic relative you still want to love you.* Friendships and relationships were forged out of this shared desperation, gripes that metastasized into anxiety over ordering a second drink at a bar.

This camaraderie was an adjustment, because I had grown up accustomed to spending time with people who were flush and therefore ambivalent about money. People who treated their finances like I'd treated those walls in my Bushwick building: something they didn't need to look at too closely, a given that would always be there. The other families who summered (a verb for their type) in Watch Hill were different from mine—*different* being a euphemism for *richer*. It was a seasonal zip code for the Kennedy-adjacent and kids whose last names were on buildings at their alma maters, not general contractors/aspiring novelists (my dad) and third grade teachers (my mom). Our place, named Ginger House for its small proportions and exterior reminiscent of the Swiss Alps, was passed down from my paternal grandfather. He'd made a decent fortune working in advertising, but the money started dying when he did, before I was born. My dad's whims and fantastical mind weren't conducive to stable finances. He spent money he didn't have on things he didn't need: a kayak, wine and hot sauce subscriptions, a vintage dollhouse for my birthday, day trips to Newport with me and Virginia where he'd buy us matching dresses and rope bracelets and take us to the bookstore to fill up our libraries with *The Baby-Sitters Club*.

Virginia and I had known each other since we were infants, oblivious to the striations of wealth that banded and separated Watch Hill. I knew her house, Idyll Wind, was bigger than anything I'd ever been inside—a structure that could've digested Ginger House—but this realization didn't intimidate me. We became so close that Idyll Wind soon started to feel like my home, too. At the end of the summer, we'd go back to our separate Connecticut towns—she to New Canaan, me to New Haven—and have quarterly sleepovers and weekly landline calls, picking up right where we left off every Memorial Day.

We ended up going to college together at Brown, where her dad was on the board, shifting our special summer friendship into a year-round best friendship. I'd subconsciously absorbed the Murphys' Providence propaganda after borrowing a series of university sweatshirts so worn they felt like velvet. I listened to their stories about themed parties (some half nude), art exhibits (some fully nude), and a legendary deli (sandwiches so thick and delicious they made you never want to get nude again). Mimi and her husband, Walter, drove us to Providence from Watch Hill the summer after our freshman year of high school "just to see," and I liked—no, loved—what I saw: a vibrant, artistic campus nestled inside a manageable city; an hour drive to Watch Hill; excellent pre-med, English, and art programs. My application wouldn't get preferential treatment like Virginia's—I wasn't technically family and applied the same year as her—but I decided to go for it anyways. I cried when I got a scholarship, a tight ache in my chest blooming into an open, fulfilled longing.

We'd been out of college for seven years and hadn't experienced one of those stretched-out Watch Hill summers in almost a decade, but I still considered Virginia my best friend—despite the time lags between our texts and the uneven ratio of blue to gray, my updates and questions going unanswered for days when she was on the West Coast. I often heard people talk about their childhood friends by saying, "If we met now, we wouldn't get along," and that was probably true for us, too. But she'd been there for me during the worst time of my life, with a fierce protectiveness that was only possible for someone with her confidence and what I'd always thought of as essential goodness.

I took the stairs halfway but still somehow beat Virginia and Mimi to the eleventh floor. Virginia mumbled about her mom stopping to talk to a woman named Connie about fabric swatches.

"Voilà! Your new home," Mimi said.

The door knocker was in the shape of a horseshoe, a kitschy nod to their Connecticut horse farm and Mr. Murphy (the protestations to call him Walter hadn't yet stuck like

Mimi's had) and his racehorse Liquid Courage, runner-up in the 2010 Kentucky Derby.

As we fell through the door with our backpacks and carry-ons and other soft cases that would've been crushed in the jigsaw of the moving truck, Virginia tapped the knocker three times.

"Making sure the ghosts know you're here?" I said.

"It's good luck."

"Like you need it."

"Up here, I do." She pulled up her baggy mom jeans, a trend that only thin people could pull off. "We do."

She gave me the conspiratorial look—mouth in a side twist, eyebrow slightly raised—that used to force me into dares like running around Idyll Wind in my underwear at night, sending an AIM message to a crush, and stealing a pack of peach ring gummies from the general store. Histori-cally, that look had been punctuated by a thrilling or sinister agenda, and I wondered how that spirit would function now that we were *adults,* a word that still didn't sit right with me, no matter how much I resented being one of those millenni-als who acted like my age was an elaborate cosplay, a scam I pulled over everyone. The idea of "adulting" was dumbly ubiquitous, but it still resonated.

The Murphys' entry foyer was simple, but I had seen and bought enough cheap furniture to know that this was *nice,* the kind of side table that, dimension and style-wise, looked close to what you'd find at Pottery Barn, but with an extra $5K on the price tag. A massive deep blue porcelain vase held a curve of orchids.

We walked into the living room and sat down on the cream couch. The movers were filing in, and we wanted to get out of their way, but really, we just wanted to sit down. Nothing better than when inaction is a directive.

"Home sweet home, not in Kansas anymore?" Mimi said.

She often spoke in Frankensteinian platitudes, Mad Libs of common phrases that always elicited light laughter from her audience, regardless of whether they made sense.

"I'm just happy to have consistent hot water," I said. "Seriously, Mimi. This is incredibly generous."

"I wasn't going to strand Virg up here alone. This will be good for you girls. When I was your age—"

"The Upper East Side was like the West Village, we know, Mom."

"All I'm saying is it's cyclical. Trends come back."

"I'm not sure gentrification and bell-bottoms are the same thing."

"That reminds me." She fished through her purse, pulled out a pouch, and doled out a pair of earrings with the nonchalance of shaking pills from a canister. "I got these from a store up here the day I moved to the city for the first time. They're so seventies, but, you know, the seventies are back. They were from this hole-in-the-wall jeweler, the man who owned it was so sweet. I remember he was eating homemade hummus the day I got the earrings, and I thought, *Huh, you can make hummus?* I don't think I'd ever made anything but scrambled eggs!"

"I love them," Virginia said, tracing the design. They were bright turquoise drops set in silver, delicate yet funky, and jewelry she'd actually wear. "Thank you so much." They hugged. This gift was peak Mimi: making something look spontaneous that she'd probably planned and anticipated for months.

I commented on how special the earrings were, trying to stave off the creeping, gut-deep ache that I didn't get to have this, the transfer of talismans and stories. I couldn't wake up one day—with horror or gratitude or a mixture of both—and realize I was becoming my mother. I didn't even know what that meant anymore.

.

I hadn't seen my mom in over a year, and my dad died the month before my seventeenth birthday. Multiple myeloma. The disintegration happened so quickly, I barely had time to Ask Jeeves about his chances. After he passed away, we had to give up Ginger House. He'd mismanaged our finances to the point of foreclosure. My mom was so angry with him, a kind of blunt resentment that blinded her to my grief. I still couldn't understand why she'd curdled toward my dad after his death and dwelled on the mess he left behind instead of his full, living memory. She shut down, preferring to avoid mentioning him, and I resented her repression. She moved to Maine, where she got a different teaching job, a catering gig, and a failed relationship with a gardener. She'd lost touch with the Murphys, and I sensed tension whenever I mentioned them. We caught up on the phone every few months, limp conversations that always ended with unfulfilled promises to make plans. During our last call, I'd told her I was reading *Leviathan* by Paul Auster. My dad's copy was annotated on almost every page, tight scribbles tracing a map of what was inside his head. "You need to stop dwelling," she'd said. "It's unhealthy." If she knew about my other habits, she'd realize that reading good books was the least of my problems.

Once the movers walked out to bring up their second haul, Mimi offered to give us "the grand tour," heavy on the sarcasm because she thought the place was tiny. We walked a circle around the living room, which contained a piano, a faded Persian rug, the cream couch, and leather club chairs that looked comfortable enough to disappear into. An impressionist painting I vaguely recognized from the one art history class Virginia had forced me to take in college hung above the fireplace.

The dining room had an antique-looking mirror and table, plus thick curtains in a toile pattern. It opened into an actually small kitchen—"The prewar compromise," Mimi said—that was still bigger than my living room–kitchen combo in Bushwick.

Down a hallway that led to the bedrooms, Virginia's art was all over the walls. She'd been a painting fiend since we were kids, finger growing into watercolor and graduating to oil. Her official reason for moving to New York was to get an MFA with a painting concentration at Columbia. But I suspected she also missed her family and wanted a good excuse to come back, an explanation that wouldn't foreground her homesickness.

Photographs were interspersed with Virginia's paintings. Most of them were taken by her cousin Ollie, a professional photographer who got assignments in places like Fiji and Australia for *National Geographic*. I quickly averted my eyes. I couldn't look at the pictures without seeing his face behind a camera, too. It hurt to look at that face because I'd known it so well: the open-mouthed laugh that showed his crooked bottom teeth, those bowed lips, the thick eyebrows I traced in the middle of the night after drinking wine I didn't have the tolerance for yet. I'd been trying to blur it for years, and here it was, coming to me fully formed in the middle of a black-and-white image of the Great Barrier Reef. I kept walking and looked ahead.

Virginia would live in the guest bedroom, a designation that attempted to conceal the room's intended occupant: Virginia. Mimi had framed a Picasso print they'd gotten her for graduation, and her face looked out from almost a dozen silver frames: Virginia in front of an easel; Virginia and her younger sister, Gray, in ketchup and mustard costumes for Halloween; Virginia jumping off a diving board in Watch Hill; Virginia and me smiling on the porch of Idyll Wind, teeth white against sunburns we tried to will into tans. Aside from the pictures, Mimi had decorated the room sparsely, knowing that Virginia would recoil at anything she hadn't picked out herself. These generic light green pillows would be replaced by flea market finds within two weeks.

"Last but not least, the grand finale," Mimi said, leading us out of Virginia's room and to a door at the end of the hallway. "Callie's crib!"

It was, indeed, a crib. The room could fit nothing but a double bed and dresser. Oddly, this calmed me. It was like I'd copy-pasted my Bushwick bedroom onto this separate stratosphere of the city—minus the mice and clicking radiator and landlord who'd look me up and down as he stood in my doorway eating a mysterious sandwich pungent with Russian dressing. I was used to tight spaces. I could fold myself into them nicely, and after so many years of monitoring my weight, I liked feeling small. A Girlboss panel would find this idea appalling, rows of size 2 founders telling us to "take up space" as they saved half of their Sweetgreen salads for later.

Mimi explained that my bedroom had been the servant's quarters, "how cozy," sounding like a Zillow write-up that used *charming* as a euphemism for *tiny*. She didn't apologize, which I'd always liked about her. Growing up, my mom would say sorry before we started eating dinner, claiming that she'd messed up the sauce or overcooked the meat, only to have it all end up tasting delicious. This was the parental equivalent of a kid insisting she was going to fail a test she'd studied hard for, and I found the impulse disingenuous.

On my bedside table, a single framed picture: my parents and the Murphys in Watch Hill, holding baby me and

Virginia. It was hard to distinguish between the two of us all swollen and swaddled, but I noticed with a twisted sense of pride that Virginia looked chubbier. Mimi and my dad held the two of us like heaps of laundry to their chests. My mom was laughing in the image; I couldn't remember ever seeing her so happy.

The master bedroom door was open, revealing a perfectly made bed with tight white sheets, a baby blue duvet, and *M*-monogrammed pillows. It probably hadn't been used in over a year. I asked Mimi what was behind a door next to the master, the largest and least-used bedroom in the apartment.

"Walter's office." She rolled her eyes. "It's a mess in there."

Mr. Murphy ran a major pharmaceutical company, Murphy Inc., the eponymous giant passed down from his great-great-grandfather. Boss by inheritance, not by design. In his case, that meant he worked twice as hard to prove himself, Mimi had emphasized to me in the past, making it sound as quaint as if he were trying out for a soccer team. They'd bought the uptown pied-à-terre because Mimi wanted a place to go on "adventures" while Walter was holed up in his office all night. It didn't hurt that they had one daughter to lure home and another, Gray, who was planning a wedding and living in Gramercy. Everyone agreed that it wouldn't work for Virginia and Gray to move in together; they'd end up hating or hurting each other—or both. Gray's engagement party next month (along with Virginia's reluctant maid of honor status) was already threatening to upend their relationship. Enter: me and my grateful bank account, conflicted yet eager to pack myself into the servant's quarters in exchange for free rent.

Mimi left us with a box of fancy chocolates, some Poo-Pourri spray, and a faint pink lipstick mark on both of our cheeks, an optical illusion of a pout—I could see Virginia's only when she sat on the sunniest square of the couch, illuminated by a concentrated beam of light that came from the street-facing window.

We were drinking rosé because it was Thursday afternoon and we were twenty-nine with the day off and a new address in a luxe building, grown-up and tipsy Eloises. The light started dipping below the rows of skyscrapers in the window, our postage stamp view of the city. The sun became an orange dot in the distance, and Virginia and I stared at it together, watching it turn the tips of buildings gold.

I swirled the rosé around my mouth like the fine wine that it wasn't and let the taste coat my tongue. I remembered the diagram of the tongue from some long-ago science class: salty, sweet, bitter, sour, districted with the precision of county lines. If only emotions were that distinct. I yearned for a GPS to navigate my internal landscape, a rubric to tell me how I was feeling, how to proceed. From up here, the whole city looked knowable, cut into clear lines. The *grid,* like the posts on my feed, worlds portioned out for consumption.

"Should we go out to celebrate tonight?" Virginia shouted from the living room. "Dorrian's, for old time's?"

"Maybe I'll tell Whit to come," I said, trying to mask my nerves over introducing her to the new guy I'd been seeing.

I took a picture of the view from my new window and upped the saturation. I went to lie down and decided to broadcast the move. *Instant* was baked into the name and premise of the app, but it was rare to actually post something in the moment. I tried to embrace my occasional impulses toward spontaneity because I was usually so careful and controlled. I captioned the skyline sunset with **uptown girls** and tagged Virginia, hinting at my physical (and hopefully mental) relocation. It was January and it would be my—our—best year yet.

mimimurph new digs, old friends!! 🐾

bexjones jeal

whitty_ waiting for my invite 👀

meet.virginia uptown is the new downtown

2 December

whitty_ Old-fashioned, New York. One is silver
and the other's a highball 🥃

I met Whit on the subway. People's reaction to this fact says
a lot about them. I've gotten everything from horny to horror, from ecstatic requests to meet his friends to urgent pleas
to do a background check and hire a PI.

Two weeks before Christmas, the F train: he was wearing
a suit, sitting across from me with an open book. I invented
a story about him, of course. His inner life was being sti-
fled by his work—at Goldman or Morgan Stanley or another
rich robot factory—and he used his commute to let his true
self seep into the cracks of the morning. He was reading Au-
dre Lorde or bell hooks or even Sally Rooney—something
deep or deeply trendy, I wasn't sure which I preferred. He
planned on getting out of finance after he made enough to
open a restaurant upstate, farm to table, with an extensive
natural wine list.

Because the thing was, he was beautiful, and we're wired
to give beauty the benefit of the doubt.

He wasn't your typical pretty boy, either. He had a sharp
jaw, a large nose, and a full head of dark hair just long
enough to hint at a latent artistic side. Light wrinkles fanned
out from his eyes and his lips were thin and those slouched

shoulders didn't match the suit, and yet—good bones. Like that Maggie Smith poem, his foundation was attractive and solid, undeniable enough to read like a kind of beauty.

Objectifying him like he was a woman in a skirt at a bar in the fucking 1950s made me feel powerful. I pulled out my phone before I got carried away, pretended to read on it while staring at the numbers on the clock—8:16, 8:17—and thinking about what he'd look like without clothes and then without skin, those good bones rattling along with the F train. I didn't tell people that detail because it was weird and probably deranged, but this next part was always included in the story, the poetic climax that never failed to stir an audience:

I looked up and he was looking back.

I immediately flicked my gaze down again, an urgent readjustment like my eyes were a hand on a burning stove. He didn't look as cute head-on, did he? His face wasn't quite as symmetrical as it appeared reading the book, but maybe I didn't have enough time to take it in, and before I could decide where to rate him on some internalized scale whose awful nature I dismissed, because men had always done this to us, after all, the subway had pulled up to Twenty-Third Street.

I walked out the doors, and before I made it to the steps—a hand on my shoulder. I didn't flinch; I knew it was him before I turned around.

"Sorry," he said. The apology was his first strike, but I let him continue. "I swear I've never done this before, but would you want to get a drink sometime?"

He had a slight lisp, which I found endearing. It was critical to find endearing traits in a stranger I was agreeing to drink with before I'd even had a cup of coffee.

I told him I'd go out with him if he could find me based on my first name and industry. This seemed both flirtatious and self-protective.

"End of life," I said, when he asked where I worked.

"That's the company name?"

"Not going to make it that easy. The industry." I paused and glanced down at his hands, which were unlined and pale, probably from staring at a Bloomberg portal indoors all day. "What were you reading?"

"*Thinking, Fast and Slow*. It's this business book—"

"I know," I interrupted before he could go on, wishing he'd been reading a book by a female author or a novel. "Good luck on your mission."

Two days later, I got an email at my work address:

> **Mission complete. See you 7pm next Thursday at Anfora on 8th.**

Cocky and direct, which was increasingly rare in my dating life. The month before, I'd talked to two guys on apps for weeks, tepid back-and-forths about our weekend plans that never materialized into real plans. I was sick of the digital dance. I'd finally met a real live man who wanted to take me out at a specific time and place. This should've been baseline for a date, but shocking insight: being single in the city isn't all cosmopolitans and rainbows and hailing the same cab as your soulmate. Sometimes it's urging a stranger on a subway platform to stalk you.

We ordered old-fashioneds as a nod to the way we met.

He was excitable and much chattier than the narrative I'd crafted for him on the subway. I had trouble getting a word in at first, but as the date went on, he relaxed into a flow, pausing at appropriate times and shoehorning fewer jokes into his stories.

His name was Whit Harris and he was thirty-four. Grew up in Philly, went to Syracuse. He worked in health care venture capital, meaning he was forever looking for important drugs to throw money behind. Clinical trial results sounded like auditions to him, opportunities to discover the Next Big Thing in pharma. Cancer was his latest obsession, all those black molds that ruined anatomies. Breast. Pancreatic. Lung. Prostate. The list of cell therapies in Whit's inbox sounded like a heat map of the body, touching on all the major parts.

I told him that these site-specific organ cancers seemed less threatening than blood cancer—multiple myeloma, which killed my dad, formed in plasma. It was mobile from the beginning, something in the water that ran through him. Whit said it didn't work like that; any old cancer could spread. But I liked to think of my dad's diagnosis as distinctly evil, uniquely quick.

I found Whit's work interesting because I was a medical nerd, too. Whit and I discovered that we'd both been premed in college, but neither of us had actually become a doctor. I'd abandoned it when my GPA dropped low enough to threaten my academic scholarship; he pivoted when he realized he could make more money elsewhere. I'd let go of my twin dreams—first art, then medicine—for the former's improbability and the latter's difficulty. Instead of making me practical and realistic, I worried this surrender made me cowardly and inadequate.

I didn't dislike my job, but I often disliked explaining it. Whit joked that together, we were the spin doctors of death. I worked at Composure, a start-up aimed at disrupting the "end-of-life industry." The company's body decomposition technology turned human remains into soil. Instead of shooting up a corpse with embalming fluid and trying to preserve a simulacrum of life in a lifeless box, Composure turned your loved one into an eventual tree or bush or place to piss. It also turned the "what do you do?" question into a long answer.

I was a communications manager at Composure, meaning I was paid to spread the word about this corporeal glow-up. My to-do list included securing placement in publications, getting the founder onto panels, and partnering with brands to raise the company's profile and convince the public that this technology could upend a staid, dead industry—a pun I would try to avoid in story pitches. Before Composure, I'd worked in corporate communications at NBC, a job I'd disliked for its cog-in-the-wheel anonymity. I was on a huge team, tasked with KPIs and circling back and targets that could've been hit by any one of the hundreds of communications majors lining up for these jobs every year. When one of my best friends from Brown, Bex, mentioned she knew the founder of this "death start-up" who was hiring for a comms director, I'd felt a kick in my gut. I had more impact at Composure—we were a team of twenty people total—and the product fascinated me. I'd learned that embalming—fluid replacing blood, organs getting aspirated like drained pools—was an outdated practice. The ancient Egyptians started it, but the idea of making the dead look as lifelike as possible was an American scheme. It became popular after the Civil War, when dead bodies were transported on slow, hot trains so that families could get a last look at their fallen soldiers. It was essentially human taxidermy. When framed that way, human composting didn't seem like an insurmountable mental leap.

Whit laughed at my canned details, honed from overexplaining my strange job. He talked about his work with an urgency that I found sexy, an earned buoyancy in opposition to the apathy I heard from a lot of my peers, the "it's a job" pushback against capitalism's tendency to make work our lives. It reminded me of an older generation. It reminded me of Walter Murphy. I pushed the thought out of my head, not wanting to picture a sixty-year-old bald dude when I inevitably kissed this new guy outside the bar.

After a few dates, I decided that the tone of Whit's initial email was a ruse, and I liked him better for it. He couldn't keep up a confident or mysterious performance for long. His goofy sense of humor and neurotic foot tapping and shameless four texts at a time could read as him giving too many fucks or no fucks at all. Did his inability to maintain a cool veneer show that he was self-conscious, or secure enough to be openly anxious in a new relationship?

I didn't think he was "the one," but I also didn't believe in the type of brick-from-the-sky love that rendered partnership involuntary, the clarifying soulmate stuff that made you discover yourself through the skin of someone else. After what happened with Ollie, I didn't even want that if it really existed. I wouldn't mention this comparison to Virginia, though—she didn't know about my history with her cousin.

Whit posted a picture from our first date: an old-fashioned in mood lighting and a silly, somewhat witty (@whitty_) caption. The randomness and spirit of the post hinted at his overall persona: unapologetic in his urge to connect. This trait was a little off-putting and ultimately charming. If he'd been less attractive, I probably would've found it annoying.

michael.stephens15 who ya with?

graham_cooke good one, bro

drewfeelz one is silver and the other's . . .
wasted

calliememaybe hot d8 😏

3 January

Camera Roll
A square of skin covered in raised red bumps

Alone in the apartment, I scanned the bookshelves.

They were stacked with historical bricks and beach reads: Winston Churchill and Elin Hilderbrand, Sally Bedell Smith and John Grisham. They'd been sorted by color, a method I opposed. My dad had taught me that sorting books by anything other than alphabetical order amounted to a type of monarchy, a useless practice that was all for show. As an aspiring writer, he'd been personally invested in this belief and used these colorful (and flawed) comparisons to make his point. Bookshelf order should function as anarchy or democracy: pure chaos or organized by a technique as egalitarian as the alphabet.

Unlike tortured artists who discuss writer's block as if it's an unavoidable epidemic, my dad never had an issue generating material. Concepts came to him with muscular force, and he said it was like a possession, with writing as the exorcism. His day job as a general contractor was what he did to pay for life; writing, by his estimation, was closer to what he did with his hours. He was unpublished, but a lack of recognition didn't deter him. He said it was a long game and generated new book concepts with the frequency that Mimi bought new clothes. A partial sample of his ideas:

- A man who works the front desk at a whaling museum in Nantucket witnesses a child abduction outside the ice-cream store. Tentative title: *I Scream.*

- An NYC couple moves to Vermont and becomes involved in a throuple with a local woman who sells honey. Tentative title: *The Hive.*

- King Henry VIII, but make it a queen who beheads her husbands.

- The polio outbreak. Add a disgruntled marriage.

I was biased, but I thought his work was good. Lively. He had an ear for rhythm and an imagination for metaphor. Some of the relationships were surface level, but he always assured me that would be fixed in subsequent drafts, depth applied like paint layers. The issue was he never got to those later drafts. He got too excited about new ideas before he could put a single novel to bed. He was a creative bachelor, unable to commit to one project. When he died, he'd been working on something new. He said it was his best yet, but he always said that. This time, though, I'd felt a shift. Up until he became too weak to move, he was typing away, picking at the keys with two fingers. He guarded this idea and didn't excitedly pitch it to strangers like he had with the others.

Days before he passed away, when his skin was all shadows, he asked me to find and finish the novel. "You're a good writer," he said. "And you know me better than anyone."

I'd taken this with me—the "you're a good writer," the dying wish to complete his work—when I decided to minor in English. It didn't feel as noble as medicine or as fulfilling as painting, but it had a purpose. If I could ever find those pages, the degree might help me finish them.

If. Because after he died, I opened the computer to the exact location he'd shown me days earlier.

The file had disappeared.

I searched and searched, sifting through his email for the document name, thinking he might have sent it to himself or someone else. My mom told me to forget about the novel; it would only bring more pain, and we didn't know anything about the story anyways. But that unknowing was the reason I needed to find it, as if the document could contain his resurrection—work that was so clearly him, he'd climb out of the computer. Or maybe it would be full of wisdom, words to soften the abrupt way he'd been taken from us. I knew that cancer wasn't homicide, that it struck indiscriminately and without motive. But it still felt targeted and personal. Why him, why now? He'd taught me that fiction allows room for questions, makes it all right to live with the mystery of humanity. Maybe his novel could help me come to terms with the randomness of his death or preserve part of his spirit that lived on outside his body.

I thought about the novel obsessively for years, but like all fixations, it was stretched by time. Multiple times a day turned to once a day, once a day turned to once a week. After a few years, I could go into a bookstore without crying.

On the bottom shelf, an unfamiliar spine peeked out from a row of dictionaries: *Skin Conditions: Diagnosis and Treatment.* I picked it up and started flipping through the pages full of rashes and spots, skin photographed close-up so that it looked more like fabric swatches than flesh. A header for how to treat eczema was followed by a patchwork of raised pink spots. "Keratosis pilaris (chicken skin)" was accompanied by constellations of tiny red bumps, which were apparently just hair follicles clogged with dead skin.

This was the least erotic skin-centric book on the market, and yet I couldn't look away. I took a picture of the chicken skin and then examined my forearm: barely visible light hairs, a cratered mole with small white dots inside the larger brown circle. How strange that the material that contained us could change so quickly and inexplicably that we needed a book (or a WebMD spiral) to decode its shifts. The ugly markings that cropped up on us all could be extracted—Dr. Pimple Popper was one of my favorite accounts—but it wasn't until I started working at Composure that I understood the wide range of comfort levels people had with their own bodies. Most people cringed when I explained the concept, the term *human composting* making them lose their appetites or scrunch their noses. But Virginia understood it immediately when I'd taken the job a few months ago. Maybe it was the artist in her that allowed for an imagined future, the reframing of death as an extension of life instead of an imitation of it. Waxy, embalmed dolls replaced by nourishing soil.

I continued flipping through the skin book, page after page of bolded ailments and declarative tips for how to treat them (my favorite: "take a deep breath"). I looked at my feed, full of bachelorettes and selfies and **that feeling when**s. A college acquaintance put up a picture of Carbone spicy rigatoni vodka with the caption **shot of vodka**. A news account described a tsunami in Thailand, a friend of a friend vacationed in Barbados. My cousin let us all in on her January detox, some combination of honey, cayenne, and deranged hope. A coworker was selling a mauve couch and polished nickel tables. People tried to leave behind past selves, the shedding we all did for a chance at feeling new.

Virginia came back into the apartment, wet dots decorating her beanie.

"It's snowing," she said. "I have so much fucking work to do."

"Good weather to get cozy."

"Or off myself. Bury me in a snowbank."

"What are you working on?"

"Same old. The paintings for the end-of-semester show. I'm worried my pieces just aren't resonating."

"With your professor or with you?"

She paused. "Both."

Virginia painted in old master style, trying to imitate life with photographic precision. Ceramic vases, fields of wheat, apples on tables. In a world where everyone with an iPhone fancied themselves a photographer, I could understand why she was questioning her approximations.

She sat down on the cream couch and curled her feet up underneath her legs. She was wearing a T-shirt and sweatpants but still managed to look cool—even more so because of the casual clothing. The shirt, a worn blue tee Swiss-cheesed with holes around the neckline, hung loose over her nonexistent hips and flat stomach. Her body was a tight bracket compared with my wide parentheses.

"Would you try something new?" I said.

"I can't figure out *what*. And all this maid of honor shit."

"I can help with that. Go listen to some music, get weird, come up with a wild and fresh idea."

"Good idea." She stood up and riffled around a silver bowl for her AirPods case, the plastic beetle she'd already misplaced twice since we'd moved in, and started gearing up for another walk.

"Maybe you'll meet someone on the street," I said.

"Or the subway. We've started to think you made him up." It was always *we* with the Murphys. Whit hadn't ended up coming to Dorrian's the week before, and Virginia, Mimi, and Gray's pleas to meet him were getting louder every day.

"I told you, I'm bringing him to Gray's engagement party."

"Believe it when I see it."

"Bon voyage," I said as she walked out the door.

"You sound like my mother."

"I'll take it."

Because for all of Mimi's eye-roll-inducing behavior, she was still charming and joyful, a version of adulthood that didn't involve knit brows and traffic anxiety and endless phone calls with insurance companies. Her money was a kind of Lexapro, smoothing over the hard edges of being alive.

The door shut behind Virginia and it was just me again. Alone. Living in a space that's not your own, you start to take risks. Daily negotiations over how much snooping is normal versus creepy, trying to justify or dissuade yourself from opening drawers and riffling through closets. I'd convinced myself that this was a universal human impulse—*right?*—and could almost hear my internal monologue curling with insecure pleas for assurance. Two weeks in, I was playing it safe. I'd mentally circled the areas ripest for intrigue: the set of drawers underneath the living room TV, Mimi and Walter's closet, the cupboards in Walter's wood-paneled office. I knew they were probably full of manila folders stuffed with tax forms and stained menus for already-shuttered restaurants, but the presence of unexcavated surfaces made me buzz with anticipation. Like the urge to squeeze, pick, and diagnose my skin, I wanted the interior to turn exterior.

The TV drawers were the easiest to explain (*I was looking for the remote*) and likely the most harmless. I opened the bottom drawer. The big reveal: a single hammer and a rubber band. I slid open the top drawer, preemptively reacting with disappointment and boredom, to find a manila folder and a box. The folder contained some of Virginia's childhood art. She'd drawn the hydrangeas in the front yard of Idyll Wind, her early talent—I guessed she'd been twelve or thirteen—coming to life in the periwinkle shading. In the next picture, she'd drawn herself, Gray, and Ollie sitting on

Adirondack chairs. I was cartwheeling on the lawn in front of them. The proportions were off and the faces weren't there yet—we all wore identical, cartoonish expressions—but the slope of the lawn and the croquet set coming up from the grass were rendered beautifully. The sky was hazy and perfectly imperfect, looser than the rest of the drawing, and my initials (*C.H.*) were scribbled inside a cloud. I remembered now: I'd drawn the sky. We worked on this together, sitting on beach towels on their wraparound porch. Back then, I also loved drawing and had some talent to back up the enthusiasm. My inclinations were wilder and more abstract than Virginia's faithful adherence to reality, and our instructor at beach camp favored my creativity over Virginia's precision. I'd won some silly camp art competition at the end of the season in August before fifth grade, my submission a picture of the pond next to Ginger House—bright ripples in Picasso-like curves, trees with swirls for leaves, and a blueberry pie in place of the sun. I'd always been a hungry motherfucker. Virginia hadn't talked to me for a day after I'd won, saying she was just "confused" about why they'd pick something as weird and unrealistic as my drawing, especially since *I* didn't want to be an artist—she did.

I couldn't say this out loud, but it wasn't about desire; it was a matter of possibility. I didn't have the financial freedom to pursue a career so fickle and impractical. Even before my dad died, I knew that money was tight. I'd once gone downstairs in the middle of the night to find my mom awake, coffeepot drained, face knotted over a stack of bills. My parents fought in the car every summer driving to Rhode Island when they thought I was asleep. I picked up phrases like "overdrawn" and "credit card debt" over the sound of the Rolling Stones on classic rock radio. Then once we arrived in Watch Hill, I'd listen to Virginia and Gray talk about their ballet classes and squash lessons and after-school math tutors, patiently nodding and acting like I could relate. My parents and the Murphys became close because of my friendship with Virginia, but I sensed that they wouldn't have otherwise socialized, even though Watch Hill was small—one square mile, three restaurants, and house names that everyone knows small.

Whit could relate to this insider-outsider dynamic. I'd described my summers to him, and he'd told me he felt the same in his Philadelphia suburb. His dad was the cook at his all-boys private school, so his tuition was covered, allowing him to rub elbows with the sons of corporate lawyers and investment bankers, the little shits who didn't flinch when they lost their $400 Barbour jackets and showed up hungover to expensive lacrosse camps that were supposed to get them into college (even though everyone knew Dad's annual donation would do the trick). Maybe we both had chips on our shoulders, but it was nice to date someone whose chip clicked into my own—jigsaw pieces that wouldn't have lined up with a person who'd always belonged.

The apartment door opened behind me, and I managed to close the drawer before I heard Virginia's voice. I'd have to check out the contents of the box later.

"How was the walk?" I asked.

"Well, I talked to Gray on the phone about her engagement party for half of it. So it was *hashtag bridal*."

4 February

The bride and groom had no faces.

Dozens of them stood on rows of cupcakes, light blue frosting lapping at their feet. I could make out the curve of a nose and the suggestion of an upper lip, but they lacked the requisite holes for a face. Their poreless plastic skin looked better than the results of any serum or surgery.

The cupcakes were on a table full of untouched food: homemade chips, crudités and hummus, four different cheeses and a tangle of prosciutto, cornichons and mini tartines, and guacamole. Custom blue napkins featuring the wedding hashtag, plus cups printed with their crest. It was Gray's engagement party, and I was starving. The Murphys had rented out a popular West Village restaurant known for its first-date-to-barstool ratio (high), jalapeño margaritas (high on spice), and rooftop garden that grew its own vegetables, aided by the exhaust of Manhattan air (highly suspect).

I dipped a celery stick in hummus. We were early, even though we'd walked halfway so I could get my steps in. Whit had insisted on getting there on time because he wanted a chance to "connect" with Mr. Murphy. I was nervous about

Whit coming on too strong—there was a fine line between familial and sleazy, the hairline fractures of opportunity.

"Should I go talk to him now?" A half-moon of sweat had formed in the armpit of his blue button-down shirt.

"Give it a minute."

Walter Murphy stood in the far corner of the restaurant. He rarely moved at events, preferring people to come to him like he was hosting office hours. His khakis were two sizes too big and his jacket looked limp and his enormous bald head shone with dots of light from the restaurant's chandelier, but none of these superficial markers mattered. He was still the most respected, most moneyed, most *somebody* person in the room. I wondered if he got away with it because he was a man or a boss, neither of which should've impressed anyone because he was born into both. Still, even after all these years, I was intimidated by how well he wore those roles, despite how poorly he wore actual clothes.

Gray and I hugged, said our hellos and our "you look amazings." She'd done something to her face to make it appear filtered (one of the micros: -dermabrasion, -blading, or -needling), and her high-waisted silver pants and white cropped sweater glowed in the low light of the bar.

I introduced her to Whit, and she barely said hello, instead turning toward me to ask where Virginia was. I had no idea; I hadn't seen her since that morning.

"She was supposed to be here a half hour early for a family champagne toast and to stuff goodie bags. Jesus," Gray said. She took a long sip of her Boskerita, a forced melding of her fiancé's last name and her favorite drink.

I said she'd be here soon, even though I wasn't sure about anything except that Virg would need Xanax to get through the night. Gray bit her thumbnail, a habit she'd had since middle school and failed to cure with vinegar polishes and a bout of hypnosis. Gray was always five steps or years ahead of herself, worried about fourth grade math in third, college acceptance before high school, kids' names during wedding planning. No wonder she couldn't stop biting her hands, to keep them from clawing at an invisible future.

Virginia's lateness insulted the core of Gray's personality, but they'd never have an irrevocable blowout. Their shared DNA gave them tacit permission to talk to each other the way I talked to myself. Sometimes I felt a flare of jealousy over that careless security, the quiet constancy of someone orbiting you no matter how forcefully you pushed them away.

I told Gray I'd "let her go," the classiest and easiest way to get out of a conversation.

Mimi was holding court at the bar, talking to three friends from her garden club and double fisting drinks like Edward Martini-hands, a joke Whit would make. After two months of dating, were we already morphing into one person? I thought of the social account that made you guess whether two people were siblings or dating. So many couples looked alike, a combination of narcissism, growing into each other, and staying within your league. I didn't have to worry about that with Whit. He was unquestionably better looking than me.

Once she finished talking to her friends, I introduced Mimi and Whit. She clinked her martini glasses together and squealed like he was a dog who'd just performed a delightful trick.

"The famous Whit! Don't mind the double vision," she said, looking down at her two martinis. "I'm bringing one to the bride-to-be. Do you have any friends for my other daughter?"

"No one good enough."

"I just love how you two met, god, so *romantic*. Never thought I'd say that about our subway system. You know, the last time I took the subway I saw Dennis Quaid in a beanie."

I'd heard this story multiple times. Whit made a bad joke about Meg Ryan being his "one that got away."

Mimi chuckled politely, a laugh like a punctuation mark. "He's a funny one," she said.

"He's a funny one" was a poor substitute for real laughter. Whit's compulsion to connect made him try out material that wasn't always sharp or natural. The thing was, I didn't mind his not-so-subtle desperation. It was refreshing to be with someone with bald needs, his social desires an above-water structure with a discernible shape. It was easy to get to know him, which was more than I could say for some of my past relationships.

Exes like to appear at inopportune moments—in physical form or as a song playing in a bar, a street sign they'd find funny, an ad for a show you watched together. This usually happens right when you haven't thought of them in hours or days or weeks and are finally breathing free of the ghost.

Mine walked into the party with Virginia and a woman I didn't recognize. His hair was longer, golden-brown curls hitting just below his ears. He wore a denim jacket, jeans, and slip-on boots that were more suited for a spring rainstorm than a twenty-five-degree February night. His clothes invited commentary—when we were kids, it was because they were more unusual than everyone else's polos and khakis. But in the city, no one was unusual. Here, they raised questions for their impracticality, the arrogant assumption that he didn't need to play by the weather's rules. *I run hot,* I imagined him saying to me with a blank expression, his face refusing to close the loop of innuendo.

Why was I imagining what he would say? He was right in front of me; I could talk to him in person. Whit was in the bathroom, and I scrambled to make myself look engaged or busy or interesting. I walked toward the bar because my hands needed an outlet and my brain needed another drink or four, but before I could safely wedge myself into ordering position, I felt him behind me.

"Callie," he said.

Before turning around, I tugged my top down a bit and had the sudden, superficial regret that I hadn't been able to afford highlights in almost a year. He liked me blond. "Ollie."

We hugged. My cheek pushed against his denim jacket, which still held the cold from outside like a stone. I'd forgotten that I lined up exactly with his shoulder, and I almost moved to rest my head under his chin. Stubble surrounded his mouth, a scruffy look he leaned into a few times a year. It had brought a fresh tension to kissing, the texture elevating instead of dimming the sensation of his lips.

"Long time," he said.

"Since what—Virginia's birthday?" I turned a statement into a question. I didn't need confirmation. "When did you move back?"

"Last week." It had been three weeks ago, and I wondered if he rounded down to make his silence seem shorter. "I'm still adjusting to the whole other people thing. I could go days without talking to someone else there."

"Was it lonely?"

"Alone"—he paused—"but not lonely."

Ollie had an enviable ability to fill his hours with nothing but himself. He'd been away for over a year—a photography assignment had taken him to India, and he'd decided to stay. He got lost in his work and thoughts: taking, retaking, and developing photographs; gazing at them for days on end, squinting at each angle like he was translating a foreign text. He was fascinated by the world, or by his way of seeing the world, and I couldn't decide if he was expansive or self-involved.

"What are you up to now?" I said.

"Reading, mostly. Taking pictures on the street. Trying to avoid getting sued by strangers."

"Unwilling Humans of New York."

"I had coffee with that guy the other week. Good dude."

Of course he had coffee with the person behind one of the most popular photography accounts in the world. Ollie's access used to thrill me, especially when we were at Brown and he was already rubbing elbows with big-time artists; now his nonchalant tone just depressed me. It was so far removed from my plebeian enthusiasm. I'd text everyone I knew if I saw a Real Housewife in a restaurant, while he treated actual celebrities like peers. I resisted asking follow-up questions about his coffee date.

"How was the food in India?" I asked. The predictability of the question pained me, but I wanted him to make me taste a dish from seven thousand miles away.

"I think I broke through another layer of the Scoville scale. You know, the different levels to describe spice."

"Just like how in German there are six different ways to express love?" I'd read it somewhere or someone had mentioned it to me. Was it a different language, maybe Greek? I felt the prickly regret of hitting "send" on an email too early.

"Really? Pretty sure *ich liebe dich* is the only one." He pronounced the phrase with a perfect German accent, or my imperfect idea of a perfect German accent.

"I thought I read it somewhere. How in English our idea of love is binary, but in other languages it's more nuanced. Like instead of saying the lame 'I really like you,' there's a word for it with a sort of distinct meaning. I don't know."

"German words are funny. *Kummerspeck*," he said. "Do you know that one?"

"Something about getting drunk at Oktoberfest?"

"Means 'grief bacon.' Eating your feelings when you're sad."

"So, Sundays."

He laughed. "Or like how I had a milkshake every night in eighth grade."

"Mine was doughnut holes. I can barely look at them now."

"We had a good excuse." His eyes wandered to the bar. "I'm going to grab a drink." He squeezed my upper arm once before walking away.

"The famous Virginia!" Whit said, hugging her with an enveloping embrace for someone he'd never met. "Oh my god, I'm sorry!" A wet trail of margarita snaked down her velvet blazer.

She removed the jacket and shook the liquid from it. Smiling, she lightly pushed his shoulder. "You clumsy motherfucker."

"I can get that dry-cleaned for you? I'm so sorry."

"You can barely see it. The beauty of wearing black." And the beauty of having so much money that you can easily pay for dry cleaning or a new blazer altogether.

Whit looked like he'd committed a grave offense, and I could tell he was spiraling over his slip. In such a quick exchange, I saw the contrast between the two of them: Whit's effort chafed at her effortlessness. They wouldn't butt heads, because they didn't remind each other of their own worst qualities, but would instead interact with baffled fumbling, unable to close the wide gap between their ways of responding to the world.

Whit asked Virginia about her sister's wedding—summer in Italy, how dreamy—and Virginia told a story about Gray requesting glass tumblers from Spain to be flown in for the reception in Positano.

I gave my phone to Whit to get a picture of us. Virginia and I posed with the lips of our margarita glasses touching, heads cocked and soft smiles straining for the best versions of ourselves. It was strange; the universal advice to avoid standing next to someone better looking in pictures didn't hold with me and Virginia. I took my best photos next to her, the most striking woman in most rooms. It was like her looks rubbed off on me, an odd sort of spell.

The woman Virginia had walked in with, the one I didn't recognize, came up and said hi. She was short and dressed plainly, but was pretty enough that you'd notice her on the street. Her black hair, thick and long like Virginia's, bracketed her face with a darkness that made her lips and eyes stand out.

"I just met your mother," she said to Virginia. "She's lovely."

"Oh, Callie, meet Anika," Virginia said. "Ollie's girlfriend he met in . . . where, Jaipur?"

"It feels like we've known each other for years," Anika said. "That Rumi quote about knowing each other all along."

"I know it," I said.

"Lovers have known each other all along," she said, looking like she'd just woken up from a sex dream. Her eyelids hovered, birdlike.

"'They're in each other all along,'" I said.

"Same thing." Anika sipped her drink and looked past me.

"Not really," I said. Virginia narrowed her eyes. Maybe I'd overcorrected. "No, it's just that you kind of need the full quote to really appreciate it, you know? Out of context it's sort of cheesy. The full thing is better: 'The minute I heard my first love story I started looking for you, not knowing how blind that was. Lovers don't finally meet somewhere. They're in each other all along.'"

"Now I know how you two spend your free time," Virginia said, looking at Whit. "Whispering sweet nothings plagiarized from dead poets."

"I've never heard that before," Whit said. "Are you going to start posting inspirational quotes soon? Roses are red, Whit is feeling blue, I love him so much—"

"And a big fuck you," I said, smiling wide enough that I

could feel my chapped lips split. Even Anika laughed, her big, straight teeth flashing. I'd been the one to show Ollie the Rumi quote, and now she was walking around botching it, claiming it as theirs.

I said I had to go to the bathroom and walked across the restaurant, dodging people I knew. On the way, I grabbed three salmon tartines, a mini slider juicy with bright yellow cheese, a shrimp skewer, tuna tacos, and a bunch of mac and cheese bites, all wrapped up in two napkins.

The single-stall bathroom was the size of a coffin. I sat down on the porcelain lid fully clothed and placed my fake snakeskin boots against the door. With appetizers swaddled in my lap, I looked for Anika on Ollie's feed. Two possible accounts popped up in his followers, one with an uncomfortable-looking yoga pose in the profile picture, and one with a woman and a child. I clicked on the contortionist—too old. I clicked on the mother. It was her.

There's a dark space at the intersection of who we are and how we appear. Some call this ravine self-awareness, or a lack thereof. I call it social media. The vessel for our projections and distortions, the posts we choose reveal our priorities. People say it's a mirage or only part of the story—but for me, it is the story. Self-selections become your reflection. Like a conversation, what you conceal speaks just as loudly as what you reveal. Anika, I could tell from a brief glance, thought she was above it all and had the slim 313 follower count to reflect her low level of participation. She didn't concern herself with polished digital representations, but favored a raw, spontaneous affect that was still an affect. Every other picture featured her kid, a two- or three-year-old girl she liked to photograph wearing pink bows in a play kitchen, a somewhat retro choice for someone who'd attended two

Women's Marches and posted a text-on-screen image lamenting restrictive US abortion laws. She wore her long, thick hair piled on top of her head, down in sheets over her face, or otherwise behind a small mollusk of an ear, which, I noticed, had no piercings. Tattoos crawled up her arms in the single beach picture on her feed (one-piece). She wore a silver-and-turquoise ring on her left pointer finger, chunky and lined like a fourth knuckle. In a picture of a slice of Funfetti cake taken two years ago, the caption read **Still fun at 31**. So she was thirty-three now? With a child and unmarried? Dating a younger commitment-phobe? Each question breathed more questions, filmy unknowns that concealed her from me.

I enlarged the cake image, her left hand resting over a cloth napkin, to check her skin for wear. Her hands were smooth but veiny, the raised strands suggesting a nearly translucent layer between her inside and outside. She wasn't particularly thin—her curves were attractive, you'd call them *healthy,* but not in a condescending way—so this felt like a metaphorical conclusion. But she didn't strike me as "thin-skinned." She'd fit more neatly into the "heart on her sleeve" cliché, its blood pushing up against the roof of her palm.

I'd looked at the pictures of her face and body first, but noticed that an unusual number of her posts showcased objects instead of people or nature. One of them, taken recently, looked at first glance like an advertisement for her true crime obsession, a fixation that every millennial woman thought made her darker and more interesting than she actually was. An image of forensic tools or a crime scene, eerily filtered, stood against a white backdrop. I clicked on it. **Adult school supplies #residency.** The location tag: Mount Sinai.

She couldn't be a doctor. It must have been part of a Halloween costume. I scanned furiously, willing it to be false, hoping with the force of a desperate wish that no more evidence would present itself. A few images after the cake picture, she stood in a white coat at her Penn Med graduation. **The doctor will see you now,** she'd written with a heart emoji, suggesting the heart that it took to get her there and the hearts she'd handle in strangers' chests. After reading the comments, though, it appeared she wouldn't be handling internal organs; she was a dermatologist, expert at the outer layer. I zoomed in to see the full name printed on her white coat and held the image down with my thumb.

Fuck, I accidentally clicked it twice. I "liked" it, even though I hated it. I wanted to flush myself down the toilet. I unliked it quickly, hoping she wouldn't see but knowing that she would.

One by one, I shoved the rest of the appetizers into my mouth and threw out the napkin, destroying the evidence.

PUT A RING ON IT cutouts hung from a corner wall, the party planner's version of pin the tail on the donkey, accompanied by an unspoken nudge to post your results, hashtag graysanatommy—a nod to Gray and her fiancé, Tommy, and to the show I'd watched obsessively through college, the Hollywood version of my original goal to tag *MD* on my name.

Virginia was talking to Bex. As I got closer to them, I pretended to look at my phone. Bex had her rant face on. Recently, she'd been in a perpetual state of woke rage and had started arguing with people who already agreed with her. Before I could walk away, she saw me and waved.

"Can you believe it?" she said, grabbing my wrist. She launched into a story about her fiancé's sister requesting a suite for herself at the hotel in Miami where we were staying for Bex's bachelorette next month. Bex had met her fiancé (né boyfriend), Greg, about a year ago, and it seemed sudden. But Bex didn't see any reason in waiting once she found someone who checked her boxes; she excelled at following rules and making her own rules for others to follow. After graduation, she'd worked as an investment banking analyst and star associate, then left to start an investing platform called Wemen with the goal of closing the gender investment gap. I still didn't fully understand everything Wemen did (its "value prop" or "mission," she'd say), but its app downloads and PR placements were impressive. Two years in, and she'd already been on CNBC, Bloomberg, Fox Business, and *GMA,* on top of glossy features in *Forbes* and *Inc.*

The sound of knife on champagne flute rang through the space. Tommy gave a short toast that said nothing—thank you to the Murphys, um, excited to marry this woman, blah.

I plucked a cupcake from a tray making the rounds, bit into it and felt the sugar dissolve on my tongue. I imagined the frosting and its spongy foundation traveling down my esophagus, into the slick pocketbook of my stomach, and through a maze of intestines.

Whit found me. He talked about his five-minute conversation with Walter, giddy over the Big Man's reaction to a drug Whit's firm was considering for an investment. Ollie and Anika were standing at a high-top table. Their elbows leaned on the metal, his right hand threaded through her left. He brushed a piece of hair behind her ear and said something that made her mouth open wide with laughter.

I grabbed Whit's hand and squeezed it, leaned into him. Kissed him on the mouth and tasted tequila. I was just as bad as the girls who rushed to get engaged right after their exes did, posting long captions about the man of their dreams in between refreshing the profile of someone they hadn't shared a bed with in years.

"Cutie," Whit said. "There must be something in the tequila."

He thought the engagement party was making me sentimental, but I wasn't full of love. I was full of mini carb bombs and questions—over whether Ollie's hair would feel the same between my fingers, whether Anika had graduated at the top of her class, whether I was so full I'd need to throw up later, whether I could ever have a clavicle that looked like Virginia's in that blazer.

Anika made eye contact with me over Ollie's shoulder and rubbed the left side of her chest. Was she trying to tell me she was in love? I looked toward Whit to distract myself from her confusing movements. My boyfriend's protractor-perfect chin almost made me less confused, convinced me I was in the right place.

Anika was still trying to catch my eye. I cocked my head and raised my eyebrows, hoping to convey the friendliest possible version of a very unfriendly question: *What the hell are you doing?*

"You have a mark on your shirt," Whit said. "It looks like shit."

Over the left pocket of my white silk shirt: a grainy yellow-brown stain in the exact spot Anika had been rubbing.

"Mustard."

"My little honey Dijon." He kissed my neck, and I nodded at Anika over his shoulder.

My favorite condiment had betrayed me. Nothing was safe.

I went to the bathroom again and scrubbed the mustard stain, probably making it worse. I considered throwing up. The music and conversation would drown out the retching and I'd feel so much better. I kneeled onto the ground and pitched my body forward, curved toward the toilet bowl like a question mark. I stuck my pointer and middle finger down my throat, wriggling for that fleshy button. Leaning, pushing, trying—to turn myself inside out, to erase the past hour. An acidic trickle of margarita mixed with errant crumbs came up, but nothing with real weight.

I stood up and washed my hands furiously. I needed

something to happen—a reversal of ingestion, a penetration, another drink. A "like." I flipped through the pictures Whit had taken of me and Virginia and filtered one so that the margaritas turned fluorescent and our faces became nearly, but not quite, poreless.

bexjones dynamic duo 👯 ♀

mimimurph gorgeous!

whitty_ photo cred @me

anikaaa loved meeting you!

5 March

I stared at Ollie over the swell of Virginia's hiked-up knees. We were in our apartment watching an unreleased Korean movie. Ollie had an early screener because, of course, he had a friend who knew a guy.

Virginia and I were supposed to be in Miami for Bex's bachelorette, but our flight had been delayed and then canceled. "Bad weather, good luck," Virginia had said, trying to get me to ditch the trip altogether. I ignored her and booked us on a six a.m. flight the next morning. Whit was on a golf weekend with coworkers, and Ollie was an unexpected guest, invited over because he had access to what would allegedly become the buzziest movie of the year.

It was about a poor Korean family and their increasingly weird relationship with a super wealthy family in the same city. The subtitles demanded attention; it was hard to look away. Yet, I managed to sneak glances at Ollie's profile. Virginia, sitting between us, had her knees up under her nightgown, so his face emerged over a roll of silk. He still had the same dark freckle on his right cheek, the same faint scar above his upper lip. Of course he still had them. It was a breakup, not a body swap.

I wondered if he felt the same swallowed tension, a bloated

knowing, when he was with me and Virginia. She didn't know that we'd dated or hooked up or whatever unlabeled thing we'd done in college and then on and off for years afterward. Ollie had felt strongly that we shouldn't tell her or anyone in the family, because he didn't want to make things awkward and said that Virginia wouldn't react well. I agreed, but it still made me feel like a bad friend and a bad fuck.

On-screen, the wealthy daughter kissed her tutor. I found myself thinking that she was a slut, even though we weren't supposed to use terms like that anymore. I reached my right hand over my head and stretched my neck, so that my eyes turning toward Ollie would appear like the natural result of an unrelated movement. He was looking at his phone, smiling. He wasn't even there.

I first met Ollie Moskowitz-Murphy when I was eleven years old. He was an odd Murphy family footnote then. He'd moved in with Virginia's family when he was twelve, after his mom died in a car accident and his dad's method of grieving involved starting a new family in a different zip code. I can picture Ollie scaling the Idyll Wind staircase two steps at a time, running to his room, and slamming the door. I chalked up his emo attitude to the tragedy he'd lived through and the fact that he was a year older. His angst seemed exotic and untouchable, but also a little scary. A TRY AGAIN LATER sign hung on his doorknob, a Hanukkah gift from Mimi that she probably regretted. The Murphys started celebrating Jewish holidays in addition to Christian ones when he moved in, because his mom was Jewish and they wanted to provide him with some sense of normalcy. I was jealous of their additional opportunities for presents. Their loot was already far better than mine, and this seemed like an unfair advantage in a rigged system. I remember feeling bad for Ollie about his mom, but mostly just happy that it hadn't happened to me.

Then it did happen to me. When my dad died, the Murphys tried to make me and Ollie talk to each other about our losses, but I was still interested in looking cool in front of older kids, not breaking down in front of them. Even after the unimaginable happened, being a teenager was still being a teenager. It wasn't the easiest time to sift out sadness over a dead parent from sadness over an unrequited crush or a failed algebra test. It all felt sad and impossibly consequential.

On-screen, the poor family was sitting around a table in their underground apartment. The tie-dye sweat suit I was wearing had ridden up around my belly button, exposing a thin strip of skin. I thought again about the year my dad passed away, how I became obsessed with fitting into a medium, wearing sack dresses the saleslady called "forgiving," as if stretched-out cotton could provide absolution. In between my disappointing trips to the Gap, Ollie and I eventually sort of acknowledged our shared losses. The summer before he went off to college—to Brown, where Virginia and I would follow—he pulled me aside when I was at the Murphys' for a sleepover. "Call me if you ever want to talk," Ollie said. "About . . . you know." He squeezed my hand and his usually alert eyes softened. I was caught off guard by how connected I felt to this person whose presence had confounded me for years.

The movie subtitles increased in abstraction as they tried to describe drunken hilarity using words. *[Commotion] [Laughter] [Excitement]* The poor family rolled around on the wealthy family's couch, drunk on expensive wine that didn't belong to them. I pictured Idyll Wind, the light blue shingles, over-hang ("porte cochere," as Mimi called it in a French accent), and row of hydrangeas lit up by tiki torches during annual summer barbecues. Speckled lights outside gave way to honeyed light inside on the grand staircase that Ollie ran up, where I'd sit braiding Virginia's hair. "A prom staircase," Mimi called it, and it was—we all took pictures on it, lined up like a pimply little infantry in our tankinis and board shorts. I pictured Norma, their housekeeper, secretly inviting her Jamaican family over when the Murphys went to Europe for a week every few summers, her mother and three kids roll-ing around on the living room couch and laughing, laughing, laughing—this time, in on the joke. I imagined me and Ol-lie alone in the cavernous kitchen, setting off the fire alarm while trying to cook a meal so rich it would've made our stomachs turn.

The phone in the Korean mansion rang. Someone was coming.

"Just wait," Ollie said. He had the luxury of knowing how this ended.

Ollie and I had been alone in a house only once, but we'd been alone for an extended period of time on a campus of eight thousand people. My junior year, Virginia went to Paris for what was supposed to be a semester but turned into an entire school year. Neither Ollie nor I realized how much we relied on her until she was gone. Ollie ran in a different circle—he became obsessed with photography and exclu-sively hung out with the other art majors. Virginia was an art major, too, but her social life straddled painting and par-ties where people wore glow-in-the-dark body paint. Halfheartedly artistic and reluctantly fratty, her resistance to go steady with either world made her even more appealing to both the art boys and the frat boys (must have been nice). I'd taken a painting class with her freshman year, when I was still deciding between art and premed, and watched her get asked out by a sweaty, pale classmate while sitting in front of her easel, a dot of green paint on her cheek like a beauty mark.

Ollie, missing Virginia, asked me to stand in for her at one of their weekly dinners. It was September and she'd been gone for weeks. He emailed my student address.

Callie,
Or are you going by Cal these days?
Long time no see. V and I used to get dinner on
Thursdays and I miss it. R u free this Thurs?
—Ollie

> Ollie,
> Yes, let's. Where to?
> —Cal(lie), choose your own
> adventure

Cal,
Have craving for Thai place downtown.
7:30 good for you?
—O

> O,
> Good for me. Pad see yew then.
> —C

Caught up in photo lab. Want to meet me there and I'll drive us over?

I'd fired off my responses without thinking—I cringed remembering the noodle pun—but the day before the scheduled dinner, I had a foreign thought: Was this a date? People didn't do dates in college. I was overthinking it. Ollie was like a surrogate relative, and he wanted me there as a family understudy, a body double. This would be painless, and Thai sounded delicious. That semester, I'd unwittingly embraced the freshman fifteen two years late and had been oscillating between damage control and indulgence. The week before my dinner with Ollie, every other meal had consisted of bone broth. I'd abandoned the diet after two days of light-headedness, but still—I deserved a treat.

The photo lab was in a part of campus where I rarely ventured, and I stood outside the closed door, waiting. Five minutes passed, then ten, fifteen. I cracked open the door expecting it to be empty, thinking maybe I'd gotten the time wrong.

"Come in," he said. "I forgot. We can go in a few minutes." He'd been so absorbed that he forgot to eat. I never forgot to eat.

Ollie stood over a container full of water, whose glow lit up his face and cast shadows across his forehead. I had the sense that we were underwater; the windowless room had a suffocating finality. Cylinders lining the walls emerged from the darkness slowly, as if rising up from the ocean.

"Film," he said, catching me squinting. "Come look."

I stood next to him and watched his hands probe the photo paper with pliers. An image emerged: a naked model, sprawled on a chaise longue. Her hand was behind her head. Her body, thin with a soft swell at the hips and breasts that couldn't fit in one hand, made a comma against the curve of the lounge chair.

"Was it weird to take pictures of a stranger like this?" I asked.

"How do you know she's a stranger?"

"Oh, I thought it must have been an assignment."

"I'm just kidding." His mouth opened into a half laugh. He had full lips—I'd never noticed them before—accentuated by the bluish light of the water. We both stared at the woman rising to the surface, her body parts sharpening into a person: her hip rising, breasts swelling, face resting. Even though she was still, her skin held the suggestion of activity like a paused television. She flickered briefly in my mind, an X-ray, as I imagined what her bones looked like underneath that tight expanse. They rose across her like haunted columns, blurry at the edges.

Ollie was still looking at her when I turned toward him. We were so close—when did we get so close?—that I could smell him. Sweat with an undertow of pine. There was a strange sealing of the room, a dreamlike atmosphere that made it feel elsewhere. The rules we concerned ourselves with outside were suddenly irrelevant. I was staring at a person I'd known for almost ten years yet seeing someone strangely new.

He looked at me, really looked at me, and moved his hand onto my waist. I moved mine to cover his, but it felt like the hand moved itself, separate from brain signals. It was simply a body part reaching for another part. Ollie pulled me toward him so that our torsos touched. His belt buckle was a hard knot, and I felt a shift in the softness underneath it. With his index finger, he traced my chin up to the curve of my ear.

"How did I miss it?"

"What?" I asked.

"You."

We were on the floor of the photo lab. I was on top, pinning his hands against the ground as the kisses got deeper and more desperate. He bit my bottom lip and lifted himself up so that we were sitting face-to-face. He wrapped his hands around my waist and pulled me into him, our legs open to each other.

I lifted his shirt above his head and put my hands on his bare shoulders. I didn't say a word, fearing it could slacken the quiet tautness in the room, the line that strung us both. We stared at each other, and I could barely make out his eyes in the dark.

On-screen, the wealthy family came home, and the poor family hid under a table to protect themselves. The rich mom and dad started having sex on the couch, and the poor parents and kids heard them writhing and grunting, something natural made unnatural. The rich dad commented on the poor dad's smell.

"This is so fucked up," Virginia said.

Ollie didn't say anything, but I heard it anyways: *Just wait*.

A few scenes later, the Korean home exploded in brutality. Blood covered the placid, mowed lawn. It was the first time the moneyed family had been shocked by tragedy, jolted out of autopilot by the force of secrets.

"Crazy, right?" Ollie said. "Just insane."

I was on my side with Ollie's hands around my waist, his naked body lined up with mine. He put his fingers inside me, cold but soft, and I slipped around him. His hands moved farther up, swirling and sending small but forceful shocks through me, all the way up into my chest.

"Inside," I said. "Inside."

He flipped me onto my back and pushed into me. My shoulders chafed against the floor, a sensation that was overwhelmed by his rocking. I'd had sex, sure, but I hadn't had sex in months with someone sober or ever with someone who could properly locate the clitoris or ever with someone I'd known forever. He moved in me like he'd always been there, and I had the embarrassing thought that we'd found a home that, until then, had eluded us both.

"Well, that was a successful dinner," Ollie said as he stepped back into his jeans. The room didn't look dark anymore. My eyes had fully adjusted.

"Five stars," I said. The idea of going out to dinner with someone right after sex felt radically adult. I turned away from him and pulled my jeans back on quickly, trying to hide the extra roll of skin that hung above the space he'd just entered.

"It's kind of late," he said. "Let's rain check Thai?"

"Yeah," I said. "Good idea."

Hours after the movie ended, I woke up in the middle of the night and had to pee.

I walked down the hallway, floorboards creaking underneath my socked feet. This would be the moment in the horror film when I'd hear a strange noise, when the shadow of a hidden murderer or monster or mooching family would pass across my line of sight. When the camera would pan behind my shoulder to show the glint of a knife and then—I'd fall. Cut to my body being chopped into disparate pieces. Fade to a bright day with a close-up of another whole, unsuspecting body awaiting its involuntary separation.

Back in the real world, a tapping noise was coming from the kitchen.

This had to be my mind projecting the horror fantasy, an auditory hallucination. I tried to remember a snatch of information from my premed days, a fact that would make it clear that this was a psychosomatic fake.

I held my phone like the weapon that it wasn't, prepared to bash someone over the head with it, and then—

A curly-headed halo illuminated by the refrigerator light. It was Ollie, standing in front of the food stocked by someone on the Murphy staff.

"Holt," he said.

"Moskowitz-Murphy."

We laughed. People had always joked that his hyphenated last name was a tongue twister—long and clunky, it excluded him from the standard male surname club, so many boys whose given names I couldn't recall. But everyone knew he was Ollie. When we'd been whatever we were, I was fixated on the symmetry of our first names: Callie, Ollie, two lines or people standing side by side.

"Why are you up?" he said, still holding the fridge door open like it was an entrance he could usher me inside.

"Couldn't sleep."

"No tea?"

"Still off the sauce."

"Does Winn appreciate it?"

"Whit."

He remembered the tea. Ollie once said that my Sleepytime habit reminded him of his uncle, the chamomile smell immediately invoking the hum of cable news washed down with Celestial Seasonings. "Dad breath," he called it, laughing with our legs poured around each other in his off-campus full bed, considered spacious at the time. He thought it was hilarious, but I stopped drinking the stuff, thinking that abandoning various preferences could make him love me.

"Midnight snack?" I said.

"Leftover lo mein. Two a.m. delicacy."

He let the door swing behind him and brought only one

fork to the banquette table. I wanted a bite—but more than the taste, I wanted him to want to share it.

"I thought you went home."

"Passed out on the couch," he said, glancing at his phone. "And then crawled into Mimi and Walter's bed."

"Home invader."

"Says the woman who squats here full-time."

"I'm a legitimate tenant, even if I don't pay rent."

"How's it been, playing house?"

"Fun. Weird. Both?"

"I don't know how you live up here. It's so *far*."

"From Williamsburg, Center of the Universe?"

"I told them I couldn't do it." He looked at his phone, smiling at a screen I couldn't see.

"They asked." It came out less like a question, more like a statement of resignation.

"Sure. Family."

It shouldn't have surprised me that the Murphys asked Ollie to live here first. But for some reason—self-protection, narcissism, an inflated sense of my position in their orbit—I imagined that I'd been the only choice. That Virginia had suggested it, telling her mom that she couldn't live with anyone except me. I wasn't family, but I was less inevitable. I was a decision. When I moved into the apartment, my mother had cautioned me that they would never treat me like real family. "The Murphys take care of themselves first," she said. "Just be careful not to get too close." I laughed and told her my life wasn't a season of *Succession*. While I couldn't say this out loud, Mimi had been pulling more parental weight than my actual mom, checking in on job updates, taking me out to lunch when Virg was living in L.A., inviting me out to Connecticut for a weekend to get out of the city. And, of course, offering me the rent-free room. Mimi turned my trust into a default setting.

Ollie slurped his lo mein while looking at his phone. A

noodle fell onto the screen, and he picked it up like nothing had happened, not self-deprecating it away like I would have.

"Do you still delete everything?" I said.

"Yep. No text left behind."

"No mess, no stress."

"Only noodles," he said, wetting his finger and wiping the lo mein residue from the screen.

"Noods."

"Send noods." He laughed. "That's good." I could tell he thought he'd come up with this association, even though I'd said it first and had taken it from a bunch of recycled memes. I wondered if his tendency to delete everything from his phone—texts, emails, calendar events, photos—was a deliberate lightening of his load like he'd always claimed, or a strategy to make all his impulses feel original.

I sipped a glass of water, fighting an urge to grab the fork from his hand and take a sloppy, full bite. The next night I'd go to bed in Miami, too lucid for my high blood alcohol content, thinking about everything I didn't say. It could fill a whole stomach.

whitty_ yas queens 👑

calliememaybe ily! Best weekend ever

officialgregwilliams 🔥

meet.virginia hi, I'd like to place an order for mozzarella sticks and an IV drip

6 April

olliemmphoto sand | bubbles #35mm

The apartment refrigerator was transparent.

You could see everything: the expiration date on the milk, dewy berries, dimpled egg cartons, precut melon, turkey wrapped in plastic, a full jug of no-pulp orange juice, nearly neon in its insistence. *Drink me. Eat me. We are Whole Foods' prodigal sons.* It was a little slutty. The glass fridge made our skin seem almost prudish, covering up so much bounty— organs gleaming like fruit.

I stood in front of it trying to decide what to make for a snack. I was meeting Whit for dinner in two hours, but I hadn't eaten anything all day. It had been a week since my encounter with Ollie, and I'd been falling back into old patterns ever since, monitoring my food intake like I hadn't been through years of therapy to rid myself of that default. I took out a carton of eggs, cracked one against the rim of a metal bowl, and cleaved the whole in half with a satisfying pull. Eggs were a rung of adulting closer to Easy-Bake Oven than open-plan chef's kitchen. But in the Park Avenue apartment, even a sad scrambled plate had an air of classy maturity.

I made a single egg. I hated that I still knew the caloric evaluations of so many foods and could guess someone's weight by a simple once-over. I bet Anika was 133 but rounded up to 135, while I was 150 but rounded down to 145. Virginia was in the high 120s, which, with her height, was a different species of body altogether. Her bones asserted themselves, let you know they were there.

Whit had some pudge on him, which I appreciated. I couldn't handle a man who cared about his weight as much as I did. Worse, a man who didn't need to care. A man who ate a ton but remained thin signified that my state was unfixable. I could stop obsessing, but I could not stop the way the calories clung.

I sat down on the couch and opened my email. One of my neighbors had written the apartment listserv about a health food delivery service for Gwyneth acolytes that cost more than a whole nest of yoni eggs. I went to the website and read copy that sounded like disordered eating purified into buzzwords: *cleanse, reset, shed.* At least my fucked-up relationship with food wasn't hidden underneath a haze of sans serif, muted earth tones, and bright pictures of gluten-free, dairy-free, taste-free breakfasts.

I had three emails from Composure's founder, Maxine. The annoyance in her messages—**plz, checking in, looping back**—might have been manufactured in my head. Even though I'd been in the position for only a few months, I could already anticipate her reactions. As communications manager, half my job was knowing Maxine and her story. The SparkNotes: MIT, worked at SpaceX, lost both her parents in a car crash. Researched cremation and found it environmentally dubious. Started talking to the inventors of the mushroom vest (too expensive) and the freeze-dry method (too *Austin Powers*) and discovered a gap in the market. Enter: body composting.

I was pulling late nights and early mornings trying to prove myself in the new role. Whit and I fell into a relationship rhythm: heads down all day, meet for dinner at night a few times a week, wake up with morning sex, repeat. We were successfully separate yet together, a duality that felt grown-up. Monotonous but also realistic and sustainable.

Mario's at 8? he texted. **Pasta la vista!**

On the feed, @mimimurph had posted a picture of her garden in Watch Hill. **Everything's coming up hydrangeas!** A jewelry brand shilled Lucite hoop earrings, an acquaintance from college got engaged at the top of a mountain, a loungewear company pushed $175 silk pajamas. My former boss was at the Union Square farmers market getting tomatoes and a bouquet of cilantro with some **cheese plz** thrown in. Bex had put a *New Yorker* cartoon on her stories, something she'd started doing at least once a week because an employee leadership survey revealed that 71 percent of the We-men staff thought she was harsh and unapproachable.

Then a new picture from @olliemmphoto popped up.

The boredom that compels me to scroll is usually shadowed by a more sinister impulse. I'm looking for an image that will upset me enough to stop, a picture that pulls tight on a hard, internal knot and initiates a shuddering shutdown, a logging off, an attempt to pacify the reaction with a menu of real or imagined remedies (meditation, food, yoga, manifesting, food, crystals, detox, more food).

Ollie's pictures could do this to me—an impressive feat, since his professional account mostly featured inanimate objects. He didn't have a personal feed. The perpetual scroll didn't mesh with his digitally light philosophy, his idea that memories were a burden. He was bad with names but good on his feet; inept at recall but adept at creation; clever at the expense of thoughtfulness.

He'd location tagged the picture with Bondi Beach, where he'd gone on assignment for a hotel chain years ago. The shot: two size 0 women in striped bikinis with their legs propped up in the sand, sharing a bottle of champagne and a pizza. His captions were always a simple inventory of nouns, because he was too sophisticated for a wit-measuring contest. This one read **sand | bubbles**. This sparseness was like his long silences, the way he stayed quiet in large groups and then interjected with a single, cutting line—a tendency that, on him, read as depth instead of reticence.

The women he'd photographed were so tiny they looked like they could be folded, beach chairs stacked on top of the beach chairs they drank champagne from, probably before fucking him together in a hotel room with ocean views. I noticed, with a dark sense of glee, that the one with her leg in the air had ugly feet. Thank God. There was justice in those gnarly toes.

But the curve of those shoulders, the pinch of the waists, the chests that had no time for gravity. No matter how many meals I skipped or cayenne drinks I inhaled, this was genetic perfection I couldn't attain.

Before I knew what I was doing, my hands were inside the fridge. I rolled up sheets of turkey and stuffed them into my mouth, layer upon layer like I was packing a valuable to ensure it wouldn't break. I took out a pint of ice cream and drizzled it with chocolate sauce. Chased it with five Oreos, plus an entire sleeve of saltines with peanut butter. A handful of almonds—healthy, to counteract the damage. Water, water, water, to dilute it all inside me, and then—

The release.

My fingers pushed to undo the ingestion, a hasty rewind, an unfurling that almost felt like a cleansing, the acidic burn in my throat and churning emptiness in my stomach disguising the knowledge that I couldn't have possibly excised it all. Then the shame, hot like the tears in the corners of my eyes, one of which was still marked by the faint red trail of a vessel I'd popped doing this same thing in college.

The term *muscle memory* usually refers to positive or formative habits, like riding a bike or working out. But the bad habits were coded, too. I came back to this place with a swiftness that made me want to scrub my insides free from a force more permanent than food.

Swamped, I texted Whit. **Can we rain check?**

Virginia texted that she was out helping Ollie with a man-on-the-street photo series that day.

Doesn't he have an assistant for that? I'd responded.

Not anymore, she said. **Nat Geo and Conde didn't renew his contracts. Budget cuts, etc. Media's a bitch.**

Ollie wouldn't struggle financially—the Murphy fortune would always cushion his professional blows—but the hit to his ego would be sizable. I'd seen his lip curl with suppressed pride when asked what he did. Being "a *National Geographic* photographer" sounded sexy; being "a photographer" sounded unemployed.

That sucks, I responded to Virginia's text, secretly pleased that a Murphy was having trouble making it.

meet.virginia dope pic

anikaaa love this, my love 🐶💕

jess_fitzsimmons sweeeeet 🙌

officialtaylorweill take me back!

will_mcdunn ma dude

bexjones the boy's got skillz 🔥

graymurphy15 these gals are def drinking on empty stomachs

7 May

Mimi and Virginia were riffling through a box of pictures.

"I completely forgot about this treasure trove," Mimi said.

Virginia had found a box of old photographs in a drawer while "looking for the remote." Snooping was apparently irresistible even when—perhaps especially when—the victims were your own family. Mimi was in the city for a "doctor's appointment," which she'd then admitted was dermatology and Virginia had guessed was Botox. Gray was with her, getting a facial, aka a Botox consultation. For $500, one could get embalmed while still alive.

"Are you seeing Anika?" Virginia asked.

"Yep," Gray said, pulling at the split ends of her blond ponytail. "She's giving us a free consult."

Gray looked thinner than I'd ever seen her. "Shedding for the wedding," a phrase that made me think of sunburned skin peeling. Gray couldn't eat Nutella-smeared bagels for breakfast and spaghetti carbonara for dinner while maintaining a stick figure like Virginia, so she ran and juiced herself into the body her sister was born into. Gray would be the type of bride who drove herself crazy in post-wedding years with how little her reflection matched the person trapped in picture frames all over Idyll Wind and squares on her feed.

"God, look at my *skin*," Mimi said, holding up a picture of herself wearing a green dress at a wedding. "I thought I was old. I was a spring fucking chicken! Excuse my French."

"Excused," Virginia said, laughing.

"Let me see that." Gray took the picture, and as she squinted, I mapped her skin for folds and creases, knowing they were about to get made into tight corners like a bed that would remain undisturbed for months. "Mom, you were gorgeous. How old were you?"

"This wedding was the month after Janet's thirty-fifth and I'm a year younger than her, so . . . thirty-four."

"And you had both of us already?" Gray asked. She looked concerned.

"It's amazing I ever managed to look put together with the two of you running around."

"So how old were we?"

"Why do you care so much?" Virginia asked.

"Eight and six," Mimi said, eyes upward toward the pendant light in the hallway and the edge where the wallpaper frayed slightly at the seam. "No, seven and five."

"I have to get going," Gray declared.

"I'm driving us," Mimi said.

"I mean, you'd already had Virginia at my age."

There wasn't a discernible line on her face, not a crinkle of jest, of *just kidding, I was being psycho and playing the type A part you've always ascribed to me.*

"Call the biological clock police," Virginia said. "We have an emergency at 1100 Park Avenue."

"Haven't things changed a bit?" I ventured.

"Maybe culturally, yeah," Gray said. "But fertility-wise, no."

My referee alarm started going off. Between Virginia and Gray, I was often a translator: softening Virginia's digs and decoding Gray's passive aggression to try to expose the anxious heart running underneath. Or I just played the common denominator, bringing up a related point we could all agree on to divert the conversation.

"It sucks that our most fertile years are when we're like nineteen," I offered.

"Well, thank god you're about to get married," Virginia said, turning to Gray. "You can start barreling toward the next major life event so you don't fall behind your mother or your peers, because god forbid you had time to just get to know yourself."

"Virgie," Mimi chided, bringing out a childhood nickname she used only when she was trying to appease. "That's not very nice."

"I think Virg means that, well, *we* aren't married or engaged," I hastened to say. "So it's kind of hard to hear Gray say she's falling behind."

"It's not hard," Virginia said. "It's ridiculous."

"Not my fault you won't date anyone," Gray shot back. "Tommy's tried to set you up with his friends and you refused."

"No offense to Tommy, but 'New Jersey lax bro in private wealth management' wasn't the sale of the century."

"I know you don't like him," Gray said. "Tommy. My therapist says this could be jealousy manifesting, but I told her she definitely didn't know you if she thought you'd ever be jealous of me."

"Girls, girls. If anyone is jealous, it's me! Look at your skin! Gray, we're going to be late if we don't leave now."

Mimi was the most superficial kind of peacemaker; she steered away from discord with breezy distractions instead of unearthing the root of the issue. Her strategy was helpful in the short term but useless in the long term.

"You two are perfect together, G," Virginia allowed in a rare moment of surrender. She knew better than to strike at Gray's insecurity over Tommy. "His friends just sounded lame."

"I'm going to take a few of these pictures with me," Mimi said. Turning to Gray as they walked out of the apartment, she added, "I want to put up a *hashtag tbt*."

A series of old pictures that Mimi left with us:

- Me, Virginia, and Gray in a tent on the beach in Watch Hill. We'd spent the night at the water's edge as part of an end-of-summer camp excursion. The stars like sand scattered on a dark surface, the sleeping bags cold in the midnight wind. Gray had Mimi pick her up in the middle of the night, claiming she couldn't sleep unless she had a specific silk pillowcase. She was ten years old.

- Teen Ollie and Virginia eating Chipwiches on pool chairs. Ollie's hair to his shoulders, the smile I didn't yet love wider than it had ever stretched for me. A trail of ice cream bright white against Virginia's tanned, bony knee.

- My mother smiling in a shapeless black shirt dress, Mimi's finger pointing toward the unexciting clothing and the exciting news it contained. I'd never seen an image from this time, the months when my mom thought I was going to have a sibling. She'd miscarried late, at five months. I was only two then, too young to remember the devastation and shame. Of course it wasn't her fault, she'd reflexively told me later. This happened to so many women. Still, she blamed herself at the time—was it that one glass of wine, that sleepless night, cosmic retribution for screaming at me when she was having a bad day?

She'd opened up to me about it once, but otherwise my baby brother was another unspeakable—like my dad, a topic too raw for her to fully broach. Mimi had gotten pregnant a few weeks before my mother's miscarriage, and Gray was born while my mom struggled through failed rounds of IVF.

Mimi's feed hours later: a throwback of my parents and the Murphys in the Idyll Wind pool. The shallow end, elbows propped up on the concrete, each reading a thick book except for Walter, who holds up a huge, unfolded page of *The Wall Street Journal*. I couldn't make out the book choices, but my dad's was probably fiction—one of his beloved Toni Morrisons, Paul Austers, Zadie Smiths, or Anne Carsons. In the picture, the four of them look peaceful, at equilibrium. Together while swimming through four separate worlds in their hands.

That night, I woke up sweating at three thirty a.m. The underarms of my old Brown T-shirt were fecund with heat. Manhattan was edging into summer, but this wasn't just seasonal. I sweated under duvets but loved their weighted assurance, the way they pressed sleep into me. Familiar rituals that felt good could quickly turn suffocating in the small, dark hours when even the city quieted to a hum.

Down the hallway—pulled by an automated force or thirst—my footsteps creaked on the floorboards as I clocked the shiny frames of Ollie's photographs, the images just barely visible in the dark. I looked at the picture of market stalls in Beijing and my own face stared back, thin lips eclipsing a container of dead fish against a smog-filled sky.

After gulping ice-cold water, I felt too awake for the hour. Virginia would be deep in her REM cycle; I had an opening for Project Creep. I hadn't tackled Mimi and Walter's room yet. I approached on my toes and opened the door to a space five times the size of my crib.

The four-poster king bed sat undisturbed. The duvet had only slight ripples and tugs, like tiny rocks had been thrown into a still lake. I could see the room through open curtains, the city's pulsing light pouring its dregs through the window.

First, the closet. Mimi's wardrobe was vast, but she kept most of her stuff in Connecticut and Watch Hill, so I was curious to see what she deemed practical enough (for walking) or glamorous enough (for walking into charity galas) to store here. PETA would have a field day. Five furs and a row of silk gowns hung lazily on the rack immediately visible in the walk-in closet. I imagined her petting them, nicknaming each fur like a wildly expensive pet. A sapphire gown grazed the top of a cardboard box. I pulled it out from under the dresses.

I took out folders one by one: tax forms, real estate documents, Virginia's and Gray's first and second grade finger paintings. Ticket stubs, television instruction manuals, printed restaurant menus. All junk, all old, all hoarded. Mimi couldn't bear throwing anything away because "you never know."

Then, at the back of the box, a manila folder of printer pages. Most of the folders contained a skyline of paper heights, standard size followed by an envelope, a loose picture, a crusty legal pad. This one was neater, with *T.H.* written in a tiny scrawl on the front.

I slid the pages out and was too shocked to scream.

"OFF-SEASON"
   by Teddy Holt

My dad's missing novel.

It took me a beat to realize I wasn't hallucinating—this was really it, the manuscript that had haunted me for a decade.

I started reading. The book took place in the late 1800s in Watch Hill and New York. It borrowed from Edith Wharton's settings and themes: upper-crust society, repression, the suffocation and expectation of marriage. Some of the prose was overly flowery and inconsistent, like he'd performed a botched surgery to meld *The Age of Innocence* with twenty-first-century sensibilities. But I was instantly drawn to the main character, Sterling Barnett, and his caustic observations.

I read the first few pages, exhilarated by my discovery. I briefly wondered why it had been hiding in this box for so long, but knew there must be a simple explanation. Walter and Mimi sometimes read my dad's work for feedback and, in Walter's case, grammar policing. He was a stickler for the correct use of a semicolon. I could ask them, but then I'd have to admit I'd been snooping in their closet. I slid the manuscript under my arm, half expecting the pages to curl into themselves and sleep. It felt that alive to me.

graymurphy15 babies!

nancywallace12 hi mimi—been too long. How are the kids? Older than you are here by now, I bet! Louisa is at Duke med school and Connor works at Morgan Stanley. Oh how time flies!

meet.virginia nerds 🤓

bexjones perfect tbt. A+ 🙌

8 May

Camera Roll
Lines of text on a page

We headed to the Murphys' house in Watch Hill for Memorial Day. Our friend Leila, whose family had a house down the street, was getting married. I was excited that Leila had given me a plus-one, until I realized it likely meant she'd given Ollie one, too, and I'd have to see him and Anika drunk in love on the dance floor.

Whit and I arrived before sunset Friday night and drove up to the house in all its summer glory. Idyll Wind, set at the end of Larkin Road, was a manicured green slope on top of a cliff. It was hemmed in by the Flying Horse Carousel, a landmark merry-go-round where kids on metal ponies reached out to try to grab the elusive brass ring, and Holiday House, Taylor Swift's mansion/Fourth of July social media set and the unintentional nucleus of town. Tourists posed in front of the PRIVATE PROPERTY and I KNEW YOU WERE TROUBLE WHEN YOU WALKED IN signs, and Mimi loved every second of it. "Taylor's made us fame-adjacent," she'd say, shooing off outcries of overcrowding and congested foot traffic. The "porte cochere" overhang opened into a stone courtyard crisscrossed with planted grass. The shingle-style house was painted white, buffered by hydrangeas, and separated from the water by a rolling lawn with Adirondack chairs and a croquet set.

"Holy shit," Whit said over the sound of gravel crunching under our wheels. "I knew they were rich, but this is . . . I don't know, Rockefeller vibes."

"It's tasteful, though," I said, parroting the line I'd heard the Murphys' friends whisper at countless summer barbecues. I had an unexpected swell of ownership over the place, wanting Whit to love the house, too, and treat it as an oasis instead of a testament to their wealth. The sentimental pang of bringing him home was shadowed by the bitter truth: this wasn't my home. Ginger House, only a few minutes down the street, had been knocked down and replaced by a modern eyesore.

"It's a dream," Whit said.

Ollie's car, the Jeep Wrangler he'd had since college, was already in the driveway. This was, by design, a long weekend, but I had a feeling I was in for three days that felt like thirty.

Mimi rushed to the door in her bathrobe.

"Welcome, welcome!" She patted Whit's shoulders with excited ease, like he was a pillow she was fluffing. "Your drive was okay? How do you two look gorgeous after hours in the car? My ride here was god-awful, traffic all the way up and an accident near Exit 54. We're heating up lasagnas tonight. Bon appétit."

"Your home is so beautiful," Whit said.

"Thank you, isn't that sweet. Well, we just love it here." Mimi knew how to take a compliment, especially one she'd heard hundreds of times. Something in her frenzied, lovable presence made me want to tell her about discovering my dad's manuscript—I longed to hear her thoughts and maybe read it together like a book club—but a stronger instinct told me to guard the discovery. Not only would it indict me in snooping through their closet, but it was also unfinished business between me and my dad alone.

We set down our bags and walked through the high-ceilinged entryway, which was flanked by two large-scale beach paintings from local artists and a table with a leather-bound guest book and candy jar. The pile of mini Snickers, Peppermint Patties, Milky Ways, and Jolly Ranchers made my stomach flip, remembering those college summers when I'd crept downstairs and binged, throwing up sugary sewage in the guest bathroom.

Ollie was sitting shirtless at the kitchen table. Of course he was shirtless at the kitchen table. Anika had on jeans and a white top, gauzy and chic, and a tiny human perched on her lap. Her daughter.

"Noorie, say hi to Callie and Whit," she directed.

"Hi, CALIFORNIA," Noorie screamed.

"She's learning the US states in preschool," Anika explained.

Virginia walked into the room wearing a sweat suit. "Pretty sure I was learning animal sounds at her age. Impressive."

"A convincing *moo* is tough," Whit offered. Mimi and I laughed.

"Isn't she just the cutest little muffin," Mimi cooed. "She reminds me of Cal at that age. Precocious *af,* as the kids would say."

"Mom, do not say that," Virginia said, pouring herself a glass of rosé.

Gray stuck out her almost-empty glass for Virginia to top off. "She used to think it stood for *and fabulous.*"

"Muffin!" Noorie shouted. "Yum muffin."

"How old is she?" I asked.

"How old are you?" Anika repeated my question to the muffin enthusiast, whose face had since twisted from glee into a verge-of-tears grimace.

Instead of responding, she screamed: an unexplained, spontaneous combustion. I knew this was typical toddler behavior, but it was still jarring to see it play out in person. I didn't have any friends with kids yet. Ollie picked her up and bounced on his heels as she grabbed at his chest.

"Pec!" she wailed through tears. "Breast!"

"She's obsessed with the human body," Anika said. "Three and a half and can't get enough of that coloring book." She pointed toward a bright yellow rectangle on the counter. The book, which was bigger than a placemat, featured a skeleton layered with muscles and organs like an anatomical tiramisu. The cover sacrificed visual accuracy for kiddie aesthetics—the exaggerated piling of the muscles, a clown-red heart, and a liver shaped like a cartoon lima bean—but it was arresting, especially since I thought kids read only about magical goats and goodnight moons.

"Like you," Ollie remarked, looking at me for the first time since I arrived. "A little science nerd."

"Women in STEM," Gray said. "The future is female, baby. You're going to make a lot of money someday, aren't you?"

Ollie's eyes were still on me. Anika, the unsolicited arbiter of all things fair and good, gave Gray a withering look. "We don't really like to talk about—"

"She was kidding, love," Ollie said. He pulled his gaze away from mine and rubbed Anika's back, his hand dancing on her spine. I wanted to take each lean, elegant finger and put it inside me, twist them around my mucosal tissue and clench hard enough to mark his pruned knuckle skin.

"What's it like?" Gray asked. "Being a mom."

"Because you want to get knocked up as soon as you burn your wedding planning bible?" Virginia mocked. "You all should see this thing. It's a fucking brick."

"The biggest responsibility of my life," Anika replied. "A different level of love. Terrifying. All the things you hear, they're true, but you can't internalize them until it's yours, you know?"

"My coworker says the same thing," Gray said. "That your entire world shifts under the weight of this new person."

"The weight is right," Mimi quipped. "Virg was ten and a half pounds with a full head of hair, and yes, I deserve another glass of chardonnay."

"It's a gift," Anika said, "being a mom."

"With no return policy," Virginia retorted.

Mimi was placing another bottle of white in the wine fridge while cutting herself a slice of Brie, expert-level WASP maneuvering. "You'll feel differently someday," she said knowingly.

"Yeah, not going to happen."

"You will find someone!" Gray promised. "If you're open to it at *all*. Two dates a month for over a year on the godforsaken apps, and here I am."

"Where is the T-Man, by the way?" Whit asked.

Virginia ignored Whit and laughed at her sister in a challenging bark—a laugh of derision, not of joy. "Not the issue."

"It's fine not to focus on dating," Anika said. "It all happens when you least expect it."

Anika's platitudes about motherhood and relationships gave me more evidence to mount against her in an internal trial that would convict her as basic. I'd bring these scraps to Virginia so we could deliberate later, though mentioning Ollie was a delicate dance. I couldn't let on that I cared.

"How did Leila and Graham meet again?" I asked, trying to reroute the conversation before Virginia blew up at her family and made dinner awkward.

"'At a bar,'" Gray said in air quotes. "Code for Hinge, then a first date at a bar."

Virginia said she didn't want kids and everyone else said she would change her mind. In Murphy world, it was filed under "unspeakable until further notice," and we circled the topic semi-frequently without diving in. Mimi and Gray willfully ignored Virginia's claims, saying she just hadn't met the right person yet. Hadn't grown up. Hadn't experienced the heady drug of being called "Mommy."

Though her art stayed within the bounds of a genre, Virg liked painting outside the lines in her personal life. She didn't want what other people wanted—typical for her downtown art scene, atypical for her traditional upbringing. It was hard to tell whether this child-free plan was spurred by a desire to rile up her family or a real, bone-deep conviction. I leaned toward the latter. Virginia was so self-contained, it was tough to imagine her fully sharing herself with anyone, let alone a little life that required sustaining. She relished her freedom. It wasn't selfishness; it was self-awareness.

In bed after our lasagna dinner, I read my dad's novel while Whit snored. I wanted to tell him about the book, but our relationship was still in a tender, new space; announcing my dead dad's presence in bed seemed ill-advised. My book light made the turning pages cast shadows, dark wedges marking my progress.

Sterling Barnett arrived at the Cahills' home in Watch Hill at five after noon. Dorothea was still in Manhattan—she insisted on seeing her hairdresser before

the trip—and would meet him there early the next day.
The Cahills should be settled in by now, their trunks
unpacked and hats removed to reveal pale faces primed
for summer to change their color like leaves.

The Cahill home, where Sterling and Dorothea would
stay for the weekend, was the most magnificent in Watch
Hill. Edgecliff, set at the end of Larkin Road, boasted
sweeping views of the Atlantic. The shingled exterior
appeared intentionally weathered, a badge of honor
like money worn through generations. A porte cochere
covered in vines housed Fred Cahill's Ford Studebaker,
crouched on the concrete. A guest cottage, which looked
as if a piece of the main house had broken off like an
island, rose against the horizon in the distance. The
driveway opened into a pristine courtyard of grassy
diamonds and Ionic columns that held up the shingled
home, built under Fred's scrupulous oversight. As the
young, freshly minted CEO of his family shipping
empire, with a vast inherited fortune underpinning his
rise, Fred's success was born into him, as undeniable a
trait as eye color or height.

Sterling approached the entrance with trepidation. He
and Dorothea were close with Fred and Amelia, about
as close as you could be to people whose blood did not
mingle with your own. Yet, the Cahills' societal standing
and vast wealth gave him pause when presented in such
a flagrant manner as the Watch Hill house. It was a
fortress of accomplishment that prevented anyone from
achieving assimilation.

The house was quiet inside. A gold mirror greeted him
on his right, bookended by two glass sconces, punctuated
with a table that held a thick leather guest book. A
crystal chandelier hung in the middle of the entryway,
throwing glittering handfuls of light onto the wallpaper.

A voice rung out from the kitchen. "Dorothea? Welcome!"

Amelia Cahill rounded the corner of the sitting room and entered the space Sterling occupied. Her cheeks were flushed, and she wore a pair of loose-fitting pants and a turtleneck. Her hands were covered in dirt.

"Oh, Sterling. Heavens, I look a fright! I didn't know you were arriving early, too. I would've cleaned up."

"Nonsense."

He'd only ever seen Amelia with her face made up, wearing dresses, corsets, and the other fineries that turn women into presents. This felt as intimate as seeing her without clothes, and he blushed at the intrusion.

I put down the pages once my eyes started to involuntarily flicker. I hadn't read Edith Wharton or Henry James since high school, but my dad had clearly borrowed heavily from the formality and pomp of those styles. It was more obvious, though, that he'd borrowed from Idyll Wind. The house he described was unquestionably the Murphys', down to the porte cochere and guest book in the entryway. I took a picture of the page so I could compare notes the next day, hold up the house in his head to the floors under my feet.

9 The next morning

calliememaybe dark and stormy in cups only
🍹 #athousandmiles

Saturday cracked over Idyll Wind in a yolky spread, illuminating the grass, ocean foam, and seaweed-slick rocks. The reward of watching the sunrise almost made up for poor sleep. My multiple wake-ups hadn't managed to stir Whit, aside from a zombie pet he gave my tangled hair after I turned into his chest.

The window seat was the best viewing spot. I wrapped myself in a waffle robe with the house name embroidered in delicate script as if I were a guest at a five-star hotel and leaned back into the powder-blue pillows—cold after pressing up against glass all night. The roof sloped toward the sea, and the shingles—what did my dad write?—looked "intentionally weathered." Like old money, that unattainable comfort that didn't need polishing.

On the stone-lined path that cut from the back lawn to the beach, a human head bobbed into view like a body rising to the surface of water. Wet, matted hair. Male. Ollie. He'd gone for a morning swim, his remedy for a sleepless night. We had our sporadic insomnia in common, but his coping mechanism was a cold cleanse, while mine was a hot phone in my palm.

He sat down on a rock. Trying to make sense of his

movements was like attempting to track an exotic animal, because he didn't gravitate toward comfort. His tendency to sit when I would've moved and move when I would've sat both thrilled and confounded me. He'd lived in four different cities, while I'd remained in New York; he luxuriated in a wet bathing suit on a cold morning, while I watched him in my cozy robe on a plush window seat.

"Morning, babe," Whit slurred, half asleep.

"Come here." I patted a space for him, and he ambled toward me.

A swell in his boxer shorts, a draft from the window. My hands on his chest, touching the crop of hair. Ollie didn't grow chest hair, his frame too thin and lanky to sprout anything worth stroking. I sat in Whit's lap, wrapped my legs around him, and pushed his back up against the window: a perfect position to watch Ollie watch the water.

I slid myself onto Whit and let him fill me. He drew circles on my nipples, pulling them lightly and licking the tender skin, sending a wave down my torso and between my legs. He thrust and moved his hand lower, warmer, yes, as I watched Ollie get up from the rock and turn toward the house. Gaze up to the salt-streaked shingles and—

His eyes clipped on me.

I couldn't make out his blue irises from above, but I saw them anyways, remembered visions filling his faraway face. Whit's hands were clutching my sides, and I worried that Ollie would see fat poking between fingers, the untamed spill of me against the window like a body of water threatening to flood. I moved Whit's hands to my shoulders and rode him with both palms pressed against the glass. A rising current, eyes still latched on Ollie, who raised his eyebrows once before walking back into the house. I crested over thinking of his tongue; when I peeled off Whit, my clit beat like an external heart.

.

Noon at the pool: Gray and Virginia were playing backgammon while Whit read a biography of Abraham Lincoln, because straight men lived in a constant state of preparation for a trivia night focused on dead presidents. One had to remain vigilant.

I went to use the bathroom in the guest cottage because it was closer to the pool and absent from rules about hosing off like the main house. It did look like an island that had broken off from the main house, as my dad had written. The Murphys called it "the Eye," as in "the eye of the storm," and Mimi had outfitted the place with brightly colored evil eye pendants. My dad used to write in this space because he craved privacy and also because, I suspected, the Murphys supported his creative dreams more than my mother did. My mom had always described my dad's writing as a "hobby," a word that conjured children with Play-Doh and senior citizens with pottery wheels. It was a point of contention between my parents that my dad was less concerned with making mortgage payments than he was with the character arc of a horny British monarch. "You don't support me," I heard him say during one of those Rhode Island drives. "No—" my mom nearly screamed, then paused for an unnatural stretch. "You don't support us." She'd gone on to talk about how her teaching salary alone couldn't keep them afloat if he didn't pick up more work on the new builds and renovations rising up like dinosaur skeletons along the Watch Hill coast. He'd argued that money wasn't everything; my mom resented him for making her out to be some aspirational social climber. She didn't want the sailing lessons and golf memberships, she said. She wanted the roof over our goddamn heads.

I remembered the intrigue the guest cottage once held

for me—every unopened drawer contained the possibility of finding my dad's missing novel. Now that I'd found it, the Eye had lost its allure, but this weekend, its guests piqued my interest instead. Anika, Ollie, and Noorie were staying in the cottage but currently on a Watch Hill tour with Mimi. A dresser in the entry hallway was piled with a stack of Noorie's coloring books. The body books were on top: *My First Anatomy Book* and *Human Anatomy for Kids*. She'd colored outside the lines with abandon, bleeding the lungs into the trachea into the larynx. Yellow crayon slashes marked a red blood cell like haphazardly applied caution tape. Underneath her scribbles, the text was simple: "What is blood? Mostly water and cells. It travels around and around your body in tubes large and small. It delivers nutrients to your cells and picks up cell waste." A diagram of the chest instructed kids on how breathing works: ribs move up and out, chest and lungs get larger, diaphragm moves down and flattens. Her hot-pink crayon had darted across the page like it was in a hurry. On a page dedicated to digestion, Noorie had diligently filled in the small intestine, red as meat. Her mother's profession concerned the skin, that sensitive wrapping, but here was a child curious about the mess it covered.

Midnight at the wedding reception: Virginia and I stood outside the tent on Leila's family's lawn, bored of speeches that mentioned the groom's alma mater (the one that rhymes with *kale*) and conversations about apartment locations and job titles that felt like bad first dates with people we already knew.

So bored that we were about to take mushrooms.

The thing I know now about mushrooms, almost a year after that night, is that they warp the external but reveal the internal. You interpret what you're seeing as a hidden reality, like a power grid running underneath a city. But really, they tell you nothing about the world: only truths about the buried landscape inside your own head.

We ate them as chocolates. Virginia went first. She'd bought them from an artist friend and claimed that they were different and better than what we'd done in Mexico years ago with a bunch of frat boys. This meant that she'd done them without me and without telling me, and I tried not to dwell on that point. After so much time orbiting the exact same universe, the Venn diagram of our friendship had started getting wider in its outer circles, growing hips.

We both ate our pre-portioned shroom halves. Virginia then held up another half and looked at me. "You want?"

"I think I'm going to stick with the proper dosage."

"You might not feel anything at all." Virginia swallowed the second half. When she turned to walk back into the tent from our place in the shadows outside, an urge came over me. The urge to match her.

"Give me the chocolates." I ate another half and walked in with her, waiting for the moment the tent would tilt. I looked at the waterfront house, a clapboard structure with evergreen shingles. Even at night, I could see the salt seeping into the facade like sweat dried on skin. In a half hour, would the shrooms prompt a different vision—a tiered cake, a crouching monster?

Virginia went to use the restroom, and I paced the periphery of the tent, looking for people I should say hi to before I started tripping.

On Adirondack chairs outside, I spotted Ollie and Anika. I'd managed to mostly avoid them all night, rattled by our eye contact that morning and semi-disturbed by my refusal to break it—was I trying to taunt him, make him jealous, fuck him through transitive property? Out in the harbor, a boat cut through the water, getting briefly swallowed by Ollie's and Anika's sitting forms until it emerged whole on the other side of them. It was headed toward a rock at the edge of the view. If Ollie got up from the chair before the boat passed out of sight, I would talk to him tonight. I'd tell him that he kept showing up in my head. That the whole time we'd been watching the Korean movie, I'd been thinking about our first time in the photo lab. That I missed the way he'd tugged at the belt loop of my jeans, the texture of his eyebrows under my thumb, the sparse mini fridge in his off-campus room that he'd called his top-shelf bar. I would break up with Whit and finally tell Ollie how I felt, because our initial ending was just an error in the code, a random mutation rather than a genetic fate.

He uncrossed his legs. I started assembling the order of words, how I'd start: *Listen, I still think about you.* No. *Do you ever wonder . . . ?* No. He crossed his legs again. Was he getting up or just shifting his weight? This distinction mattered; my self-imposed test had taken on a finality, as if my mind's randomly administered games had tapped into an undercurrent of destiny. The boat looked like it had stopped right before the place where it would be subsumed by the rock and the distance.

Then it started moving again, passing behind the rock. It happened slowly then all at once, like a sun falling into the horizon. Ollie sat in the chair, oblivious to the decision his immobility had made. I thought of what he'd said to me during one of our first discussions about our dead parents: "Sometimes I want to feel it all at once. Horrible and incredible at the same time." I'd responded with a line like "Isn't that what drugs are for?" and he'd laughed, the sound I craved. I realized then that I would do anything for that laugh. I still couldn't feel anything from the mushrooms—horrible or incredible or a combination—and I waited for the second they would hit, the moment I'd travel without moving.

.

Virginia and I danced to the band's version of "Mr. Bright-side," coming out of our cages and doing just fine. She swayed with her eyes closed, waving her arms in the air. Technically, we were both bad dancers, but her movements had enough enthusiasm and abandon to convince people that she was magic on the floor.

"I don't feel anything yet," I said so that only she could hear, even though I was screaming.

"Patience, Cal!" She shook her hair in front of her face. She was talking about our specific drug trip, but I realized that Virginia had a general patience. She trusted that things would work out—whether with an emerging picture on her easel or a life she hadn't planned beyond her most recent bout of inspiration. Ollie lived this way, too. Maybe this was the nicest result of their kind of wealth: the security to sink into the present.

She grabbed my hand and twirled, opening up her eager eyes at the Killers' instructions. We danced like this together to the next two songs, letting the party fade into the background. The colored lights behind the bandstand started bleeding into one another. She looked up at the tent with childlike wonder and anticipation, like she used to react to a big wave at the beach. I was hit with an appreciation for the length of our friendship, the externalized reminder of the stages of our lives. When I looked at Virginia, I saw a twenty-nine-year-old, but I could also see her at five, ten, eighteen, the past selves she'd shed. This was probably a diluted version of what it felt like to have a child. An old guilt crept up in me, the secret I'd kept from her about my history with Ollie. The omission became bigger and stranger the longer it went on, but Ollie had stood his ground over the years, claiming that it would complicate the dynamics between us all.

"Can you believe that no one else knows?" Virginia shouted.

"What?" Could she read my mind?

"How good this feels right now."

The poles of the tent started moving slightly and a lightness fizzed in me. *"Do you remember . . . the twenty-seventh night of May?"* the singer belted, changing the lyrics to match the date.

Whit came up from behind and squeezed my shoulders. I looked at Virginia and smiled, trying to make sure she knew this night was still ours.

"Never was a cloudy day!" Whit screamed. He danced with alternating elbow pulses at his hips, as if he were running a towel along his lower back. His cuff links, monogrammed with his initials, caught the blue light from the stage, and his drunken giddiness didn't match our shape-shifting trip. Virginia stared at him, probably agreeing that his vibe was off. She walked away, saying she'd be right back, and I worried she was lying.

Ollie and Anika had moved from the Adirondack chairs to sit at an abandoned table near the dance floor. Their foreheads almost touched. She talked while Ollie listened, and the dynamic seemed at odds with the person I knew. I had been Ollie's audience, tracking and classifying his words to dissect later. Anika must be one of those people who liked to fill silence, who preferred her own voice to a wordless buzz.

Whit twirled me. The twenty-seventh night of May faded into summer as the singer told us about a woman with her hair combed back and her sunglasses on, baby. Ollie and Anika had moved even closer, her knee slipped into the open V of his legs. His hands ran up and down her arms, over and over, like his skin had fused with hers and he was warming himself up on a cold day. He touched a necklace on her chest, fingered its small gold charms.

Her neck lit up from the inside.

I don't mean this metaphorically—I could see through her skin, past her dermis, and into the trapezius muscle snaking into her neck. My eyes had become an unwilling X-ray machine. The mushrooms had hit in a way I'd never experienced them before. Anika's trachea pulsed red, and Ollie's brain wavered into view. I could see it curled up inside his skull, as small and defenseless as a naked baby animal.

"Are you okay?" Whit asked. "Want some coffee?"

"Just tired," I managed.

Whit's lungs were yellow. It seemed odd that they weren't pink, though it was stranger that I could see them at all. They filled with air in desperate bursts.

"I'm going to grab us some caffeine," he said. "You look like you're going to pass out."

I sat down at an empty table and looked out at the dance floor, which had turned into an anatomical map. Different body parts lit up inside people, a below-skin light show. I had to find Virginia and tell her what I was seeing. I walked through a clump of lungs, hearts, livers, and latissimus dorsi, all glowing red, blue, and green, looking for her long hair and lavender dress.

I found her knuckle bone first, the interphalangeal joint. It glowed neon orange, hooked in the hair of a woman I'd seen her talking to earlier at the bar. They were kissing in the dark at one of the cocktail hour high-tops outside the tent. The stranger's pubis bone stood out under her dress, flashing lime green. Was I imagining it? Virginia had always been into men. Seeing under someone's skin should feel more intimate than catching two people pawing at each other's outer layers. But watching Virginia with this woman, anatomy aside, was too much for my eyes to handle. I wondered if the mushrooms had manufactured the vision, if I was producing bodies instead of just seeing through them.

I walked away, hoping they didn't see me staring. I thought of the bodies inside the Composure vessels, their chalky rigidity, the opposite of this flowing current inside the tent. I danced alone like the manifestation of that Robyn song, watching organs light up all around me. I imagined kissing someone with their skin removed, touching the pulpy forms underneath. What if we all walked around with our insides showing? *She has a really sexy liver,* someone would say. *A toned uterus.* Or maybe it would mean that we were all just templates, our tissue collections indistinguishable.

An hour later, the body parts had faded. A lingering lung here, half a heart there, but their brilliance had been turned down, the work of some invisible dimmer. Ollie was leaning against the coffee stand. His eyebrow bone, the superciliary arch, still glowed red, lighting fire to thick, uneven lines of hair. I remembered what Bex had said to me after she met her fiancé, Greg: "Have you ever loved someone so much that you want to zip yourself inside them?" I hadn't known what she was talking about, but now I did. I wanted to merge with Ollie's insides, stencil myself over his form.

My post from that night: a picture of me and Virginia holding dark and stormy cocktails, portrait mode blurring the boats behind us.

It took me less than ten minutes to edit and caption the picture. For the next hour, I sketched the image on a legal pad—except with our anatomies visible, like they'd been during my mushroom trip. I wasn't an artist, but mapping what was inside us soothed me like filling in one of Noorie's coloring books.

whitty_ miss steal yo girl @meet.virginia

meet.virginia I had her first @whitty_

lbmofficial awww love this! Thanks for celebrating with us

bexjones @lbmofficial new handle

10 June

In eighteenth-century Europe, medical school tuition could be paid in corpses.

Christianity and all its attendant anxieties ruled that dissecting a body was considered sacrilegious, a scarlet letter at the gates of heaven. God wouldn't accept you with your insides all scrambled. He admitted only fully assembled structures, because who has the time to rebuild all those humans from scratch, Ikea style? So, anatomists had to improvise. *Body snatching* became part of the criminal lexicon, and instructors provided aspiring anatomy students with an incentive: education in exchange for a body. You do the underground work, and we'll explore the underground of a human together.

I read about this practice when I started dreaming about cadavers and going down morbid Google holes. In one dream after Leila's wedding, I imagined myself showing up at the dean's office at Brown, Ollie draped around my shoulders with his eyes closed, looking like just another passed out drunk kid. *I don't need the scholarship money anymore,* I said to the dean. *I can pay.* I dropped his dead body at her feet, and she smiled.

.

Between dreams, I drew.

I took pictures from weddings—ones I'd attended and ones on my feed—and sketched the couples, exposing their insides. The results looked like bodies tattooed with their own anatomy. The tangled-wire tissue sprawl appeared charmingly messy next to perfectly curated cakes, altars, and veils. Sometimes I turned organs into objects: a heart would become a wedding cupcake, a tendon a string of tent lights.

One night after drawing my parents at their wedding, intestines out and brains sitting pretty, I took a photo of the sketch. It appeared intentionally raw, even stylish. Or maybe I was just drunk on my newfound outlet, excited to have a hobby that wasn't flicking my thumbs over a phone—so excited that I wanted to share my creations, which contradicted the idea of a screenless habit. *Yes, I contradict myself,* I thought. *I am large, I contain multitudes*—the Walt Whitman quote that had made me feel special until I saw it crop up in two high school classmates' yearbook quotes and an AIM away message from laxstar430.

I followed a handful of illustration accounts, most of them cartoonists. But I hadn't seen anatomy drawings on social media, though I'm sure they existed somewhere in the two-dimensional universe in our palms. I'd heard about "finstagram," or fake Instagram: Gen Z's version of a diary. The idea of having a secret account with everyday, scandalous, or simply strange pictures had never appealed to me before. But now that I was producing images that didn't fit into the standard boxes—images that were, really, the hidden content of those squares—I had a perverse urge to put them out into the world without telling anyone.

I created a new account called @bridalbodyyy (*body* with one *y* was taken) and uploaded a few of my drawings. I paired them with punny captions to make the sketches less grotesque, more palatable to people who might find the account while looking for ten-minute booty-blaster routines.

Social media put me outside my body while consuming bodies. I flicked and flicked, unmoving, watching people dance down my screen. But until now, I hadn't imagined these images as bodies beneath the skin. They were personalities and outfits and glow-ups. Bikinis and captions and aspirations. Panelists and cultural commentators and POV memes. With their anatomy obscured, it was easy to forget what they really were: trillions of cells, teeming and surviving. A collection of tissue vulnerable to interruptions—disease, injury, mutation—that couldn't be quelled by followers, photo editing, or one-liners.

My dad's book provided me with another point of entry. Back in the late nineteenth century, people gussied themselves up for an in-person audience, projecting versions of themselves to other flesh cages covered in layers of fabric. The stitching on one's jacket telegraphed social standing, income, and earning potential, while people ignored the growing anxieties or maladies underneath. Growing up, I'd inspected the tags in Virginia's and Gray's Watch Hill closets—Gap grew into Abercrombie, followed by Vince, Veronica Beard, and Ulla Johnson—and googled the prices, my eyes widening with each new brand. They added outfits to their carts with the nonchalance of buying lunch. But cut through those outer dressings, and we were all the same—hell, my pancreas might've been glowier than Gray's epidermis after her latest laser facial. Anatomy, the great equalizer.

As I sketched and uploaded, my perception of our anatomical ignorance shifted from epiphany to mild indignation. If bodies were like houses, we all walked around looking exclusively out the top window, without real knowledge or curiosity about the floors within.

> **willkandcookies** came here for workouts, wtf?
>
> **magglesss88** rad
>
> **zptheking** who are u?

11 Now

I give my thumbs a scrolling break.

Outside the honeymoon suite bathroom window, the Atlantic's foamy tips rise and fall. The waxing moon makes the shore partially visible, shadowy forms like an ultrasound of the beach. It's empty, of course—the guests who braved the cold for pictures during cocktail hour and smoke breaks during dinner now curl up underneath duvets in rooms below me. The ballroom should be packed up by now, the cadaver of my wedding hollowed out.

My body project was supposed to be fun. A low-stakes secret, a coping mechanism for a screen that refreshed without my permission. But controlling a small corner of your phone is an illusion; the feed can always turn its appetite toward you. Taming it, like washing down pre-portioned almonds with water and a smug smile, can unravel faster than it takes to flick to a new image.

My stomach houses half a large pizza. I have about two hours to throw it up—if I wait any longer, the cheesy mass will have traveled from the stomach to the small intestine, too far gone to turn back. Peristalsis, the contractions that move food through the digestive tract, will whisk away the wreckage. An inexplicable need to sit with it all comes over me in the bathtub, vomiting a too-easy way out.

My phone, faceup next to the soap dish. A light:

Can you talk? It's from Virginia.

My feed beckons with distractions, curated moments that serve as a portal to the messier memories. People say the past is out of our grasp and the future is in our hands, but that isn't quite right. We project our futures with a tenuous, private filter—one that can be deleted swiftly due to external forces—while we're able to edit our pasts, enhance or darken or saturate the narrative to fit our needs. No wonder so many of us live inside memories; it's safer to reside in a place that can be re-uploaded or excised.

Instead of responding to Virginia, I go back to the camera roll and feed, rewinding with a futile compulsion to undo the past not unlike the thrust of a meal from my mouth.

12 June

Camera Roll
Lines of text on a page

We cooked for Mimi and Walter at the apartment. New York hadn't yet descended into its heat spiral, and color clung to the full trees on Park Avenue and the tulip boxes dotting the street dividers. Nature in New York felt singular, even showy—it stood out in contrast to all the man-made gray, those green and pink and yellow growths that, unlike people, became more remarkable when stacked up against the city.

Mimi arrived early, before sunset. She was shouting about the tulips.

"Summer has sprung, ladies! Where are your fresh flowers?"

"Where's Dad?" Virginia asked. She was finishing up a cheese plate while Whit and I prepped shrimp scampi ingredients.

"Work, shmerk. Driving me berserk!" Her bright voice undermined her alleged frustration. She walked around the dining table, touching the head of each chair like she was playing duck-duck-goose with invisible friends. "Girls, did I tell you about where I got these chairs?"

She had. Before I could lie and say I wasn't sure, Whit replied.

"I haven't heard, Mrs. M! They're beautiful."

"Call me Mimi!" she shouted. "Callie, you've passed this old affliction on to your significant other and I refuse to be aged one hundred years."

"Did you black out the first twenty years of my life when every single one of my friends called you Mrs. Murphy?" Virginia asked.

"Selective hearing."

"Explains so much."

Virginia had shifted from a bent position over the cheese plate to a reclined sprawl on the couch, indicating that her work was finished. We hadn't even started cooking, and I felt the particular sense of dread associated with public performances of multitasking. Could I sauté shrimp and make sure the noodles were properly al dente while also following Mimi's story about antiquing in the Berkshires?

"The man in the store had the same birthday as me. Down to the year and the time. Can you believe it?" she was saying. "And he sat down on this chair, this very one, and said, 'Listen—let me tell you about us.'"

Mimi started talking about zodiac signs and how this man with the chairs unlocked parts of her personality she hadn't explored yet. Leo with Gemini rising and a Cancer moon became her religion. She now spoke to this man every year on their birthday and whenever she was going through a "mini crisis" or a big change in her life.

"I know, I know," she said, rolling her eyes with cartoon-like exaggeration. "I'm a sucker. But this stuff works, I'm telling you. He knows things."

Her faith in astrology didn't rub me the way it did when people my age subscribed to it, seemingly to fit with the dusty-pink aesthetic of their feeds. Mimi was part of the generation that avoided therapy and thought that analysis was a form of weakness. She'd once told Virginia and me that ruminating can lead to an emotional cul-de-sac, a thought loop that turns in on itself. So, for her, astrology—codified self-reflection—was a revelation.

The garlic skins popped off in one piece under my knife and I thought they looked like cicada shells. I almost said it out loud but stopped myself to avoid ruining appetites. It would be nice if we could peel off our own skin with similar neatness. I wondered if Anika might have some ideas for how to accomplish this; sheet masks and chemical peels were amateurish compared to the type of full-body shedding I craved.

"I told Ollie to come over for a drink after dinner," Virginia said. Like at Leila's wedding, I had the sense that she was reading my mind.

"Fabulous," Mimi said, biting down on a cheese stick. "I hope he brings that girlfriend of his, I need to get to know her better."

"She's great," Whit supplied. "Really smart."

I laughed, but it came out more like a cough. "You've spoken to her for what, thirty seconds?"

"We talked for a while at Gray's party. The dermatology field is super competitive these days. Getting into any residency, let alone your top residency, is like getting an average white kid into Harvard undergrad. Nearly impossible."

Mimi laughed nervously. Gray had gone to Harvard, and her test scores had been questionable at best. I thought Whit's *comment* was questionable at best. Was he against affirmative action? Or was he just trying to be funny? This had become a recent pattern: Whit would say something that made me cringe, then I'd wonder if I'd overreacted.

The water was boiling. I dumped in the uncooked pasta and watched it go from rigid to comatose in seconds. Mimi was asking Whit about his line of work, wondering why he was knowledgeable about the medical profession. He rambled about his pharmaceutical venture firm with an enthusiasm that couldn't manage to pique Mimi's interest.

"You and Walter will have a lot to talk about. Where is that stranger? You know, I've seen him once in the last week. Once. Holed up in his work bunker." She said this with an odd note of pride, in the same tone she always used when talking about Walter's overworking: feigned annoyance that failed to mask a deeper sense of rightness that he—and, by extension, she—had earned everything they had. Never mind that they were born with most of it prebaked.

"The only time I've seen him all week was over a turkey sandwich, and he took the last bit of aioli from that new market in town, the place that wraps everything in gingham. It's darling. The owner is from Louisiana, and god, her biscuits. You know, I once made biscuits that were so hard, I chipped my roommate's tooth." And we were off.

Whit made martinis and asked Mimi questions about her anecdotes, leading her down a web of tangents. Stories bred more stories until the room was overpopulated with her history. Virginia came to peer over my shoulder at the shrimp bathing in butter.

"A regular ole Ina. Who knew you'd be domesticated so quickly?"

Her emphasis on *domesticated*—pronounced like the word was unsavory, lowly—annoyed me. I was cooking for her family, not launching a *Stepford Wives* reboot.

"Someone has to."

"It's a gift to everyone that I'm not in charge."

Virginia did this with tedious tasks like cooking, driving, and check splitting: she used self-deprecation to exempt herself from responsibility.

The door opened, and I could hear Walter scuffing his boots against the welcome mat.

"Honey, you're home!" Mimi shouted.

Virginia went to hug her dad as Whit stood up and brushed his button-down for lint. He pushed his shoulders back too far, like a teenage girl trying to show off her chest. I imagined the muscles straining underneath his shirt, slabs of deltoids that might have been indistinguishable in a butcher's shop.

Walter asked how I'd been liking the apartment. I said it was great, so generous of them, and cursed myself for not coming up with a more descriptive response. I was distracted by his head. It had been a while since I'd gotten a good look at it in bright lighting. I wondered if I could see my face in it if I perched on a step stool. Perhaps this was the secret to his success: he quite literally mirrored people back to themselves.

Whit shook his hand. "Great to see you again. We met briefly at Gray's engagement party."

"The young man at the upstart firm—"

"Guilty as charged!"

Walter flared his nostrils slightly, a tic I'd noticed that meant he wanted to remove himself from a conversation. I realized that Whit hadn't supplied his name or made any move toward a more permanent recall from Walter, and that they'd likely have this exchange all over again in a few weeks depending on how dinner went.

Mimi insisted that I serve the scampi in her wedding china.

"I left it here because it was just so formal for the suburbs, you know? It has a sort of New York glamour, doesn't it?"

I nodded. "Very Edith Wharton."

She was already on her second martini. Mimi's drinking wasn't out of control, but it was consistent. Her days seemed to unspool in half-hour increments, time doled out with the precision of a medication schedule: 50 mg of parenting, 10 mg of self-care, wash down with a liter of affirmations. Maybe she drank to break up the dosages, let the hours become less measurable at the end of the day. Virginia leaned over my shoulder to crack pepper on the pasta, a last-ditch effort at collaboration, and we brought out the serving bowl together, one of us on each side like we were singing "Happy Birthday." It wasn't a heavy bowl and I could've carried it myself.

I'd forgotten to make a salad. Virginia had assured me that greens were superfluous, more of a decorative suggestion than a food item. But the omission still felt like a giveaway. We were more like children at show-and-tell than dinner party hosts.

Mimi disagreed. "If only Maggie Mendelson could see you now."

"Who's that?" Whit asked.

"Their art camp teacher. She sent them both home after they flung paint at that poor girl's new bikini." Mimi looked up at the ceiling, trying to remember. "Kelly Yeatman!" she exclaimed, like she'd solved a complex math problem. "I wonder where she is now."

"Works at Goldman," I announced.

Virginia rolled her eyes. "Of course she does."

Everyone served themselves and started eating immediately. Walter had instilled an "eat it while it's hot" compulsion in his kids and colleagues that left no time for prayers or waiting until everyone was served.

Mimi complimented the food and said that my dad had loved shrimp scampi. Walter gave her a chiding look that translated to: *Let's not bring up the dead guy first thing at the dinner table.*

"What?" Mimi challenged. "It's not taboo to talk about him. We're all adults here."

Her eyes started to glaze with tears. She was getting drunk—alcohol gave her permission to indulge darker emotions that were usually pushed down in favor of buoyancy.

"I wish I could've met him," Whit said.

"You would've loved him." Mimi reached over the table and squeezed my hand. "Everyone did."

"Scampi. Good taste," Virginia said. "He liked to fish, didn't he?"

"Teddy was good on the water," Walter said.

"Better than good. He's like a merman. He always said he wanted to live on the water someday, and that's why, you know, his grave—"

"I still think it would've been better to cremate and scatter his ashes in the ocean."

I'd interrupted, but I couldn't let her keep veering into the present tense and talking about my dad like he was alive. I knew that for some people, including Mimi, this type of magical thinking was palliative. But for me, these recollections were followed by the hangover of a good dream—a jarring, haunted push back into a bleaker reality.

"You're right, sweetie," Mimi said, addressing me with her pet name for Virginia. "We should've let you do whatever you thought he wanted."

"It's okay. We were all just doing our best."

Glancing at my phone as if I were reading a text message, I opened my camera roll to a passage from my dad's book. I'd taken a picture of it last night, for the overwrought yet striking way he described Sterling's obsession with the ocean: "Sterling succumbed to nature's bubble bath with a reverence most men of his ilk reserved for club sports. The sea was a vat of possibility: swimming, boating, diving, conjugal evenings after a picnic on the beach. There were few masses that stirred his spirit like the Atlantic's deep blue, foam-flecked and undulating." It's reductive to assume that a protagonist is based solely on the author, but it was difficult to overlook the similarities between Sterling Barnett and Teddy Holt.

As I looked up from my phone, I realized the pause at the table had veered into awkward territory. Whit rushed to fill it, fixing his eyes on the face he'd been circling all night.

"Walter, I've been meaning to say congratulations on the encephalitis vaccine approval."

"I can't take credit, but thank you."

"Top-down."

"Sounds like a Matt Damon spy thriller," Mimi chirped.

Whit laughed but couldn't resist mansplaining. "It's an organizational philosophy. Success starts at the top and trickles down to the rest of the company."

"I think she knows what it means," I said, rubbing his back so my reproach didn't come off too harshly.

"Because trickle-down always works out so well for everyone," Virginia quipped.

"No politics at the dinner table," Mimi warned, invoking a slogan from a simpler time. Before she could launch into a topic-changing story, the door opened.

Ollie and Anika had arrived. They were wet.

"You poor things!" Mimi exclaimed, spotting Anika's dripping hair that, by some cruel genetic trick, managed to look lustrous instead of stringy.

"It's raining?" Whit asked.

"What are we drinking?" Ollie picked up the bottle and squinted at its label, and I couldn't help but read his nonreply as a slight to Whit's stupid question.

"You tell us," Virginia said. "It's a red."

He poured a glass for himself and Anika while Mimi rushed to get extra chairs. They stood there holding their drinks, her head tucked into his shoulder. She was around my height but thinner, the perfect size for folding into him. I thought of pulling her forearm, yanking it like a weed, until her radial bone separated from her humerus with a satisfying, hollow *pop*.

Since the eye contact—eye fucking, really—a week ago in Watch Hill, I'd been replaying the moment. Did he actually see me, or were his eyes fixed on a seagull outside the window? Putting words to the incident, especially out loud to his face, would ruin the memory. It existed only in our heads, those seconds where we might have had sex from yards and floors away.

I shoveled the scampi into my mouth. I always ate too quickly, treating food like evidence to be buried. Unfortunately, my body didn't function as an alibi. My stomach strained against the band of my jeans.

"Are you keeping this boy in line?" Walter asked Anika.

"Not at all." She smiled with all her big white teeth. "Any tips?"

"Sour Patch Kids," Mimi said.

"More of a sour belts guy myself," Whit offered in a somber tone that was meant to come off as sarcastic but read as earnest.

"Now Aunt Mimi's secrets are revealed." Ollie traced a finger down the stem of his wineglass. "All that time, I was being trained like a dog."

"Like a boy." Mimi turned to Whit. "You understand, boys are just, well, different. Of course, I came in at a later stage with this one. All that pent-up physical energy. Sometimes you just need to give them the sugar and run."

"That explains why my mother ran away with the gardener," Whit joked. He laughed, trying to prompt the rest of the table to join in. The silence was weighty, the thick pause after a poorly timed joke, and his sarcasm was delivered clumsily enough that I wondered if the group would take him seriously.

"I'm sorry," Mimi said. "I want to hear about that another time. Poor thing."

I forced a laugh and said Whit was kidding, but she didn't hear me because she'd already turned her attention to Ollie.

"How was MoMA?" she asked. "Did you send Ellen my love?"

Ollie talked about a Junior Associates meeting at the

museum led by Ellen Kennedy Strauss, American royalty and Mimi's acquaintance. Virginia mentioned a digital art exhibit there, saying that it was more of a technology showcase than art, CES in a museum.

"Is there a difference now, though?" Ollie prompted. "Between art and technology? Take Hockney's iPad stuff or NFTs. All of that qualifies."

"God, NFTs," Virginia said. "The acronym stands for No Fucking Time, right? Because I can't be bothered to learn about them."

"It's interesting to think about digital art in terms of heists," Anika said. "Like what happened at the Isabella Stewart Gardner Museum in the nineties could be accomplished by hackers on their couches."

I hated her for contributing an informed comment even more than I resented her perfect hair.

"I read something the other day," I piped up. "About Banksy's art shredding." All their eyes were on me, and I had nothing more to say on the topic. I'd brought up a half-relevant news item that I had half-baked knowledge of, for what? To prove that I could read? I tried to remember details from the article. The infamous Banksy had built a shredder into a piece of art that went for over $1 million. The second it sold, the piece self-destructed. That was all I knew, so instead of summarizing the event, I improvised. "It was about how feelings are fleeting, like art. Art is supposed to be an experience, so I guess it's valid that you buy the experience."

"And then what?" Whit asked. "Mount a tape of people watching it disappear? Ridiculous."

"You could put the shredded pieces back together," I ventured. "It's probably going to be worth even more now."

"If he wanted to make a real statement, he would've totally destroyed the art," Ollie said. "What he did was less of a social commentary and more of a self-promoting publicity stunt."

Ollie talked with authority about anything related to arts and culture. I was tempted to blow up his legitimacy and bring up his expired contracts, the fact that no one was currently paying him for his expertise.

"Ellen just went on the most fabulous trip to Japan," Mimi chimed in. "Did you see her pictures?" Here it was, her reason for bringing up Ellen in the first place. She'd been trying to convince Walter to go to Japan for years.

Ollie nodded. "She emailed me for recs before she left. I hooked her up with a reservation at the sushi spot in a subway station."

"We need to go there!" Whit said, squeezing my shoulder. "Our meeting place."

"I can't take two weeks off right now," Walter said. "Why don't you just go with the kids?"

"I feel a visceral need to visit Japan." Mimi started talking about Gray's wedding in Italy, where we were all headed in a month. She was craving a trip after so much planning and mother-of-the-bride business. Never mind that Italy, for most, was the vacation of a lifetime. She wanted new geography. She wanted Japan.

"*Fernweh,*" Ollie supplied. "The German word for being homesick for a place you've never been." Another German word reference to make us all feel inferior without our consent.

Mimi looked at Anika. "You're lucky to have this walking Wikipedia."

"I'm the lucky one," Ollie said. He kissed her cheek, and I wanted to throw my single remaining shrimp at them.

The bathroom floor called. After discreetly chugging water during dessert, I headed to the powder room with the soundtrack of drunk Mimi attempting to force charades trailing from the kitchen. She'd outpaced us all during dinner and was pushing to play a celebrity version of the game, perhaps so she could act out Dennis Quaid in his beanie.

Since my crib of a bedroom did not have its own bathroom, the powder room had become my default space to pee and preen and turn myself inside out. A candle masked the smell, and I was adept at a quick session: knees to the ground, fingers down the throat, light match, emerge. But first, I looked up the phrase Ollie had said at dinner: "less of a social commentary and more of a self-promoting publicity stunt." An article in *Smithsonian Magazine* popped up with that exact phrasing. It was benign enough and could've been a coincidence. Did he even realize he'd put this writer's words in his mouth? Or was all information up for grabs, no transfer restrictions apply?

As I faced the porcelain hole, the door creaked. I'd forgotten to lock it.

"Sorry." Fuck, it was Ollie. "Sorry, sorry, sorry." He continued like the word was a stubborn "eject" button that could undo his intrusion if he pressed hard enough.

"Anyone else sick from that shrimp?" I said to no one. I opened the door, but he'd already walked away.

He'd know I was lying. I was never good enough at hiding my habits—and after all, the whole unsavory routine had started with him.

13 September—nine years earlier

Camera Roll
A drawing of a heart, veins and aorta included

The first picture in my phone: a notebook doodle from an English class I took with Ollie my junior year. I'm amazed that the cloud has carried it through multiple years and software updates.

That day, our teacher got heady:

"Who owns a story?"

Brown's Advanced Creative Writing Workshop was held in a windowless room in the humanities building. By our first class, Ollie and I had already had sex in the photo lab, my room, his room, and the bowels of the library at three a.m. I'd stopped keeping tally after that.

We sat on opposite sides of the table so we could make eye contact without anyone noticing. Our teacher, Professor Randall, was a legend in the English department. He'd published six books: one a magical realism World War I novel that had been nominated for the Pulitzer, another a slim memoir that *The New York Times* said "reinvented the state of literature." I'd read three of his books in preparation for the class, while Ollie had read none, claiming he wanted to "read his energy" instead.

Lauren Hollis raised her hand to answer Randall's question. "The author."

Randall didn't move or say anything. When he agreed with a student, he nodded his small head almost imperceptibly and made a soft cooing noise like he'd just eaten something pleasing.

"It's more than that," Ollie said. He hadn't raised his hand. "Stories ultimately belong to the person who shapes and finds meaning from them. That might mean the author and the editor—or reader."

"Does a story exist without a listener?" Randall asked.

I raised my hand yes. Mountains existed without a climber. Food existed without an eater. A story could live in a head or on a page free from consumption. My dad's drafts were still stories even if no one read them.

Ollie and one other girl were the only people whose hands didn't shoot up.

"I have to agree with Oliver and Gillian," Randall said. "You must write to bridge a gap between yourself and a reader. Literary stories are not a play-by-play of what happens outside these walls. They're edited to keep an audience's attention, sifted for the richness and humanity behind every interaction. Everything you hear is up for grabs, whether you experienced it yourself or thought of it first." Here, he got excited, his voice rising with the growing tenor of a stump speech. "Don't just tell me what happened. Make me care."

I'd been doodling a realistic heart on the side of my notebook, the four chambers with an aorta emerging from the top like a thick straw. It was funny that the heart got all the credit for love. It had nothing to do with it; it was just a convincing symbol.

•

After class—hours or days later, I couldn't be sure—we were lying in Ollie's bed watching a Canadian show I hated but pretended to like because he did. Fake laughing and sex were my workouts of choice. I was getting a lot of reps in.

I'd put on one of his button-downs. Wearing a man's shirt in bed transformed me into Carrie Bradshaw in Big's apartment, when really, I'd grabbed it to hide my belated freshman fifteen. It was a convincing cover-up, so well plotted that I almost persuaded myself to feel sexy.

He traced his fingers over my forearm. I froze, wanting to make my arm as hospitable as possible without ruining the moment or saying the wrong thing. Was I being too rigid? Should I trace his arm back? My head crowded with hypotheticals and directives, conflicting ideas about how to move and speak and live in the same space as him.

On-screen, an annoying character said something that made Ollie laugh so hard, he gripped the mattress. I'd missed the joke, and even if I caught it, I doubt I would've found it funny. I tried to join in, emitting a bark that was probably worse than silence. Thankfully, he didn't notice or call me out because he was too absorbed in the show.

His profile, his fucking beautiful profile—chin stubble, long eyelashes, dainty nose slightly upturned at the end, curls that hit his forehead in a way that suggested they'd been mussed by a photographer when really *he* was the photographer—was dangerous. How had I overlooked it for so many years? My ambivalence was self-protective, because I'd never thought someone like him could be interested in me. I'd filed him under "family friend" to avoid another embarrassing unrequited crush that seemed to be a trademark of everyone's middle school experience except Virginia's.

While men on-screen walked around in ill-fitting T-shirts,

Ollie moved his fingers over my hand. When I was a kid, my dad would talk about the *vena amoris,* or the love vein, that runs from your ring finger to your heart. He brought it up to get a rise out of my mom, who was allergic to romance and would respond with a pantomimed finger down her throat.

Ollie was still tracing my fingers, and I hoped the skin felt soft, pliable. This gesture was more intimate than kissing or sex. Could it be communicating what he couldn't say? I reminded myself to *live in the moment* and *get out of your head,* the universal instructions for happiness and attraction.

The episode ended. He closed his laptop and rolled toward me. Our foreheads were touching, and I imagined what we'd look like from above: a pair of inverted commas, two people in love.

"Plans this weekend?" he said.

"I have that Sigma Chi party."

"Ah." He reached for his phone on the nightstand. "The demanding schedule of a fraternity groupie."

"The theme's pretty funny. Astronauts and Whores."

"Absurd."

He wasn't wrong, but I also appreciated the party's no-BS take on the underlying goal of every fraternity event: less clothes, more skin. It made me and my friends feel like we were in on the joke, even when we'd ordered three versions of galactic minidresses online and agonized over which one made our boobs look perkiest.

"Why don't you come? Oh!" My voice rose with the delight of a clever idea. "You can wear my bowling ball costume from last Halloween."

"Why would I do that?"

"A black hole for the space theme. Hot."

He laughed, pulling me onto his chest and cupping my chin. "You're so fucking funny sometimes."

The kiss was bottomless; I could've stayed inside it for hours, but Ollie pulled away.

"Only sometimes?" I teased. "I need to work overtime."

"Then stay with me. Don't go to that dumb party."

A question I couldn't ask out loud flashed into my sex-sick brain: Was this about wanting to be with me or avoiding being seen with me? He still didn't want us to go public, claiming that Virginia would be upset. But her effusive emails about life abroad, Parisian nightclubs, and a pizza chef named Pierre (**you can't make this up,** she'd written) made me think that she had better, cooler, Frencher things to worry about.

I'd been looking forward to the frat party all week. It was silly, but Bex had planned a big dinner before with our girl-friends. We'd gone to Party City to buy alien headbands and glow sticks for the table.

As I considered the logistics of doing both, I caught Ollie's face in the computer light: I stood no chance.

"You're the worst," I said. "Of course I'd rather stay here."

"The beginning of season three is the best," he promised, tilting his chin toward his laptop.

The next morning, my eyes opened to Ollie squinting at the computer. I liked when his face creased and became a little less symmetrical, rumpled like a piece of clothing I'd just worn.

"This is bullshit," he said.

Familiar hieroglyphics glowed from his screen. Physics. I'd taken it the year before and gotten an A–.

"Do you have Beasley?"

He nodded. "Why the fuck do I need to know this?"

"Let me look at it."

Ah, the ole ball and ramp. Physics had satisfied a premed requirement, but I preferred the rawness of biology and organic chemistry, the flow between living things that didn't fit inside geometric shapes.

I scribbled on a stray notepad, working out the problem for him. After twenty minutes, I'd finished the set.

"Genius. Thank you." He massaged my shoulder, kneading my skin. Needing me.

We opened beers in bed and didn't flinch when foam spilled onto his sheets. Setting our lukewarm cans on the headboard that functioned like a precipitous wooden shelf, we initiated the choreography that had become familiar. The sight of him lengthening thrilled me every time. *I did that,* a physical, tangible change in the person I feared I loved.

My eyes blinked awake to Ollie's darkened room. The shapes of the space took a moment to place: an obscure anime poster and a painting from a local Watch Hill artist on the wall, T-shirts silk-screened with ironic phrases piled high on the uncomfortable university-issued desk chair, mini fridge decorated with a Deer Valley magnet and a printout of Black Keys tour dates. No Ollie.

It was five p.m.; we must've fallen asleep watching that show on the laptop. As I swung my legs out of the flannel-sheeted mess that was starting to smell like soy sauce and armpits, I heard his roommates' voices coming from the kitchen.

His roommates and I treated each other like cordial strangers: a closed-mouth smile, a hello, a limp wave. They were all art students—a painter, another photographer, and a graphic design major—who didn't seem to care about getting to know me. Their disinterest made the feeling mutual. The off-campus apartment was the one place where our relationship was public, but my discomfort in the hallways and awkward interactions over the kitchen sink weren't exactly a red carpet debut.

Matt, the graphic designer, always sounded like he was trying to be heard in a crowded bar. They were talking about an exhibit at the campus gallery and a new Japanese restaurant they wanted to try after.

"How's your side piece?" Matt asked.

"Fuck off," Ollie shot back. "She's asleep."

"Too big to be a side piece," Trevor, the one I'd thought was the nicest, said.

They all laughed, including Ollie. I listened for a hesitancy, waiting for him to rush to my defense.

"Did one of you idiots eat the sandwich I had in here?"

I made myself throw up for the first time in the dorm bathroom the following Monday, the one day of the week I could reliably avoid drunk classmates stomping in wedge heels all over the linoleum. The ramen and ice cream I'd inhaled from the minimart came up quickly.

I'd resisted texting Ollie since my eavesdropping and couldn't bring myself to accuse him of seeing other people or laughing at his roommates' cruelty. We weren't exclusive; I was supposed to be sleeping. So I continued sleeping while awake, pretending I wasn't waiting for the night-light summon of his text.

What r u up to?

I received it while brushing my teeth, the stomach acid mixing with mint to both defang the burn and poison the freshness. I went back to his apartment twenty minutes later.

14 July

calliememaybe When life gives you lemons 🍋
#graysanatommy

My wood-fired pizza contained the world. Entire continents were spread out in white shapes, oblong and uneven, intersected by a red sauce sea. Italian margherita pizza didn't let its cheese blanket the sauce; it gave the elements a refined sort of space, a geographical distance. One cheese blob looked so much like Australia that I said it out loud.

"Someone's jet-lagged," Whit observed. We'd just arrived in Positano for Gray's wedding weekend and, after spotting Virginia and her parents outside the villa lobby, decided to sit down. The day was postcard perfect, the Amalfi Coast in full bloom. My sweat stains and hair grease, fresh off an eleven-hour trip, were also in full bloom. I was an insult to Villa Treville, the five-star hotel where Gray and Tommy would say "I do" in two days. The Murphys had generously comped half of our room cost—my salary and Whit's combined could barely cover half.

"Isn't this just divine?" Mimi asked, the word *divine* stretched out like the strings of cheese that connected her mouth to the dough. I looked at my piece like an old adversary and promised myself I'd only eat one. "Walter, remember our last time here?"

"Mm-hmm," he managed while chewing his pizza.

"Tell the story. Tell it. Oh, it's so good."

"What story?"

"Bob and Sheryl!" she said.

"What about them?"

"Our trip to Italy? With them?" Mimi's face briefly flickered with annoyance that Walter had no recollection of this unforgettable tale. Before letting her husband dig himself deeper into amnesiac ignorance, she started in on the memory.

"We came here ages ago with Walter's business partner, Bob, and his second wife, Sheryl. She must have been Virginia and Callie's age! Anyways, she was this thin little thing, but she'd put on some weight during their European tour." Mimi reflexively glanced at her pizza, only two small slices taken from the pie to ensure the same would not happen to her. "Sheryl was convinced she was pregnant. Convinced! I tried to tell her, 'Honey, that's not how babies work, they don't really show themselves for the first few weeks.' Everywhere we went to dinner, she'd tell the waiters, '*Prego,*' pointing at her stomach."

"But that means—" Whit started.

"You're welcome," Mimi continued. "Yes, it means *you're welcome*. Not the brightest bulb."

"How long did that relationship last?" Virginia said.

"Still hanging on through two kids and two mistresses."

"Mimi," Walter admonished. "That's private."

"He made it public when he started blatantly sleeping with another secretary. Such a cliché, I could scream. Scream!"

For someone who'd just said "not the brightest bulb," the cliché insult was rich. But behavioral clichés were different—Mimi did everything in her power to point out when she broke from a multimillionaire norm. They'd been hands-on parents, not the type to outsource all childcare to a live-in nanny (they'd had a nanny who came every day, yes, but she slept at her own home). They were happily married and allegedly faithful after twenty-nine years of marriage (though when Virginia once complained about her high school boyfriend's lack of thoughtfulness, Mimi had told her to "take what you can get"). She'd never get plastic surgery like her mummified peers (Botox and fillers were noninvasive and therefore different). The Murphys' caveats and small hypocrisies were offset by their generosity. Even though I'd just arrived, Villa Treville was one of the most stunning places I'd ever seen; they were subsidizing our collective awe.

On the flight over, I'd dipped back into my dad's book. Sterling and Amelia had just realized that they were stuck in Watch Hill without their other halves, thanks to a brewing hurricane that prevented travel. A passage had brought up a question I didn't realize I had about the Murphys' hospitality. "The Cahills' guest room contained enough towels to dry an army. Scented soaps turned the powder room into a secret garden, an oasis of freshness, not waste. Sterling wondered whether their generosity was a result of altruism or narcissism, a desire to make people feel welcome or a longing to flaunt their wealth."

"So what's the schedule today?" Walter asked. He'd finished his pizza and radiated impatience, a man accustomed to being ushered between meetings by a secretary he would never stoop to sleeping with.

"It's all in the welcome bag and on the website, honey."

"A welcome bag? Like a party favor?" he asked. "Jesus, don't tell me."

"Party favors are a favor for attending the party," Mimi said, with the tone of someone explaining a grammatical error. "Welcome bags are a welcome to the weekend."

"Did we buy everyone a car, too?"

"Just for the night."

·

A procession of vintage Italian cars wove down the hill that led to the hotel. The Murphys had ordered enough of them to bring us all to the welcome party, a bouquet of multicolored balloons fastened to each trunk.

Whit and I got into a car toward the back of the line. I played a peripheral role in the weekend and didn't need to be close to the couple. Weddings often felt like an exercise in spatial awareness.

"*Buongiorno,* my man," Whit said to the driver. "How do you say 'holy shit, this is sweet' in Italian?"

The driver looked at him quizzically. "My English is not good."

Whit talked to drivers with gleeful abandon. He said that he liked getting to know strangers; I think he liked trying out new material on someone he'd never see again.

We finally started moving. The serpent tail of the road, the winding and claustrophobic path it cut through the mountain, was vertigo inducing or thrilling, depending on the passenger. I loved the anticipatory suspense of being inches away from falling. We turned two tight corners in quick succession, and I thought of the road as intestines turning in on themselves. The sea at the end of the long fall was so turquoise it almost hurt my eyes. I looked down at Whit's khakis and a square of blue transposed onto them, like a window.

I counted all the lemons on the welcome party porch.

Lemon trees. Lemonade. Hard lemonade. Lemon woven napkins. Lemon-painted menus. Lemon-shaped limoncello bottles. Lemons shaped like bloated livers. Lemon cocktails that destroy livers.

Gray had on a lemon-printed Dolce & Gabbana dress with a voluminous skirt and sweetheart neckline. Her hair had been gathered into a high ponytail and meticulously tousled and curled like a bouquet of yellow freesias. Her personality usually made me forget how pretty she was. Gray wasn't unbearable, but her type A tendencies (anxious, anal, ambitious) eclipsed her looks. Tommy stood with her, watching her talk. She held his hand and included him in her answers to questions, like he was a fickle houseplant that needed coaxing.

The professional photographer was busy preserving the welcome party, creating images for Gray to use in every anniversary and birthday post until the gap between herself in real life and the person in the wedding images became upsetting instead of aspirational.

By the bar waiting for a drink, I checked @bridalbodyyy, scrolling through my sketches. Most of them were based on pictures from weddings, exposed brides at the altar, but some drawings were from an imaginary vision. As I'd continued reading "Off-Season," I'd drawn the Cahills' and Barnetts' elaborate nineteenth-century costumes, then erased their outlines so the pouf of dresses and sharp punctuation of tails hovered around the hastily drawn figures. I replaced the heavy body drapery with anatomies, so that the characters wore their organs like costumes. The formal language and stilted conversations in the book made me realize a truth that should've been obvious: the human tendency to obfuscate and edit went back much further than social media. The feed just gave us a tool to commit misrepresentation at a larger scale.

The bartender handed me my dirty martini. Its liquid-quick burn, the salty plunge, buzzed bright in my mouth. I raised my phone and zoomed in on Gray and Tommy from afar, the photographer's lens in the foreground. The silent click of my thumb gave me an option to draw later. I couldn't wait to make her liver into a lemon.

Ollie sat with Anika on the uncomfortable-looking metal chairs in the garden. She'd also curled her hair. In a work-fueled Google hole, I'd discovered that hair doesn't continue to grow after death, despite what horror movies and Halloween fun facts had led me to believe. It just looks longer because the skin retracts, leaving the hair—which takes more time to break down—nesting next to bone.

I placed my phone in front of my face like I was reading a text and zoomed in on them to find that the skin on Anika's elbows was chapped and flaking. I smiled. This was bad advertising for a dermatologist.

To their right, long tables were sprawled alongside bougainvillea bushes with hand-painted pink-and-yellow menus, personalized embroidered napkins, and, of course, more lemons. Bottles of olive oil glowed like unlit lamps. Gray and Tommy stood in the middle of the center table, leading by example so that the staff could reasonably direct everyone to their seats.

An hour into dinner, Tommy stood up. I thought he was about to give a speech, but then he started walking away from the table, covering his mouth. Gray grabbed his elbow and looked into his face. He couldn't speak.

He was choking. Not the botched speech kind of choking—the real kind, the throat closing up kind. The kind that can kill you.

"Help!" Gray shrieked. "Is there a doctor?"

I almost raised my hand. I knew the Heimlich like an old prayer, one I hadn't recited in many years. I waited a beat to see if there was someone else who'd volunteer, some older man with a title to back up his expertise.

Anika rushed over to Tommy. In one fluid motion, she wrapped her arms around him and pulled him into her. It almost looked like they were spooning. She rocked him once, twice, three times. He was double her size, but she managed to steady him, clutching his body to her chest while trying to shoot out whatever he'd wedged in himself. Ollie was staring at her. I was reminded of the way I had stared at the boat during Leila's wedding with willful concentration and a belief that if I pushed hard enough with my mind, I could bend the scene in front of me.

A red, mangled piece of steak flew out of Tommy's mouth and sailed across the table onto Mimi's lap. Tommy sat down and reached for his glass of water, clutching it like it was a ledge he might fall from. Silence came over the table, so many conversations about summer plans and homes and egg freezing and master's degrees halted by the presence of mortality.

After several gulps of water and many deep breaths, Tommy looked up. "Cheers to Anika," he declared. "For saving my life and, more importantly, the wedding!"

"To Anika!" Mimi cheered, standing up and raising her glass. The steak had left a dark stain on her silk dress.

Everyone clinked glasses. Mimi ran to the bathroom, likely texting her "house manager" about the best way to get steak juice out of silk. Virginia scrawled words on a piece of paper, probably a revision to her wedding speech. Gray and Tommy posed candidly, an oxymoron frozen in open-mouthed laughs. Whit talked to one of the distant Murphy relatives about the stock market. Ollie whispered something to Anika and kissed her on the lips. I imagined her organs coming up from her mouth and into Ollie's, pouring into him like a glossy, undercooked meal.

.

The next morning, I woke up early with a light hangover. I opened my dad's manuscript before Whit started stirring.

> *Amelia descended the staircase dressed for the day while Sterling read the paper in the kitchen. The Cahills' cook couldn't make it to Watch Hill either and was stuck back in Manhattan. This resulted in an elaborate domestic play, with Amelia attempting to conceal her lack of culinary skill and Sterling pretending to enjoy the burnt toast and porridge. They played their parts with aplomb.*
>
> *"Good morning," Amelia said. "What'll we have to begin the day?"*
>
> *"Wit and repartee, with a dose of the real world." He pointed toward an unfolded copy of* The World.
>
> *"Do you often consult the papers?"*
>
> *"Every day."*
>
> *"I'll fix us some porridge."*
>
> *"A true delicacy," he said with a smile.*
>
> *Amelia swatted his arm playfully, ignoring the subtext that her porridge was as delicate as a rock.*
>
> *"Do you prefer current to past events?" she asked, looking at the open paper.*
>
> *"Of course. Don't you?"*
>
> *"I crave context. History. I'd rather look back and learn about our past to inform my present."*
>
> *"Which era?" Sterling replied, his interest piqued.*
>
> *"Ancient Egyptian. Colonial America. Belle époque. Nothing against the papers, but it can all become a bit myopic—looking at daily developments as if they're severed from their heritage."*
>
> *"I like seeing what's in front of me," Sterling said,*

suddenly feeling dim in the presence of such passionate
light.

"Which is nothing without its long, invisible tail." With
her neck bent over the coffeepot and white dressing gown
hitting at her ankles, Amelia looked like a large swan.
Sterling averted his eyes at the swell of her buttocks
underneath the gauzy fabric.

I cringed imagining my dad writing this scene. If I drew
this final image for @bridalbodyyy, gluteus maximus straining in front of brewing coffee, I'd undoubtedly get a string of
peach emojis in the comments.

I pictured my dad as Sterling, but Amelia was less distinct, a swirl of traits that didn't cohere neatly to one person
in my dad's life. My mom was a history buff, often repeating
lessons at the dinner table that she'd taught her students.
Mimi couldn't cook, outsourcing the feeding of her family to
a professional who wouldn't "burn the house and everyone's
palates." Amelia, then, was a fictional collage—the closer I
looked, the more she blurred.

I put the manuscript away and closed my eyes, trying
to fully picture the scene in the book. Whit murmured,
wrapped up in sounds without meaning. He talked in his
sleep sometimes. Once, early in our relationship, he'd said
his ex-girlfriend's name, Madison. He claimed he was having
a disturbing but mildly pleasurable dream about murdering
her. "The opposite of love is indifference," I'd said. "Not hate."
But I'd been secretly thrilled that Whit was capable of dream
murder, even if it revealed unfinished business with an ex.

Cuts of light slipped through the slats in our window. I got
up and flung open the blinds. The sun felt bright enough to
bleach us.

"Look at this day," I said. Our Murphy-subsidized room at

Villa Treville overlooked the pool and a terra-cotta-colored cabana.

"More sleep," Whit said. "Come here."

I sat at the edge of the bed and let him wrap his hands around my waist. I usually liked when Whit was warm and touchy, but I didn't want to stay in the room that morning. I wanted to carpe diem. I was already mentally dressing myself, grabbing a croissant and an espresso. Whit put his hand underneath the waistband of my pajama shorts and rubbed my upper thigh. I was busy walking through the Positano markets, taking pictures of the coastline. Whit motioned for me to move on top of him, positioned my legs on either side of his waist. What would Anika wear to the markets? I thought I'd put on a dress, but culottes might be chicer, more Italian.

I mechanically moved my hand until he was hard. I guided him inside me, pumping up and down with the reliability of a butter churn. A French press. Italian coffee, strong and dark, would soon be in my mouth. Whit panted with his eyes closed and lips parted. I remembered how it's nearly impossible to apply mascara without parting your lips. Was the act inherently sexual, or was it a vanity reflex left over from our preening ancestors?

Whit flipped me over to our favorite position. When we'd decided it was our favorite, it had seemed exotic. Now, it was like claiming Malbec as your favorite wine: pedestrian because of its ubiquity. It didn't matter, though, because it felt good. He moved his hand in small spasms that transferred to spasms through me. Behind my eyes, Ollie's head was between my legs, his tongue moving in circles. "Meissner's corpuscles," I'd read out loud to him from a flashcard while studying for a final in college. "Receptors that detect light touch, especially in erogenous zones." I was suddenly twenty-one again, naked in the library stacks with Ollie at one a.m., my back pushing up against the carrel.

"Yes."

"Yes."

"There."

"I'm done, I'm done," we both said in near unison.

Whit held me tight to him. I peeled myself from his sweaty chest.

"Baby," Whit said.

"Let's go." I kissed his cheek quickly but forcefully, a kiss that was more like a push.

Positano was a wanderlust wet dream. Whit and I walked down a street that hugged a full beach, where families crowded under orange-and-yellow umbrellas. A young girl, maybe two or three, pulled on her dad's hand as he tried to read a paperback crunchy with dried water. Vendors hawked sodas, candy, and shot glasses, bleating from the pockmarked sand, *"La vendita, la vendita."*

"It sounds so lovely," I said.

"What?"

"Whatever they're saying."

"Gelato! Let's get some."

"Don't you love the way Italian sounds?"

"They're basically begging." Whit walked toward the gelato awning. "I wouldn't call that lovely."

"They're making a living."

"Or living to make everyone miserable." He smiled, impressed by his own spontaneous turn of phrase. His light green polo highlighted the sunburn on his neck. Golf burn, he called it.

"How is that begging? They're selling goods."

"Scoop of pistachio, scoop of amaretto. Chef's kiss," he said, scrunching his face in a way that disturbingly resembled our forty-fifth president. "What are you going to get?"

"I'm fine."

"You don't want gelato?"

"Why do you call that begging?"

"Because they're harassing people for money."

"Just like homeless people in New York, right?"

"Don't get me started," he said, staring at the mounds of gelato like they were one of his spreadsheets.

"That's pretty pigheaded."

"Oh, come on," he said. "I can't say anything around you anymore!"

"The PC rant. Classic."

"Because I'm a straight white man it's suddenly like I lost all permission to speak."

"Listening wouldn't hurt," I said. "God forbid you listen to traditionally marginalized opinions. You do love your *traditional* values."

"You're not even making sense."

"You're just not listening."

Whit was a centrist conservative, or a guy who cared about taxes but hadn't voted for the reality star president in 2016. He actually hadn't voted at all in protest, a choice he'd explained to me at length and I still didn't understand. I used to agree with some of Whit's takes, his "socially liberal, fiscally conservative" defenses. But a lot of his inclinations had started to seem privileged at best and inhumane at worst. I thought of how Bex or Virginia would react to his comments and whether either could be with someone whose politics diverged so sharply from her own. I'd heard Bex discuss gun control and abortion rights armed with statistical evidence, her voice rising with each number. Meanwhile, Virginia gravitated toward global issues: the migrant and refugee crisis, the genocide in South Sudan, the HIV/AIDS epidemic in West Africa. My friends wore their chosen political stances like badges, not dissimilar to how a favorite color defined your personality as a child. It was a preference stacked up against other preferences that together made a conscientious woman. Maybe I was being unfair about their performative politics. Maybe I should just fucking care more.

"When was the last time you did anything to help these causes you're suddenly so passionate about?" Whit challenged. A drop of muted green ice cream fell from his cone.

"I'm talking about decency."

"I look way more decent than you. Look at that short dress!" He slapped my thigh playfully and laughed like this was a funny overreaction we'd repeat later, blaming a hangover or jet lag. I was too tired to fight, which was the excuse that Whit used every time I brought up a weighty topic before bed. Circadian rhythms could be useful excuses for avoiding other people's feelings.

The next day, a few hours before the ceremony, Whit took a nap as I got ready. I stared at myself in the mirror, my face too pale for July. Dr. Anika would find something to do to my skin: a laser for consistency, a chemical peel for tightening. A treatment to make me look younger, more alive, even though our outer epidermis is made up of dead skin cells. Isn't it counterintuitive that the visible part of us isn't living? We're walking cadavers covered in bright fabric. I moved my long yellow dress for tonight out of the closet, material so thin that I had to wear a slip underneath.

Wear whatever makes you feel comfortable, Gray's email to the bridesmaids, which Virginia had forwarded to me, read. **I want my girls to feel like themselves.** She'd then listed half a dozen requirements for the "choose your own" bridesmaid dresses: light blue and white florals, no navy, at least midi length, strapless discouraged.

Virginia chose a white tuxedo suit tied with a cornflower-blue silk sash. She fashioned the sash herself: went to the fabric store, measured the perfect length, cut it on a bias, and watched YouTube videos to learn how to tie a knot that looked like a cross between a flamboyant bow tie and a kimono closure. She wanted it to be a surprise for her sister.

Gray, of course, hated it. It wasn't what she asked for; if she'd wanted Diane Keaton as her maid of honor, she could've checked her availability—was it impossible for Virginia to follow the rules? Virginia had complained but capitulated. It was Gray's big day, after all. She bought a blue-and-white dress on sale, even though Mimi begged her to go high-end, and the conversation ended. Or I thought it had.

At the ceremony, Virginia walked down the aisle in the vetoed tux. I never thought I'd see it here; I half expected the blue sash to turn up in a piece of her artwork, maybe a portrait of Gray, the silk holding her severed head in place. *Beheading by Sister,* oil on canvas. The tux looked stunning. It dipped down Virginia's chest in a plunging V, an edge that could draw blood, while the blue sash coordinated with the rest of the bridal party.

The ceremony looked onto a cliff that descended into the sea. The raw cut of the coast was beautiful and reverent: colorful houses covered the hillside like so many flowers, the grass glowed gold. The Murphys weren't particularly religious, and Gray and Tommy's match wasn't ordained by anything outside the holy algorithm of a dating app, but still—it was difficult to sit in this space and refuse to believe in an unseen string-holder.

When Gray appeared at the head of the aisle, everyone stood and gasped. Her dress was huge; it looked like she'd been eaten by the fabric, digested by overly hungry lace. *Vogue* Weddings might call it her "wow factor," but it wasn't a dress; it was a statement.

Their vows were traditional, the standard "I, X, take you, Y."
I'd want to write my own, make it personalized. Your vows are
a letter to the rest of your life. Even though the @bridalbodyyy
concept railed against delusions of singularity—we're all flesh
cages, when it comes down to it—I'd try to make my promises unique. Maybe both sentiments could be true at once. *I
am large, I contain multitudes,* seventy-eight organs and thirty
trillion cells and innumerable places to live, people to meet,
choices to mess up.

Gray and Tommy were introduced by the band as Mr. and
Mrs. Thomas Bosker. They walked into the reception area,
an open porch overlooking the sea. A trellis stretched over
the length of the dining area with rows of pink-and-green
flowers hanging from the vines, nearly grazing our heads
like pots from a rustic kitchen ceiling.

"Would you ever want to do a destination wedding?" Whit
asked. The white line of a sunglasses tan had formed at his
temples.

"How many drinks have you had?" I replied.

"I'm serious!" He kissed my cheek and squeezed my hip.
"I could see us doing it in, I don't know, Maine. Florida.
Somewhere in the US, but still an escape. Watch Hill could
be perfect."

Whit's mind was far ahead of mine, his enthusiasm tugging me forward. We'd been together for less than a year,
but I could picture it: the wedding, my dress, the six-piece
band, the salted caramel cake, and the calligraphed invitations. The vision came easily because I was already living it,
enmeshed in the welcome bags and mini tacos and signature
cocktails with punny names. But I couldn't picture our life
together after the wedding, or a version of our life that would
excite me. Whit's personality was excitable, but his interests

flatlined into a single arrow: the stock market, baseball, US presidents. There were few spikes in the EKG monitor, no mountainous quirks for me to cling to. Here I was, secretly seeing organs and arteries at weddings, while he was seeing a blueprint for our own.

"This song was on her banned list!" Virginia shouted.

"Her band list?"

"BANNED. Like they were not supposed to play this song."

"Shout" blared from the singer's microphone. The band, Jessie's Girl, had been flown in from Georgia, and the lead singer sounded like she was unearthing emotion from deep inside herself, excavating everything she'd ever seen and pouring it into the room. Aside from one of Gray's Harvard classmates, the band members were the only Black people at the villa. The lack of diversity in this circle was embarrassing. I'd met more non-white people in six years of professional life than I had in my first eighteen years of life life.

Everyone on the dance floor folded into themselves at *a little bit softer now*. Virginia and I gargoyle squatted. Whit fully spread himself onto the floor, a human condiment.

At the end of the song, Virginia and I walked to the bar. Elegant sweat—she somehow made sweat look elegant—glowed at the triangle point of her chest, the part where her blazer met its sash.

"So you got away with the tux," I observed.

"Gray was cute about it after all that. Said it was more me."

"Have you been seeing anyone recently?" I asked, surprising myself. After weeks of burying the question and its implications, here it was, naked in the middle of a packed room.

"You sound like my mom."

"Just curious. Did anything happen after Leila's wedding?"

"What do you mean?"

"With that girl you were kissing."

"What the fuck, Callie. Were you spying on me?"

"She looked hot!"

"Why didn't you bring this up before?" Virginia looked into her empty cocktail glass.

"I didn't want to make it a big deal. You can hook up with girls!"

"You don't need to convince me," she said. "It's just"—she breathed in deeply—"because I'm wearing a tux you think it's a good time to bring up how you think I've been keeping some big lesbian secret from you."

"That's not it at all."

"Your timing sucks. It always has."

I didn't know what she meant by this, and I was afraid to ask. She'd known me for too long, had stored memories to unpack and twist. I was scared of being surprised by her insult. A critique I already leveled on myself, I could take. But a pointed observation outside my protective film of self-awareness might pierce. She could gouge me.

"Darling!" The wedding planner grabbed Virginia's wrist. "We need you for another set of pictures."

Virginia let herself get pulled away from me and into the center of the room.

The after-party was Moroccan themed. Are all superrich people wild for Morocco, or just the Murphys? The basement lounge was covered in brick-red curtains, huge metal carved lamps, and furry ottomans. A hookah sat untouched in one corner. Bex, Virginia, and I were dancing in a circle when Ollie walked up to us. Sweat had lightly matted his hair and glossed his face, making him shine. Elegant sweat must run in the family.

Bex grabbed tequila shots for all of us and screamed, "Let's fucking go," over the music. She wore a one-shouldered red dress with a puff sleeve and kept posing "like the flamenco emoji." Her fiancé, Greg, was covered in red lipstick marks.

Virginia and Ollie tipped their heads back in unison. They looked related only from the side—those dainty swooped noses, the sweat lining both their brows in a dewy arc. The opposite of the resting matte faces in Composure vessels.

When a relationship dies, we tend to think its heart has stopped beating—that it has entered a necrotic state so terrible, there are multiple organ failures—when in truth, some relationships die for reasons even the grimmest cut can't reveal. Morticians try to animate the detritus, but still, it's the past, not a person. Memories can't breathe.

graymbosker 😵 best weekend ever

bexjones oh HEY GB! Gorgeous Bride + new initials

mimimurph you make spiked lemonade! 🤤

whitty_ my little photographer

belindapbergin beautiful bride!!!

15 October—nine years earlier

Camera Roll
A white-blanketed beach, Ollie crouched at the shore

It snowed on Halloween in Providence that year. The jack-o'-lanterns across the street from Ollie's off-campus house grew white bangs overnight.

"Let's take a drive," Ollie said. We were naked in his bed. He traced his pointer finger over my arm, swoops and peaks that made me wonder if he was spelling out a message.

"Where to?"

"Watch Hill."

"What if Mimi and Walter—"

"They're not. It's a ghost town after Labor Day."

"You know I'm supposed to dress up as one."

"A ghost? That's lame, you can skip that." He typed something on his phone and then turned the screen toward me. "If we leave now, we can get there in less than an hour."

"A Ghost*buster*. Much more creative."

"Do you need to go back to your dorm to grab a bag?"

Why do you keep flaking? Bex's voice in my head. She'd confronted me last week for canceling on a lunch after I'd already bailed on two more parties since Astronauts and Whores. I'd been in Ollie's bed, of course, the spot I stayed when I wasn't sneaking cold cuts from his fridge in the middle of the night so he and his roommates wouldn't witness my consumption. If I bailed on Halloween plans, Bex might get angry or give up on being friends with me altogether. The latter option didn't seem that terrible—I didn't have the emotional bandwidth for friends with Ollie pushing up through every crack of my consciousness.

I went to pack a bag for an overnight and left the Ghostbusters costume curled in a sad gray heap next to a pile of dirty underwear.

The Watch Hill beach turned haunted and feral in the cold. Snow speckled the rocks like bleached moss and curved around the tidemark in a tight seam. It was the first time I'd experienced the beach after a blizzard—I'd been for Thanksgiving with my parents and a few times in the early spring, but I'd never seen it blanketed in snow.

Ollie had his fancy camera with him. I took pictures on my phone and tried to ensure he couldn't see me tracking his movements. He crouched at the water's edge, his back hunched and face jutting toward the waves as if they were prey he could consume. It was sexy, his hunger for the world.

He turned his camera toward me right after I set down my phone, avoiding an awkward lens stand-off. I posed with my hands behind my head and did my best Blue Steel, an exaggerated imitation of narcissism.

"Put your hands down," Ollie directed. "Relax your face."

I puckered my lips, then started laughing. The instruction to act natural negated itself. It was impossible to look candid on demand.

"Find something in the distance and think about a serious topic."

"AIDS!" I screamed. "Genocide!"

We laughed together then, our outburst petering with the slow-dawning realization that it was kind of fucked up.

"I can't be serious on command," I said.

"You don't realize how beautiful you are when you aren't kidding."

Well, that made me stop laughing.

I thought about my dad's final days. The tiny table next to his hospital bed stacked with old issues of *The New Yorker*. The face that thinned into an unrecognizable shadow. The way he sweet-talked the nurses into giving him more OJ, "the juice," he called it, using a Prohibition-era Mafia voice. My mother's waning attention, her impatience at his requests for legal pads and fresh pens. His late-stage focus on his book, coupled with my mom's detachment. I tried to tell her it was a good sign he was showing interest in activities that brought him joy, but she'd dismissed my optimistic takes with assertions that he should rest. I was at his side more than she was at the end, and I'd wondered with a conflicted hope whether they'd stay together if he made it. The *making it* was far more important; the potential of his death neutered other family drama.

"Wow," Ollie said. "Got the shot."

He came to sit with me on the blanket and burrowed himself into the shoulder of my puffer jacket.

"What were you thinking about?" he asked. This was always my question for him, one I often swallowed for fear of revealing my fixation, and I was honored that he reciprocated the curiosity, then vaguely sad that I felt honored by him asking a basic question.

"My dad. The end."

"It was drawn out, right?" He rubbed my back, the pressure forceful enough that I could feel it through a layer of down feathers.

"Months. I showed up every day after school and did my homework next to his bed."

"I can't believe your grades didn't slip."

"He was slipping. I didn't really have a choice to do anything but stay steady."

"I didn't get to say goodbye to my mom," he said. "But I also didn't have to watch that deterioration."

"Changing from a person to a ghost."

As if we'd conjured them, a group of young kids and a mom walked onto the sand. They were around five years old and dressed up as a ghost, a firefighter, and Nemo the fish, with mom trailing behind them wearing cat ears.

"Slacker parents," Ollie said.

We sat in silence for a minute or two, a void that didn't feel heavy despite the conversation. Forty-five degrees couldn't penetrate a puffer, a wool hat, and the warmth of Ollie's attention. Little Nemo trudged across the beach, flakes grazing the tips of his striped nylon tail.

"Why don't you talk about your mom?" Ollie asked, looking at me. There were wind tears in his eyes—or were they tears of emotion over his mom's death?

"I don't talk *to* her very much, so it always feels wrong to talk about her. We've drifted apart since my dad died."

"Because she didn't handle it well?"

"The opposite. She almost handled it too well, moved on too quickly. Things didn't seem good between them toward the end."

"Aunt Mimi said that, too."

I'd assumed that Mimi and Walter knew about my parents' issues—my dad used their guest house as a writing shed/escape portal from his married life—but I was surprised that they'd discussed it with Ollie. It made me wonder whether Virginia knew, and why she hadn't brought it up if she did. My phone calls with my mom had petered from once a month to once or twice a semester that year, and I'd noticed that she was particularly prickly when I brought up Mimi or the Murphy family. We'd never had a *Gilmore Girls*–esque relationship, but I didn't realize how much she balanced our family dynamic until my dad died and our unit turned past tense. She'd been my grounded, slightly ornery voice of reason. Without her, I was rudderless.

"I don't think my mom loves that I'm at Brown, to be honest. So much Murphy influence."

"But it's one of the best schools in the country. And she must be proud of you for the scholarship. I remember she talked about money a lot."

"Well, it was tight." An acidic bite had crept into my voice. "She didn't inherit millions like everyone else in this town." It was a delicate dance with my mother—I could talk disparagingly about her but recoiled when someone else did, particularly someone like Ollie who couldn't sympathize with the root of her faults.

"She had the house," Ollie said.

"Until she didn't."

"We should go see it. I always liked the exterior—could be cool for pictures in this weather."

"Someone new bought it last year. It might be totally changed."

"Change is good."

There it was, his obsession with motion. His deletion of memories from his phone, his desire to live around the world, to use photographs as art instead of nostalgia. Change, for me, represented a hardening of the past instead of a taffy-stretched future—a reminder that I was moving away from simplicity and toward a complicated, unsolicited understanding.

We drove to Ginger House with the windows down. The temperature rose and the sun came out; its afternoon strength made the snow sparkle like the ocean at the height of summer. Late fall shape-shifted in Rhode Island, kept me guessing and frequently refreshing my weather app.

Ollie turned on Arcade Fire, whisper-singing to the high notes. I joined in, and my voice got too loud at the chorus because those were the only words I knew. He and Virginia had gone to one of their concerts together over the summer. Indie music, like art, was an interest they shared without me, with my Taylor Swift and Colbie Caillat and other songs from high school I played on repeat until they were closer to wearing a blanket than listening to music.

On the main town strip, a woman in a pastel cardigan carried a bloated shopping bag with a jacket roped through the handles. The cardigan was the same color as her daughter's hair ribbon and the golf shirt she probably hated on her husband. I had the acute sense that generations slid into their predecessors, like a picture wedged seamlessly over another in a frame. Watch Hill and the towns people here hailed from weren't the kinds of places where people got stuck or "never made it out," even if many of them returned to raise their own families. They came back because of a certitude that it was the best way, a conviction in the quality of their own upbringing. There was the whole messy world, but you had to pick a corner to turn down, to crease and fold and surround with scented candles. Better to choose the bed you knew, one whose sheets would never be piss-stained, whose fellows would never lack job security. This made sense, but it still depressed me.

Ollie tapped his hand on the open window and hummed to a song by Arctic Monkeys, one of those band names that seemed like a manager had come up with it while playing Mad Libs over too many beers. A new song came on as we pulled up to the house.

"No," I said.

"Damn."

It had been torn down. This was inevitable—the place was divided like a kid's meal tray, portioned and cut into small rooms, when people now wanted open-plan everything—but it didn't blunt the shock of an empty hill where my house once sat. Construction tape surrounded a rectangular hole in the ground, an imprint like a giant grave.

"Can we go home?" I asked, belatedly realizing I'd called the Murphys' house my home.

But Ollie was already outside the car, taking pictures of the snow-filled negative space.

"It's like a crime scene," he said. "The tape, the eeriness."

"Yeah, it's creepy as fuck. Let's get out of here."

"Give me a few minutes."

The tree swing was still there, at least. Virginia and I had spent so many afternoons as human pendulums, competing for who could stretch her jelly sandals higher. It was the one edge my house had over hers: a piece of wood tied with ropes, the most rudimentary childhood accessory. When Virginia got a painted swing for Christmas, one that probably cost twice as much as my unadorned wooden plank, I'd been sad for a day. But we still used the swing at my place more than hers, whether out of her pity or early-onset nostalgia.

Ollie was taking his sweet time, so I called my mom. I couldn't believe she hadn't told me that the house was getting torn down. She picked up on the fourth ring.

"Hello," she said, with the preemptively annoyed tone of a person answering a robocall.

"Mom, it's Callie."

"Oh, Cal. Hi."

"Do you not have caller ID?"

"I don't look at all that stuff, you know me."

"All that stuff" meaning any form of technology. When she moved to Maine, she'd also time traveled back a couple of decades and blamed her technological ineptitude for her inability to keep in touch.

"I'm in Watch Hill. The house was torn down."

"Figures."

"You didn't know?"

"We don't own it anymore, so no. How does the new spot look?"

"There's no new spot yet. It's just a hole in the ground. It's really depressing."

"So was that house. God, it was so dark in there. That whole Alpine look gave me the creeps, especially when your dad let it crumble into disarray."

"Ramshackle chic," I said, using his term for our semi-decrepit yet charming home.

"Are you with Virginia?" my mom asked.

"Yeah," I said automatically. "She says hi."

"Hi, Virg. Her mother emailed me a few months ago, but I haven't been able to respond."

"A few months ago is a long time."

"Well, Mimi likes to keep herself busy. I don't think she's waiting by the phone. How's school?"

I filled her in on my classes and friends, leaving out the developments that took up most of my brain space: the mornings spent in a fetal position under Ollie's sheets, the nights spent hunched in a bathroom stall.

"Maybe you could come visit?" I tried. "Mimi and Walter are coming for a football game in two weeks."

"Some of us have to work," she said. "I'm sorry, I just can't get time off from catering. Weekends are the busiest."

My mom and Mimi's expired friendship was mostly unspoken and alluded to with passive-aggressive digs. I didn't know what happened between them, but ever since my dad died, my mom wanted nothing to do with the Murphys. After years of considering them extended family, they'd been relegated to picture frames in a box somewhere—my mom had no family photos at her place in Maine.

We said goodbye with empty promises to see each other and figure out holiday plans. Ollie was still focused on the grim tableau of the missing house. I waited for him to come back to the car, seconds bleeding into minutes—five, ten, fifteen—as I stared at his back, unwilling to voice my need to leave.

Back at Idyll Wind, I snooped while Ollie dozed off.

We'd made penne with canned sauce for dinner, a meal fit for our sophisticated college palates. We'd done some work—or rather, I'd done work for both of us. Ollie had given me his notes for our Randall writing assignment to "play around with," making it sound like a fun sex game. Then we'd started watching *The Big Lebowski* at Ollie's urging. When he fell asleep within the first half hour, I knew I had an opening.

Back then, I was still obsessed with finding my dad's missing manuscript. It was unlikely it would be in the house; I'd already scoured the office in the guest cottage where he wrote. But maybe Mimi could've cleaned out the writing space and stored the pages somewhere. I also just wanted to see the treasures that could be uncovered in the closet and bathroom of someone with unlimited resources.

The bathroom: jars of La Mer stocked underneath the vanity like she was running a high-end antiaging pharmacy. A stack of cotton pads in a glass container. A medicine cabinet housing three toothbrushes, floss, bottles of Jo Malone boasting garden scents. Pills including Advil, Excedrin, aspirin, and the more intriguing ones found in orange prescription bottles. I hadn't heard of the medication names. Google told me they were a mix of antinausea meds and antidepressants, neither of which I'd known Mimi was on.

The bedside table: Stephenie Meyer, spine facing the wall; Ann Patchett, facing outward. A Diptyque candle, a pair of reading glasses. The drawer contained ChapStick, hair ties, and twenty-dollar bills shoved in a corner unceremoniously like trash she meant to throw out later. I opened an unmarked envelope underneath a folder of landscaping bills and HOA papers and found a series of small pictures. They were Gray's and Virginia's elementary and middle school class photos. Gray had an awkward phase, her blond pigtails making it cute instead of tragic. Virginia managed to sail through those years, even with braces, looking like a Gap model.

After flipping through multiple pictures of them, I froze at my younger self. Mimi had saved my class pictures, too. I wondered where she'd gotten them—probably my parents? I swelled with unexpected pride at being considered part of the family, at Mimi's ownership of my little face and spirit. My smile, which cut through chubby cheeks and showed off a front tooth gap, made me ache for a time when I didn't care about my weight, when its very existence could be written off by the prefix *baby*.

A Post-it note on the backside of the envelope had a list scrawled in Mimi's chicken scratch.

Eyes
Bone structure?
Hair color (GC)
Lips X
Chin (GC)

This was a little serial killer–y. I couldn't understand the meaning of this note, written like a grocery list of body parts. Was Mimi anatomy obsessed, too?

"Cal!" Ollie shouted from downstairs. "Where'd you go?"

I scrambled to put everything back in place and shuffled out to the landing.

In the weeks after our trip, Ollie started pulling away inexplicably. He left my BBMs read without responding, turning our conversations into a poorly constructed tower with far more weight on one side of the chat. I blamed myself, thinking he'd somehow discovered my snooping in Mimi's drawers or simply decided I was "too big to be a side piece," as his roommate said. How did I manage to suffocate what was already buried?

I stopped reaching out, thinking that if I played it cool, he might warm to me again. I now believe this is one of the many lies women are fed about dating, the idea that self-protection eventually translates to mutual attraction.

After days without communication, he stopped me after class.

"Sorry I've been MIA. Shit's been busy." He peered over my shoulder as if looking for someone else. "Want to work on this assignment together tomorrow night?"

I said yes too quickly, an almost physical reflex, like he'd tapped my knee with a tiny hammer to trigger the patellar tendon's kick. *Knee-jerk,* people call it, and I couldn't see the double meaning at the time. I could only nod, agree, and show up at his off-campus doorstep the next day with words and a body to give away, fingers to type and stroke until he murmured with approval.

16 July

bridalbodyyy Tendon is the night 🌙
#bridalfitness #medical #bodygoals #anatomy
#medicaldrawings

It was after midnight at Villa Treville. Gray had changed into a white jumpsuit and light-up sneakers. She and Tommy danced in the middle of a circle, sweating, sweating, sweating. Three of Tommy's groomsmen had taken off their shirts, and everyone moved with crazed joy. One girl in a halter dress shook her head and arms like she was being electrocuted, and I imagined her kidneys as two glowing shot glasses. Waiters passed out limoncello shots, mini caprese burgers, big bowls of pasta, and tiny cheese tarts, curled up at the edges like red blood cells.

Whit sat on a furry pouf talking to Walter, one of the few adult holdouts at the after-party. I was shocked he was still awake. He probably wanted to see his money at work.

I approached Ollie at the bar. His shirt was open to the third button, exposing his hairless chest.

"Holt," Ollie said. "How are we?"

"Your date save any lives yet tonight?"

"It appears that was a one-hit wonder. Though"—he looked at the drunk, aging frat bros—"she might get another opportunity."

"They're definitely on ecstasy."

"Are you?" he asked.

"Maybe we should be."

Ollie scanned the room as if he could find the man with the drugs by the slope of his shoulders or the sweat pattern on his shirt. "I'm going to see if I can find some of what they're having."

Suddenly, it was five a.m. Gray and Tommy were already in bed, after being led out with bubbles blown from plastic lemons. Anika was done for the night, preparing to go back home to her daughter the next day. Whit was asleep, too. Walter had agreed to have an espresso with him the next morning, so he wanted to feel "on his game."

Virginia, Ollie, a shirtless groomsman, vodka kidneys girl, and I were the only ones left. The after-party DJ had stopped, so we played Spotify from inside a plastic cup on one of the wrought-iron garden tables. Robyn was in the corner, watching him kiss her, oh, oh, oh. Virginia got up and danced, her long hair sweeping over her shoulders. At the end of the song, she gathered the thick strands into a weary topknot, as if she were tucking herself in, stowing away her excess energy.

"I'm out," she said, slurring her words. "See you at brunch?"

"Overachiever. That's in four hours," Ollie said.

"Maid of honor duty calls." She walked up the dark path toward her room, her bright white tux receding into the trail like a cartoon ghost.

At some point, Shirtless Groomsman and Vodka Kidneys stumbled away from us with drunk waves. Ollie and I were alone. I closed my eyes and breathed in the salty air, listened to the hollow crash of the sea far below.

"You meditating?" Ollie asked.

"You know I can't turn off like that."

"Don't dismiss your thoughts," he advised. "Just watch them move by."

"Like fucking clouds. I know."

"You might be able to get there when you're this empty."

We closed our eyes. Our knees were angled toward each other, separated by a gap of darkness.

"Breathe in, breathe out," Ollie said. "Feel oxygen enter your lungs and exit your mouth. In, out. In, out." He was slurring his words slightly, using a faux-Zen voice. I laughed at his sloppy imitation. Technically, oxygen entered your lungs and carbon dioxide exited your mouth—Respiratory System 101—but I wasn't going to correct him. "If a thought pops up, watch it float by. Like . . ." He hesitated. "A bubble. Soapy little thought."

Breathing deeply always felt like a trite instruction for anxiety, a reflex we repeated with lame hope, like turning your computer off and on when there was a major issue you couldn't understand. But sometimes, it worked. I imagined all the branches of me, coming together to support this breath, to maintain an equilibrium even when hit with an excess of limoncello shots and pasta. I thought of the evenness of breath, how it represents the ideal modern marriage: in for four, out for four, an equitable division. I thought of the salt in the air, the salt on my lips from my final dirty martini, the smell of bougainvillea. I thought of Ollie's voice unfolding like a scroll, the one I'd always wanted to read. My thoughts weren't bubbles; they existed in a bubble. They were rooted in the moment, in the reality of feeling. I'd gone from wary to woo-woo in a minute.

"Now imagine yourself in an ocean, floating alone. You're surrounded by so much water. You're looking up at the sky and breathing in. Out. In. Out."

I cracked open my eyes. His lips were parted. His golden-brown hair looked darker against the night, a spill of curls reaching toward his closed eyes. I was breathing audibly, with an almost guttural release.

He opened his eyes. I closed mine tight, too tight—it would be obvious that they'd been open. I moved closer, or maybe he moved. We moved. My face tipped up to him. There was a brief suspension, an object thrown into the air.

Then we were kissing, his hands on my shoulders, in my hair. I put my arms around his waist, and he pulled me onto his lap, pressing hard up against the thin fabric of my dress. Our mouths were urgent, searching, digging for justification—if we moved into each other with force, we might pry loose a reason this was worth it. I didn't need a reason. His body felt like climbing back into a bed still warm from my own outline.

"This chair sucks," Ollie said.

"Here." I moved to sit in it as Ollie pulled my dress up over my head.

The wrought-iron seat dug into my skin, but I didn't mind the dual pressures: Ollie on top, metal on bottom. For the first time, I understood why people might be into BDSM. My dress was discarded, wrapped around the chair leg. I moved my head backward to give myself a better angle for eye contact. Finally, he looked at me. His eyes were blank. I felt him move inside me, and then he started pushing harder, a rising force.

"Ow," I said. I couldn't help it. With every push, the chair pushed back, a rigid skeleton. I could feel each vertebra of my spine punching into the iron, the materials too tough to mix.

Ollie pulled me toward his chest and flipped me over. I wished the motion were fluid, but it was a mess; I felt gangly and disorganized, as if it was my limbs' fault this wasn't working smoothly.

We were in my favorite position with Whit, the one that

made eye contact impossible. Ollie's pushing got faster. I gripped the sides of the chair and tried to make myself motionless. He wanted me so badly that he couldn't help himself; he'd turned into an animal. Maybe we'd recall this story privately at our own wedding, how this night reconnected us. Publicly, we'd talk about the eye contact, the Italian air, keeping the sex to ourselves. That wouldn't officially happen until later, once we'd broken it off with Whit and Anika.

A single light bulb glowed against the stone wall of the villa. I imagined it full of people, like its glass had reflected just a few hours ago, watching us. Sometimes the world gives you a loophole to live out a secret in plain sight.

maxweiner32 cool account!

jessicagreenberg wtf I came here for workouts . . .

zptheking this is weird and I'm sort of into it

passtheguac45 who are you??

17 July

calliememaybe Raising the roof 🙌
@mimimurph thanks for the perfect night!

Synonyms for *congratulations* swarmed through the Wythe Hotel roof. *Finally. Look at you. Tell me everything.* More than a hundred people—a high yield for summer in the city—stood in the outdoor space with sweeping views of Brooklyn and Manhattan, the lit-up buildings strewn like inverse constellations.

We were there for an engagement party. Virginia had sent out the invitations only two weeks before, days after the question was popped, and Mimi sprung into planning action. This time, there were cake pops instead of cupcakes, a picture of the couple printed across bulbs of hardened sugar.

My face was on the cake pops.

I was a wide-smiling head perched on dozens of plastic sticks.

Whit asked me to marry him a week after we got back from Italy. The story, which I'd now told dozens of times, spilled out of me like lyrics to a song I didn't realize I'd memorized.

It happened on Cheesy Sunday (his term), the night we usually ordered pizza. He suggested Lil' Frankie's, where we'd gone on our first dinner date. I opened the hot box and nearly missed the writing on the cardboard: *Marry me?* scrawled in permanent marker. The *yes* came automatically, like a sneeze. I screamed the answer loud and high in his apartment, and I became a bride. I wasn't prepared for the immediate interest that came along with this title. It was more noteworthy than anything I'd ever done, and I hadn't even *done* anything for it, except scream and eat pizza.

It was fast, sure. We'd been together for only seven months. But Whit was older and had always known what he wanted, and didn't I want this, too? His certainty was a salve, an invitation to live without all my hedging or alternates. I remembered another one of Mimi's mantras: "Don't stew, just do." So I did.

"This is just the beginning," people kept saying. "You don't need to make any big decisions yet."

Why did I feel like it was the end and everything had been decided?

Once the initial excitement wore off, I felt the trepidation of accepting a job after lying on your résumé. I'd had sex with someone else a week before I agreed to spend the rest of my life with Whit. Shouldn't this disqualify me from the great marital adventure? Or did this simply qualify me as human, someone who *contained multitudes*? Besides, it wasn't just someone else—a nameless, faceless body. It was Ollie, He-Who-Shall-Not-Be-Named until he was on top of me and his name slipped through my lips with a rasp. I hadn't seen him since that night in Italy; in the wedding planning frenzy, he'd taken on a phantom quality, a figure in my periphery. I told myself that there was a poetic nature to the engagement's timing. I'd needed to expel Ollie from my psyche with a literal thrust before I could commit to Whit.

I know now, after the disaster of my wedding night, that the stories we tell ourselves are a kind of brainwashing. "Follow your heart" is an empty directive—the heart is a motor without a GPS. The mind controls our path, the brain a loopy autocrat behind the wheel. At my engagement party, when I imagined everyone's organs, their minds were especially vivid. Their heads lit up like social media profiles, recalibrating, editing, and clicking through the constant feed.

Virginia was holding a tray of shots in thimbles of Italian blown glass.

"Take it, don't break it," she said, offering me a yellow-and-white swirled glass.

"These probably cost more than my engagement ring."

"Whit's a cheap bastard." She threw her head back and shook her hair behind her shoulders. "So, is this everything you ever dreamed of?"

I saw my dream from the night before. I was underwater with Ollie, his curls fanning out in the pool like tendrils of smoke. I'd been able to see him so clearly without goggles. When I reached out to touch him, I woke up.

"Dreamed?" I said, as if repeating her question could dislodge the image from my head.

"Isn't every little girl supposed to dream of her wedding and engagement party and *hashtag BrideTribe*? Where's the man of the hour?"

"Who?"

"Your husband."

"Fiancé," I corrected.

"Husband-in-training, whatever."

"I should probably go find him." We'd come to the party separately, at Whit's urging. He wanted to extend the tradition of a bride and groom cleaving on the wedding day and fusing back together at the altar.

"Godspeed," Virginia said. We clinked our empty shot glasses together, toasting to everything with nothing.

.

I saw Ollie before I saw Whit. He was talking to one of the bartenders, a guy with wall-to-wall tattooing on his arms. Ollie's curls looked longer, even though it had been only a few weeks since I was grabbing them. Since he was wrapping his arms around my waist, pulling my pelvis to mirror his. *Reroute,* I shouted inside myself. *Stop remembering.* I tried to focus on one of his nonerotic body parts, the most asexual slice of skin I could find. The ear: whorled like a shell, like the swirl of his hair, the spiral of an orgasm. Nope, that wouldn't work.

"Hors d'oeuvres?" a waiter offered, holding a tray of tartines topped with smoked salmon and chives. I popped one into my mouth and swallowed it whole.

When I'd called my mom to tell her about the engagement, the reaction had been disappointing.

"Are you sure? You barely know this guy." I heard a television in the background, probably a history documentary like the ones she'd forced my dad and me to watch when we would've preferred fantasy or horror films.

"And you don't know him at all," I'd retorted. "I'm twenty-nine. It's not that unusual for things to move quickly."

"These timelines aren't real. Doing the same thing as everyone else doesn't mean it's the right thing."

"Can you just trust me? He's a good guy."

She exhaled, her breath abrasive in my ear. "I'm sorry. I'm sure he's great. I just haven't met him, that's all."

She asked about the wedding in a resigned, dutiful tone. Where and when would it be, what would I wear, who would be paying?

I paused. I had answers for her, but she wouldn't like them. Whit and Mimi, with my half nods that registered as approval, had already mapped out a plan: Watch Hill, winter, crisp whites and greens. Mimi and Walter had generously offered to pay for half of the wedding. "We know neither of you have parental support," Mimi had said. "We'd be honored." We'd protested for less than a minute before acquiescing to their offer. Whit's savings would cover the rest.

"We're still figuring that out," I said to my mom. "But we want to have it in Watch Hill early next year. Winter."

"Why winter?"

"It's cheaper."

That shut her up.

"Mimi's throwing an engagement party in a few weeks," I added. "Can you come?"

A pause on the line. "Mimi's throwing it?"

"Yeah. She offered, which was really generous."

"You know I can't do weekends, honey." She hadn't called me *honey* in years but used to trot out this term of endearment when she was exasperated with me. "It's the busiest for catering."

"Can't you have someone cover for you?"

"Not on short notice like this. Tell you what. I'll come to the city soon and go dress shopping with you, how does that sound?"

I told her it sounded good, even though it sounded like a stressful consolation, wrapping myself up in tight lace for a woman whose presence would already make me claustrophobic.

"We're thinking February seventeenth," Mimi was saying to her friend Belinda.

"I can picture her in a regal dress, something high-necked," Belinda interjected, dreamily gesturing to indicate some vague idea of a royal wedding dress.

"We haven't even started looking," I said.

Belinda looked horrified. "Oh, darling, you need to get on that. Most ateliers require six months to tailor a dress, especially one of your caliber."

Who is paying for this high-caliber dress? I wanted to ask. *Mimi, is that on you, too?*

"We're going to Mark Ingram, Bergdorf, and Vera next month," Mimi said.

"We are?"

"Sent you an email."

She'd started an email thread with me, Whit, and Virginia (subject line: **wedding stuff**) that functioned as a disorganized repository of all her thoughts. She'd accidentally sent her grocery list to it yesterday, with **TURKEY JERKY** inexplicably in all caps. Virginia had asked to be removed from the thread multiple times, but Mimi insisted that the maid of honor should be involved in the details.

"My mom wants to go dress shopping with me, too," I said.

A flicker of surprise on Mimi's face was quickly replaced by a fake smile. "Tell her to come. We can all get lunch after."

"Whit is just so cute," Belinda cooed. "Look at how happy he is."

He was standing in a circle, gesturing to a group of his friends' girlfriends. Whit looked handsome in a navy-blue suit jacket and well-tailored pants, hair with just enough product to look groomed instead of greasy. Our engagement narratives were identical, but Whit was better at hooking an audience. In the two weeks since the engagement, he seemed calmer and more confident. He still strained for a laugh, but he did it with less desperation, more fluidity. I wondered if he'd been nervous about my saying no all this time and had relaxed with my response. Or maybe he just loved being the center of attention and not needing to work for a place in the spotlight anymore. I told Mimi and Belinda that I should go check on him.

"Future hubby!" Belinda shouted, her arms shooting up in a V, for victory, in a game I'd won without trying to play.

Maxine, the founder of Composure, was smoking a Juul in a snakeskin case. Her bright white hair stood out in the crowd. The dye job was part of her shtick: blurring the lines between youth and age, life and death. Fast Company had just published an article about us with the headline "It's Not Easy Being Green: Environmentally Friendly Burials Get an Update."

Seeing Maxine at this party felt similar to running into a teacher at the movie theater: out of place, dissociating, just plain wrong. Bex made me invite her because she said it would "engender positive communication." She was always coming up with new verbs to eliminate work-life boundaries.

"Did you say hi to my parents yet?" Whit asked.

"Where?"

"The bar."

Christine and Barry Harris stood in the middle of a crowd, blinking and looking around like children abandoned at a subway stop. I'd met them for the first time days earlier. They were staying at a hotel in Times Square and booked a reservation at Jimmy Buffett's Margaritaville. Barry ordered a fluorescent cocktail the size of a table lamp, and Christine had a dirty Shirley Temple. "How fun," I'd said, and she nodded twice, not elaborating on her choice. The dinner had gone well in terms of my performance. I asked thoughtful questions and received short, polite answers, earning laughs at a few jokes. They were sweet and good listeners, but unaccustomed to the sensory overload of both the city and their

son. Whit kept picking up their slack during dinner, supply-
ing punch lines and context to their occasional stories. Christine had talked about their dog, a German shepherd named
Rufus, and repeated an anecdote about the postman bringing
him homemade treats. Once we were back at the apartment,
Whit told me he was worried about her memory.

"Ma, say hi to the woman of honor," Whit called, nearly
pushing us together to hug.

"You look nice," Christine said.

"So do you," I lied. She had on a gray cotton sack dress
that hit below her knees.

"I met Mimi," Christine continued. "I can't believe she's
doing so much for you two. They're just family friends?"

"Mom, it's more than that," Whit said. "They're like actual
family."

"She loves planning parties," I assured her. "She'd be orga-
nizing her own half birthday if she didn't have our wedding
to keep her busy."

"Ruby from down the street went into that, party planning. You remember her, right, honey?"

"Have you tried the signature cocktail?" Whit asked. "The
Old-Fashioned, New Fiancé. Since we drank old-fashioneds
on our first date. God, she thinks of everything."

I wasn't sure whether he'd avoided his mom's question
because he didn't hear her or because he tended to dismiss
childhood memories. He wasn't in touch with anyone from
Philly. Whit came to New York, like many people, for a fresh
start—an impulse, I realized, that wasn't dissimilar to the way
Ollie deleted everything from his phone to live in the present. The city was immediate and all-encompassing enough
to render the past inconsequential, and yet I was still being
supported by a family I'd known since I was born. Pieces of
my father's book came to me as the city pulsed behind the
bar window.

*Manhattan unfolds down thousands of blocks in a grid,
but its spirit is arranged in a pattern of overlapping
circles. As one moves closer to the center, dozens of new
nuclei crop up, growths springing with the optimism of
May flowers. Social relevance is an illusion. Circles are
endless and induce dizziness. A man could be committed
by attempting to pin down the point around which the
city rotated.*

 *Fred Cahill preferred to reside in an internal
landscape where he was the perpetual city center. He
wasn't wildly off base—he'd been a looming figure in
business for more than a decade and hailed from a
lineage that had helped build Manhattan—but he knew
little of the downtown scenes blossoming just minutes
away from his town house. He had no curiosity about
alternate lives, those circles forming without and perhaps
in spite of his presence. Sterling, on the other hand,
thirsted for the ancillary knowledge of strangers, an
urban anthropologist. He went on long walks throughout
the boroughs, which Dorothea termed his "episodes." "No
need to bolt the door when you come in," she'd say to
their housekeeper. "I can sense one of Sterling's episodes
coming on."*

 *"Walking is medicine," he was telling Amelia.
They sat in the Watch Hill drawing room watching
raindrops chase down the window. "I stomped from the
Metropolitan all the way down to the Seaport last week."*

 *"I roam as well," she mused with a faraway look in
her eyes, as if she required a stronger prescription lens
to see the world. "I find people more breathtaking than
buildings."*

 *Sterling had never thought to compare the two. In New
York, especially in the year 1898, architecture reigned
supreme in the minds of their set. The Mr. Stewart Laffers*

had thrown a dinner party the weekend prior, in a new
building advertised as a Madison Avenue jewel box.
The attendees could not stop discussing the beams, the
columns, the lacquer of the crown molding. Sterling had
stared out the window at the tiny moving dots below,
wanting to discuss people instead.

"Too right," he said. "The object of my interest requires
a pulse."

"'The soul should always stand ajar, ready to welcome
the ecstatic experience.'"

"Emily Dickinson," he said, amused and pleased. He
hadn't enjoyed himself this much in weeks, even years.
Amelia's face held a placid sheen, her cheeks dewy as
if she'd recently stepped outside for a brisk walk herself,
though they'd been housebound all day as the storm
raged. Sterling noticed, for the first time, a mole on the
right side of her chin like an errant bit of chocolate. He
loved its imperfection, the way it suggested messiness
as opposed to a typical beauty mark's neat lower cheek
predictability. Her green eyes were emeralds in the light
of the drawing room.

My mom had green eyes; Mimi had a mole on her chin. Belinda liked to quote poetry unprompted to remind people she'd been an English major at Stanford. Was Amelia Cahill based on someone or an amalgamation of women he'd known, a cherry-picking of traits he found attractive? I wasn't sure which characters I should root for yet. My dad had reshuffled the tic-tac-toe grid of marriage, the immovable pieces that dictated each person's distinct placement in their social landscape.

As I spaced out staring through the window to New York,

lost in my dad's fictional world, the reflection of the party surfaced and transposed itself over the city lights. The bright, sharp sound of silverware on glass directed my attention toward Whit. He was about to give an impromptu speech.

"Some of you might know that Callie and I met on the subway seven months ago. Our relationship moved faster than de Blasio's plan to revamp the MTA." The crowd erupted in polite laughter. Walter leaned forward and gripped his thigh, a sign that he was truly amused. "From the minute I saw her staring at me like a creep across the aisle, I knew I'd want to walk down a slightly different aisle with her one day. Those of you who know Callie know she is hilarious, a little wicked, and extremely sharp. She is a woman who *knows what she wants*. And I'm a man who knows what I want: her. I want to make a family with her, because from the second I met her on that subway platform, she's been my family."

Here, multiple women clutched their chests, feeling for their hearts or their hard nipples. Ollie whispered to Maxine near the bar, and I wondered whether they'd been introduced tonight or already knew each other. Ollie seemed to have the entire thirty under thirty list in his contacts. Maxine laughed at his whispered comment, tipping up her symmetrical face and sipping her old-fashioned.

"I also want to extend a special thanks to Callie's second family, the Murphys, who have become like family to me as well. Thank you for this night and for guiding us through the wedding planning madness. We couldn't do any of it without you. Cheers!"

We all raised our glasses. His speech was the perfect length, short and heartfelt. I might've nixed the gratuitous political joke, but otherwise—no notes.

With so many eyes and smiling mouths turned toward me, I became too aware of my face. It was impossible to look natural when you were concerned about how you were appearing, like trying to listen to someone on FaceTime while sneaking glances at yourself in a suspended square.

I went to hug Whit and tell him he was fantastic, but before I got to him, Virginia stopped me. She was drunk. When she'd been overserved, her eyes didn't open all the way, which read as seductive to people who didn't know her well.

"He did good," she said. "Except . . ." Her mouth twisted to the side, the face she made when catching herself before making an offensive comment—ineffective, because this always made me desperate to know whatever she wasn't saying.

"Go on."

"You're indecisive! That 'knows what she wants' stuff. It sounds nice, but—do you?"

"We're here, aren't we?"

"I'm just fucking with you. Trolling you for never knowing what to order at restaurants."

She was right. I'd been known to chase down the waiter and switch the steak to the bass or the Caesar to the tuna tartare, usually in a last-minute calculation to cut calories. I struggled with inconsequential decisions, but did that mean I was doomed to overanalyze the big ones, too? Maybe I was just better at zooming out.

I couldn't say it out loud, but Virginia had no leg to stand on when it came to commitment. Her longest boyfriend had lasted less than a year. When I'd seen her with the woman at Leila's wedding in Watch Hill, I thought it might open up a conversation or shed some light on why she'd resisted long-term love. But so far, she'd just made me feel like a square for considering it.

"I'm going to go soon," she said. "Want to come? Ollie and I were talking about getting drinks at Lucien."

"Fun, but I don't think I can leave my own party."

"It's our party *for* you. Permission granted."

"I've barely even said hi to Whit's parents."

"Okay, well, I'm gonna go. Ollie needs this."

"He needs to drink at a restaurant?"

"A night out. After the breakup." She registered the alarm on my face and must have remembered that she'd forgotten to tell me.

When she said "the breakup," in the millisecond before it occurred to me she was talking about Anika, I pictured the breaking up of our bodies on the wrought-iron chair, the peeling away of our suctioned skin in the milky-gray early morning, the no-man's-land that counted as neither night nor day.

I'd tried to draw it. Pen-sketched arms grasping, livers pulsing with alcohol, metacarpal bones tangled in curls, and brains pumping. No hearts. All this movement in my head, translated into a shaky pen that contained some kinetic left-overs. The caption was weird, even for me: **I, XX chromosome, take you, XY chromosome, to be my lawfully bedded fuck.** My 125 loyal @bridalbodyyy followers had liked it, writing fire and devil emojis in the comments.

"When did they break up?" I managed.

"Like two weeks ago. I don't know the full story, but he's been kind of depressed."

"Alcohol's a depressant. It won't help."

"Okay, Doctor."

I flinched.

"Sorry, I didn't know that was still a sensitive subject."

"Can you just stay for another hour and help me deal with my future in-laws?"

"They're all yours," she said in a voice she meant to be light but came off barbed. "You won't even miss us."

I watched her, Ollie, and Maxine walk out the door, the fabric of Maxine's kimono and Virginia's jumpsuit touching, overlapping like grafted skin. Ollie looked back at the room one last time before they left and made eye contact with me, the shadow of a wink on his eyes.

Whit walked up, giddy and tipsy, and spun me under his arm. It felt good to be wanted, nakedly, in public.

Mimi approached us with manic urgency.

"Look," she said, gesturing to a picture she'd removed from a collage board in the far corner of the room. There were tears in her eyes. "Do you remember this night? George Hamilton's wedding. I want to post it. What should I say? *Daddy's little girl all grown up.* Oh, I can put it next to one from tonight—how do people do that? You know, make the pictures into a flipbook."

"A slideshow," I said with a laugh. "I can show you."

In the square Mimi held, I was an awkward, pudgy teen stuffed into a Delia's dress. Acne dotted my cheek; cherry-red lip gloss framed a gummy smile. My dad hugged my side, handsome and relaxed, his ill-fitting suit reading as rakish, whereas bad fits looked plain frumpy on Walter.

I traced his face on the worn photo paper, remembering that Watch Hill wedding with clarity that only came with memories I'd preserved and brightened of my dad.

mimimurph so many congrats, we love you!!

keepcomposure cheers to our @calliememaybe

bexjones LFG BRIDE!!!

graymbosker it's allllll happening 🍾 💁

18 July

mimimurph Daddy's little girl all grown up!!
♥ #tbt to her first wedding. So much fun
celebrating our @calliememaybe and her future
husband @whitty_

I danced with my dad at the first wedding I ever attended.

Virginia was my date. We were place card virgins and actual virgins, fifteen-year-old assholes simultaneously ambivalent and idealistic about marriage—a future that felt as far away as death.

The wedding was at a home in Watch Hill. We'd been invited to keep the groom's kids, who were around our age, company. I'd heard my mom whisper that the couple's age difference was "cliché," a word I already loved because of its accent and snap, the way it sounded sophisticated even though it signified the opposite.

Virginia and I were guzzling Shirley Temples and hors d'oeuvres. She dangled the cherry above her glass. "Ollie says he can teach me to do the trick. You know, when you tie the stem into a knot in your mouth."

"Isn't that like incest?"

"Ew, not like that. He's not going to *show me*."

Once we'd sampled every single hors d'oeuvre and voted

the pigs in a blanket unequivocal champion, Virginia suggested a game. Our game.

I pointed at an old guy with wiry white hair, Coke-bottle glasses, and a tie patterned with sailboats. "That dude. Go."

Virginia described how this stranger was a mad scientist working at Murphy Inc. who, unbeknownst to the wedding guests, had slipped a powerful sedative into the mustard dipping sauce. We'd all be comatose by the time the band played "Shout."

We played this guessing game everywhere back then—the beach parking lot, the movie theater, the deli downtown—and loved concocting a common theme to unite the strangers.

"What about them?" I asked, looking toward my dad and Mimi standing near the bar.

"They weren't invited," she said. "Brother and sister farmers who crashed the wedding. They're giving the couple a cow as a present, like a dowry."

"She looks fancy for a farmer."

"Dairy business is booming."

I don't remember what Mimi was wearing, but I imagine it was jewel-toned, accented with gold jewelry. I'm sure her laugh was louder and throatier than usual. A ragged bark that split wider with every cocktail, a seam opening in her mouth. Below her pink-painted lips, the large mole on her chin was punctuated by a smaller freckle, like a planet and its moon. We'd delved into the solar system in science class that year; I remembered this mole-planet comparison with a pride only afforded to the mind's early connections. I was impressed by my ability to spin a metaphor out of Mimi's chin. I was young, but the visual was arguably more arresting than my dad's "errant bit of chocolate" to describe Amelia's mole. I thought maybe I should start revising and honing the manuscript like he'd asked me to in the hospital.

Shirley Temples drained, Virginia and I headed to the bar

for a refill. I paused before breaking up my dad and Mimi's conversation. Their conspiratorial leans and loud laughter instinctively made me want to leave them alone, let my dad relax in this reprieve from his increasingly depressing days. He hadn't been feeling well lately; he took naps at two p.m. and shuffled around the house in slippers, tallying up my mom's growing list of domestic resentments. I didn't know it then, but his symptoms were a precursor to his cancer diagnosis.

"Can I try some?" Virginia asked, pointing at her mom's glass of chardonnay.

"See!" Mimi crowed to my dad, her face open and contagious with joy. "I told you they were trouble."

"Callie still drinks Capri Sun only," my dad said. "Wine is gross. Right, Cal?"

"If that's the story you want to tell yourself, Dad." In truth, I'd barely touched alcohol. Virginia, Ollie, and a bunch of other kids in town had gotten drunk off Natty Lights and Smirnoff Ices a few nights before, as I watched on over the beach bonfire's orange heat, flames turning my single Smirnoff hot while I hoped they wouldn't notice I'd been nursing the same bottle for hours.

"Speaking of stories," Mimi said, "your dad was just telling me about his new book. It sounds fabulous." She smiled at my dad and touched his wrist. "I've always loved Edith Wharton. Hopefully he'll remember us when he's famous."

Edith Wharton? Literary fame? My dad hadn't told me or my mom anything about his new idea, saying he didn't want to jinx it this time. He'd told me that ideas were always better before you tried them out—you had to kill your expectations to let a story live. I wondered if marriage was like that, too.

"Mimi's being generous," he said. "I don't have much yet."

We chatted with them idly about the ceremony ("beautiful" per Mimi, "a snooze" per my dad) and the food ("heavy" per Mimi, "incredible" per my dad). Then my dad asked me to dance, and we left Virginia and Mimi standing at the bar with empty glasses, arguing about the choker she'd chosen to wear, a black ribbon that made her head look tied on like in that scary story.

My dad spun me around the dance floor as the string lights ringing the tent flickered in his glasses. He had a kind face, the rare type of masculine good looks that weren't tainted by threat. There was nothing sinister about his chin, not an ounce of malevolence behind his dimpled smile. Sure, we glorify people after death, blunt their edges until they're symmetrical and shining, but my dad's face didn't have many edges to begin with. It had an openness that prompted me to tell him things, admissions I wouldn't put on anyone else—even Virginia or my mom.

But while I was comfortable telling him everything on my mind—a bad grade, a crush gone wrong, a fight with Virginia—his inner world remained unknowable. Adults try to protect kids from their reserves of fear, but he'd guarded truths that affected my life: our financial precarity, his man-uscript, the widening rift between himself and my mom. I wasn't aware of these specific omissions, but I'd started to notice a space he kept between himself and other people, including me. "Your father can be mysterious," my mom had said to me once when he took two hours to pick up an onion at the grocery store. "Mysterious" implied attractive intrigue but also hinted at deceit. I couldn't see the depths he hid from me—and, ultimately, from himself.

My dad flung me into the pretzel, followed by a dip that made my hair graze the floor. I felt light in his arms. Not skinny—I would never let myself wear that particular badge—but buoyant, like I could have floated up into the tent and bounced around, a helium-filled human.

He started whispering in my ear with impressions of Walter and George, the groom. Walter's lockjaw accent, George's lackluster vows. He was so good at imitating them, I felt like I was dancing with a revolving door of men. This could have made me recoil, but it just made me laugh so hard that I peed a little.

"I wonder who you'll end up with," my dad said. "I hope I can imitate him."

"What if he's *inimitable*?" I asked, using a vocab word from English class.

"Impossible."

"'Sometimes it's fun to do the impossible.'" I recited it quickly, proud of myself for procuring it at the right moment. This Walt Disney quote was my dad's favorite assurance that he wouldn't let life get boring.

I looked up at the lights and thought of the person whose name would be next to mine on invitations as thick as butter knives. Hundreds of calligraphed summons to dance under a different, but nearly identical, tent. I imagined that vague man, unaware that the man holding me would soon become vague—someone I had to remember, which would quickly start to feel like imagining.

meet.virginia hot dress #deliasforever

whitty_ love this pic so much. Thanks for an incredible night, Mimi!

belindapbergin this girl. this man!

19 Now

I take off my dress.

I've been wearing it since two p.m., this weighty, well-tailored reminder. It is an old Greek Orthodox tradition, I'd learned while researching for Composure, to bury unmarried women in wedding dresses, allowing them to leave earth fulfilled and without regrets. I would really throw those stodgy Christians for a loop.

I walk to the bathroom window naked. The trees lining the street perpendicular to the beach are bare and skeletal. My dad's novel described Watch Hill as "still in the off-season, like a film on pause," but I agree with that description only in the dark. During the day, the wind whips branches across the sand and creates a tunnel of chilled motion.

My body reflects back at me in the black window, my distended stomach a reproach. The picture of my mom at her baby shower before the miscarriage comes to me. What must it have been like to watch Mimi grow, the happy sheen of new life on her face, while emptied out? My mom, strangely, had been one of the only people I could stand tonight—the one person I'd known forever who hadn't explicitly betrayed me. Getting married in Watch Hill was a misguided attempt at closing a gap I couldn't see inside, questions about my family and the Murphys I'd never been able to articulate, even to myself. When I began reading my dad's manuscript, I had no idea that it would be one of the threads that led me here, heaped in the wreckage of the family that raised me, prematurely blowing up the family I was supposed to start.

I draft a response to Virginia's "can we talk" text and delete it. Try again. Delete. Those three bubbles pop up on her end, too, and disappear, resume, then recede. And finally, she says—

It's important.

Out the window, I treat the landscape like geographical tea leaves that will tell me what to do. I leave my decisions up to chance, like I did at Leila's wedding while watching Ollie: If a large wave hits the shore in the next thirty seconds, text her back. If you spot an animal, don't say anything.

A dark blotch appears on the shore. At first, it just looks like a moving form, a storm system traversing quickly across the beach. I squint and let my eyes adjust and realize that it's two people, arms entwined, running into the water. It's Ollie and Virginia.

I shake my head as if the movement could dislodge the image, and when I look back, they're gone. They probably weren't even there to begin with. I sit naked by the foot of the tub and go back to the images I can rely on, the ones trapped in my screen.

20 August

meet.virginia it's all in the details 👀

Virginia's only public acknowledgment of my engagement: a close-up of beaded lace, pearly braille on a white background.

We went dress shopping at Kleinfeld. Mimi had gone with Gray and said it was "an experience," which was a convenient way to avoid conferring a value judgment. She assured me I probably wouldn't find "the one" there, but it would be fun or funny and give me an idea of my look.

Virginia and Mimi sat on a chaise. My mom was running late. She was coming into New York for the day, and I was anxious about the dynamic between her and Mimi, once close friends and now near strangers.

In the dressing room, I had three new texts. From Ollie.

We'd been texting more since his breakup. I usually reached out, but he responded quickly and kept the conversation alive. I was circling a well that I could easily fall into, but for now, the mere possibility of the messages was enough to ignite a buzz under my skin. In preparation for the wedding, my life had become painfully public, every move fair game for Mimi, Whit, Virginia, and Bex's dissection. I liked having this nebulous back-and-forth to myself, the harmless texts that could turn explosive at any moment.

I'd sent him a message before the Kleinfeld appointment with a picture from the book I was reading, *American Pastoral* by Philip Roth. We'd read Roth in our college creative writing class. Was I reading the book again as an excuse to get in touch with Ollie about something substantive? Maybe, but my reading habits were instinctual: I picked up books based on my mood, and my mood lately had been frantic and painfully American. A woman on the verge of throwing a colorful party to celebrate the promise of a white picket fence.

I was ripe for revisiting old books in search of new meanings. I'd finished my dad's manuscript, which ended abruptly while Sterling and Amelia sat in front of a fire, the sunset beginning outside as the storm ebbed. I'd started to rewrite an ending, playing around with the characters and trying to imitate my dad's voice. After searching the book for clues and connections, I'd decided that Sterling was clearly autofiction and Amelia was an imaginative escape. In real life, he used this fantasy of a perfect woman to inject intrigue into days that had proceeded in a boring, repetitive march: child-rearing, house-building, pain management for an unrealized, catastrophic diagnosis. Amelia was more like a place than a person—a shore where he could bask and unclench.

In the manuscript, tension was clearly building between the two characters, but I wasn't sure if my dad wanted it to culminate in an affair, a breakup, or Sterling's return to his wedding vows with renewed dedication. Sometimes a spark elsewhere can transition to a flame back home, illuminating a darkened relationship. I cringed at making this connection with my dad's book, but sex with Whit had been better than ever the week after I cheated on him with Ollie.

An A-line dress hung in the room, the bottom of the train

rippled like the stormy ocean my dad described outside Sterling and Amelia's Watch Hill window. "Their chemistry," my dad wrote, "had been dormant for years, an invisible form at the foot of their interactions. It made one wonder about untapped beauty. How easy it could have been for them to continue missing each other in plain sight."

Instead of telling anyone about the lines echoing in my head, I texted Ollie a Roth quote I'd underlined about how getting people wrong was part of living. I'd always thought of my dad as a lively goofball, a youthful and impatient spirit whose eyes were constantly trained on his next project. The book had made me see his soft center, the content romantic lurking beneath frenzied energy.

Ollie responded, **Yeah and maybe we got him wrong,** with an article about Philip Roth being a sexual predator. He then sent a link to a historical podcast that cast events and people in a new light. **It gets into a bunch of random stuff that we, as a society, have gotten wrong. Everything from the syphilis study to Jessica Simpson. You could say it pathologizes pop culture. Also it's fucking funny.**

"Pathologizes pop culture"—who talked like this via text? Whit rarely sent me multisyllabic words, most of our history a coordinated **see you soon, k,** and **going to grocery store,** the impersonal dance of planning. Ollie was cross-pollinating, applying medical language toward entertainment. It flipped a switch inside me, or maybe it just turned me on.

I tugged a lace long-sleeved dress over my elbow, straightening the fabric so it didn't pucker. The bodice was too tight. I didn't want Virginia and Mimi to see me, so I quickly pulled the dress off.

"We're ready for you," Mimi said.

"One second." I put on a dress the saleslady had pulled for me, a massive-skirted tulle monstrosity that was loose on my stomach. It was ugly, but it wouldn't make my body look ugly. I opened the curtains to the dressing room with a laugh waiting on my lips, defenses ready.

Virginia whipped her phone out and took a picture. "So I can remind you that you dodged a bullet."

The saleslady talked about how "romantic, old-fashioned silhouettes" were all the rage, a throwback without a hashtag. Mimi said the fabric was gorgeous, so lush.

"Throw some whipped cream on me," I said. "I'm a profiterole."

Mimi laughed louder than the joke warranted, looked at the saleslady, and said, "I don't know where she comes up with this stuff." Like I was her daughter.

Where was my mom? She should be here by now. I asked if anyone had heard from her.

"She said 'en route' a little while ago," Mimi said. "Maybe she's stuck in traffic."

Even though they'd fallen out of touch, Mimi still made excuses for her, while my mom took every opportunity to criticize Mimi, never giving her the benefit of the doubt. Perhaps Mimi was so aspirational—with her magnetic charm, Hermès scarves, and wedding binders full of tips and doodles—it gave people license to latch on to any misstep.

I went behind the curtain to try on a simpler dress, low V-neck with a full skirt. As I pulled it over my head, I thought about my next text to Ollie. I wondered which scenario would be more embarrassing: if Mimi and Virginia could see me naked or unlock the contents of my phone. The iOS echocardiogram would provoke more questions. *Why are you flirting with my cousin when you're engaged? Did you and my nephew become close friends all those years ago?*

I slipped the dress over my head, felt its slick crepe cool on my skin like the fanciest sheets in the world. People always said you knew when you found the dress. I wouldn't know, not at all, but I was less repulsed by this one.

I heard my mom's voice greeting Virginia and Mimi on the other side and opened the curtain wearing my not-hideous dress.

"There she is!" my mom said. Her voice was too high, tinny and false.

I hugged my mom. She felt so small in my arms, borderline frail. She had on jeans and a worn green T-shirt reading EVENTIDE OYSTERS. It seemed like she'd dressed specifically to juxtapose Mimi, who wore a Chanel shift and slingback kitten heels.

Mimi had her hand to her chest. "This is the one."

"It's kind of amazing on you," Virginia agreed.

My mother looked unconvinced. "How many have you tried on?"

"Two."

"Well, let's not jump to conclusions."

"But this neckline," Mimi raved. "Heavenly."

"It's beautiful, but I think you should keep trying on. We have lunch in an hour."

My mom was always on a schedule, a natural instinct calcified by her catering gig. She had no time for oohing and aahing and proclamations of wonder.

"When you know, you know," Mimi proclaimed.

"Do you?" My mother's hand was on her hip, a posture of challenge. "Usually best to test out all the options, see what fits best."

Mimi turned toward my mom and squeezed her bare hands with her heavily ringed fingers. "How are you, how was your drive here?"

"Awful. Traffic all the way into the city."

Virginia had started circling the store and taking close-up pictures of the fabric, probably for artistic inspiration. I went back into the dressing room to try on another option. I could hear the patter of Mimi and my mom's conversation, catching up about Maine, catering, Gray's wedding. The transcript was light, but the inflection had subtext. My mom's "Why'd you decide to have the wedding in Italy?" sounded more like *What an unnecessary, excessive show of privilege.* Mimi's "How's business these days?" translated to *You poor thing, working in the service industry after your husband's death.* I heard their voices move farther away from me and drop to a whisper.

The next dress was bland but pretty, A-line with tiny spaghetti straps and a trail of buttons up the back. The straps were almost as thin as dental floss, rubbed between teeth that could last up to centuries in tombs. Teeth were messages from previous generations, tiny weapons letting us know how long humanity stretched.

My body stared back at me in the full-length mirror. I was a bride. I should be thinking about my first look, my veil, and my something blue, not prehistoric teeth. I took a picture of the dress, the flash briefly exploding in the mirror like the sparklers that would lead us out of the reception to the bridal suite and the honeymoon. I texted it to Bex, who'd asked me to send pictures. Her own wedding was coming up and she only wanted to speak Brideglish, the language of seating arrangements and tailoring and ceremony-to-reception transportation.

It had gone quiet outside the dressing room. I pushed back the curtain, preparing for some squeals.

Mimi was bent toward her knees with her head in her hands. It took me a moment to realize she was crying. My mom sat next to her unmoving, looking blank and drained.

I asked them what had happened, what was wrong.

"It's just emotional," Mimi said, using a handkerchief to dab her face. "To watch you girls grow up like this. I wish your father were here to see you."

"It's been a long day already," my mom said, an odd response for someone who'd arrived only ten minutes earlier.

Mimi erupted in a fresh round of tears, folding toward herself and trying to hide her puffy face. She attempted a smile. "You're going to be such a beautiful bride," she said. "I'm just so happy, that's all."

But these didn't seem like happy tears; they weren't the shiny-eyed punctuation of a proud mother figure. They were the sounds of disintegration. Did the passage of time warrant a breakdown? Sure, it was the root of most unhappiness, when the future didn't hold up to the idea of it in your head, when the permanence of the past rose up to mock the seemingly mutable present. How minutes accumulated into years and the decisions you made when you were young defined the rest of your life. But this was the simple truth of being alive, the low-grade unease we all sat with—right? We didn't break down in bridal salons over it.

I went to hug Mimi, and she sobbed on my shoulder. Virginia was still walking around the salon, taking pictures and inspecting price tags. I tried to make eye contact with her for reinforcement, but she was too far away.

My mother stood up and clapped her hands together, the physical equivalent of a period, end of sentence. End of outing. "Are we ready to go? I'm starving."

I rubbed Mimi's back and told her it would all be okay, though I wasn't sure what would be okay. I was providing comfort for an unknown calamity like an emotional insurance salesperson.

Back in the dressing room, my phone glowed with an unread text from Ollie: **Wrong number?**

I'd sent him the dress picture instead of Bex.

    mimimurph pretty!

    whitty_ sneak peek??

21 September

whitty_ Shuck it 🌽 👀

When we arrived in Watch Hill for Labor Day weekend, Mimi was drinking white wine by the pool and wearing a giant straw hat embroidered with the phrase OUT OF OFFICE.

"Don't say that she doesn't go into an office," I whispered to Whit. "It's only okay if she makes that joke."

"Friends, Romans, city folk!" she said from her lounge chair. "I had the most divine day." She told us about getting a massage at the house, going to the farmers market, and running into Randy, a magician and town celebrity. "He's sleeping with Marcie Haffenraffer," she said, making her hands into an open cave around her mouth to function as either a whisper or a megaphone, I couldn't tell which. "She told me, and I quote, 'The magic doesn't stop with his hands.'"

"Mom," Virginia said, her voice on the verge of a scream. "How much wine have you had?"

"Marcie's had a lot of partners, too. I wonder if he performs tricks in bed. Now you see it, now you don't?" Mimi erupted in laughter, and I joined in out of equal parts discomfort and amusement.

Virginia rolled her eyes and Ollie shook his head, reverting back to the disgust teenagers reserved for their parents. They both started walking inside to change. They'd arrived the day before and, from the looks of it, had been tanning by the pool all Friday while Whit and I were worsening our complexions and posture, hunched over computers like regular people with real jobs. As I'd spent more time with my side projects, drawing for @bridalbodyyy and rewriting my dad's manuscript, I was struck by how Ollie and Virginia were able to live according to their passions. Privilege was an irrevocable tie to one's past, an ancestral debt that never needed repaying—but practically, it was an opening up of one's future, the space to live based on want, not need. They already had more than they needed. Whit and I had to respond to the immediacy of our bodies—feeding, housing, insuring—while Virginia and Ollie could prioritize their minds. What would I do with that kind of freedom? Quit my job at Composure to draw and write? Drink by the pool all day?

"Bring us some Aperol, will you?" Mimi asked. "I want to make these two a spritz."

She'd pulled down the straps of her one-piece, and her sarong was draped over her lap like a dinner napkin. Her hair, usually blown out into a confectionary pouf, hung in wet, knotted strands around her face, which was blooming red despite a family-sized bottle of EltaMD sunscreen propped up on the side table.

Needless to say, she was drunk.

It was three thirty p.m. on a Friday, close to the realm of acceptable drinking hours. But when had she started? And was she alone? I asked her if Walter was at the house.

"He's in the shitty," she slurred. "HA! The city. God, that's Freudian, isn't it? He's arriving here tomorrow, allegedly."

Whit said he was excited to talk to Walter about the new deal he was working on, and I had a flicker of resentment at how often he brought up work. Walter was synonymous with the pharmaceutical business in Whit's mind, and he gabbed about his investment portfolio nearly every time the man's name came up.

Mimi had on cat-eye sunglasses that took up half her face, but I could tell she'd closed her eyes. Her body language was too passive for alertness: head lolled to the side, hat removed, leg dangling off the lounger. I put on sunscreen, hoping she'd perk up, notice, and do the same. Instead, she started humming the tune of "Born to Run" by Bruce Springsteen.

"Do you want some?" I held out the sunscreen bottle gingerly.

She didn't respond. I looked at Whit, hoping to communicate that we might need to carry a grown woman inside her own house. Then, out of a slurred fog, she said, "The sun's done for the day." She sat up straighter in her chair and pulled her glasses on top of her head. "You can't get burned after two."

And yet the sky was cloudless, the sun hanging hot and sickly yellow. Mimi's certainty was intoxicating yet deluded. How nice it would be to live according to her set of beliefs: the sun does not burn, the third martini is a good idea, the fun awaits on the corner of a street you've walked thousands of times. You never know when you'll run into a sexed-up magician. You never know when you'll wake up lucid and refreshed after a tipsy power nap.

"Shower time," she said, tying her sarong around her waist. "I hope you're hungry. We're doing scallops and corn and pies the size of your head."

Back in the guest room, I wrote:

Amelia rose to a clear horizon. The imprint of her body in the sheets reminded her of a casket lining, already primed for its inhabitant.

"Sterling!" she cried out. She nearly replaced the first syllable and said darling. After being acquainted with him at a distance for many years, he suddenly felt more intimate than her betrothed. They had not yet touched, but she'd fantasized about it, his face appearing behind her closed eyes at night, his company an aberration she wanted to turn into a forever.

With my computer hot on my lap, the lines flew from my fingertips. I'd hinted at a blossoming relationship between Sterling and Amelia, but I wouldn't write that scene. I wanted to focus on the morning-after reality behind the fantasy. I stopped to look outside: Virginia and Ollie had gone downstairs to play croquet, and Whit was typing on the porch. This image stirred a plot development; I now knew what Amelia would find.

Amelia walked downstairs, passing by gilded frames of herself and Fred. The two of them on their wedding day, the two of them sitting on the rocks. Dressed up for a charity ball, dressed down for a beach day. Her history with Fred had archival power, shadow proof that would follow her no matter how this ended. After her newfound connection with Sterling, she couldn't imagine anything but an ending to beget a new beginning.

The family photos lining the staircase were curiously absent of children. They'd been married for three years— her contemporaries who'd been married the same season were now on their third child!—but Amelia had a difficult time conceiving. After two failed pregnancies, they'd gone to see a special doctor. She was on all sorts of supplements. Perhaps the issue was not medical, but romantic, and she and Fred simply weren't meant to procreate.

"Cal, cheese!" Virginia shouted from downstairs, as if she were snapping a picture of me. I closed my computer. The ending would have to wait.

Whit and Virginia sat on plush, upholstered kitchen stools talking about police brutality. Wedges of Gouda and Brie and a box of rosemary crackers were sprawled in front of them.

"Some light predinner conversation?" I tried. A wave of panic rose in me. Whit's and Virginia's hot takes would not mix well. They both valued the idea of thinking independently, but for Virginia, that meant diverging from her parents, while for Whit, it meant breaking from the millennial Twitter mob. I had trouble listening to both of them, my instincts merging somewhere in the middle, a no-man's-land of half-formed ideas that made me feel toothless instead of balanced.

"Another shooting," Virginia said. She took a knife to the Gouda and cheese shards flew from the cut like orange shrapnel.

"I haven't even checked my phone since we got here," I announced, grateful for an easy transition into agreeable territory. "Being here makes me want to ditch it."

"It's been like twenty minutes," Whit said, and laughed. "Don't give yourself any awards yet."

Virginia's mouth was full of crackers. "You know," she said, covering her lips instead of waiting to speak, a habit that drove Mimi crazy, "we should put them in a drawer for the weekend. I'm way, way too addicted."

"Same!" Whit's voice was overeager, as if he'd just discovered they were from the same obscure town. "I read a study that it's psychologically similar to a gambling addiction."

"Social media as a slot machine, yeah," Virginia said. "But I also can't stop refreshing email."

"I read my promotions tab when I'm bored," I said.

"You do not." Virginia laughed.

"And our apartment listserv emails."

"Well, those are comedic gold."

"'Looking for a bi- or trilingual nanny,'" I said.

"'Selling organic food subscription for $500!'"

"Trying to culture your toddler?" Whit chimed in, his voice artificially high. "For just a year's college tuition, enroll little Henry or Magnolia in weekly museum visits with a tour guide and interactive art toys. Mommy and Me . . . and Matisse!"

We laughed, joyfully skewering our absurd neighbors while avoiding the acknowledgment that we lived there, too.

Virginia and I went outside to shuck corn. The back porch had ocean views for days, the green lawn morphing into deep blue with nothing but a motorboat on the immediate horizon. Off to the right, dozens of sailboats swayed in the harbor.

We pulled the rough husks off the cobs. I'd always loved freeing corn, the Russian doll reveal of the yellow beads. You knew what you were getting, but the unsheathing was still satisfying.

"We've still got it," Virginia said.

"The best chore."

Growing up, Mimi often gave us this assignment. We'd sit on the back porch steps with overalls and skinned knees, singing Backstreet Boys and using corncobs as microphones. Virginia was in it for the play, but I relished the task itself, the peeling and discarding. This impulse, I now realized, came from the same place as my current fixations, turning the inside outside. Kernels proceeding like braids of DNA, knowable and discrete.

"I think I'm going to drop out of grad school," Virginia said, looking at a frayed husk.

"Really?"

"Everyone wants to be an artist. I'm good, I know I'm good. But I don't think I'm good enough. I should be doing something more meaningful."

This admission was so out of character that I dropped my corncob and turned to her. "You're the most talented artist I know."

She laughed grimly. "You're biased and insane."

"Or I just don't know any other artists."

She hit my thigh. "Dick."

"What do you want to do instead?"

"No fucking clue."

This answer was both relieving and terrifying. If Virginia—who'd always moved forward with assuredness that bordered on cockiness—didn't have a clue, there was no hope for the rest of us. I knew the equalizing platitudes: "everyone feels imposter syndrome," "no one knows what they are doing." But those "everyones" and "no ones" were just faceless excuses to waffle in my own uncertainty. They weren't 5'10", 125 pounds, richer than most of the 1 percent with talent to beat most of the 100 percent.

"You're lucky to be able to pursue art," I said.

"Anyone can be an artist."

"Not exactly. It helps to have money."

"That only goes so far," she said. "I can't figure out what to do for my thesis show. I don't know. I've been feeling a low-grade dread about it all. It seems pointless."

"It won't feel like that once you gain some traction. I'm not an art critic or anything, but your stuff is brilliant. It's not pointless—my first assistant job at that hellhole was pointless. Your art—it can speak to people."

"Look at what you're doing, though!" she said. "Helping families remember their loved ones in a lasting way. I'm just throwing paint at a canvas and hoping people call me clever."

"Don't stop," I said. "You're too talented. Remember, art lets you travel while standing still." A Mimi-ism that she'd repeated approximately two hundred times, usually to assuage Walter's sticker shock at a new piece.

Virginia put her arm around me. She was rarely affectionate, and this made me more awkward than I ever was around her. It made me question how I should arrange my body in space. I let my head fall onto her shoulder, and we watched the orange sun hang above the water like we were an old couple in a Viagra commercial. We sat like that silently for a few minutes, a rare opening that didn't ache to be filled.

I answered work emails before dinner. Virginia's approval of my job and, by extension, my choices sent me on an excited digital scavenger hunt. Inbox maintenance, check. Light googling of the competition, check. Writing up a new idea for launch in my Notes app, check. I was buzzy with her praise and also a little high on the anxiety she'd expressed about her own trajectory. I was outpacing her in one realm, for once.

Mimi had sobered up enough to make dinner, which meant watching Mira, her housekeeper and part-time chef, make dinner as she walked around the kitchen island moving spices and glasses like a scattered game of domestic chess. The raw scallops sat on a cutting board, ready for browning. They looked as vulnerable and slimy as an open heart in an OR.

Whit excitedly showed us a picture he'd taken of me and Virginia shucking corn. I knew nothing about photography, but the dusk light, our arms working the husks as we looked out onto a gashed-open sunset—it was arresting. It almost looked professional.

Ollie glanced at the screen and nodded his head. "Good one," he said, in a tone that conveyed he did not actually think it was a good one at all.

Virginia asked where he'd been. He said he went on a run and quite literally ran into a gaggle of Swifties. We dipped into a conversation about how fandom had evolved. Mimi volunteered that she'd eye-fucked—"made intense eye contact with"—Mick Jagger at a concert in 1985.

"They used to be deities," Ollie observed. "When you remove that protective film, they're bound to break."

"We still interact with them through a screen," Virginia pointed out. "It's just a lot smaller."

"More personalized," I said. "I wonder if stalking's gotten worse now that stars are more accessible. Or maybe it's better because people can interact with them from their couch. They don't need to scale a stone wall."

"You know," Mimi said, pouring herself a glass and plucking a shrimp from a serving platter. "Your mother had a thing for stars. I think it's why she married your father. He wasn't famous, but he had star quality."

"My mom?" I asked incredulously. "Are we talking about the same person?"

"She was enthralled with artists. People who colored outside the lines. She never would herself, but she liked being in their orbit—except for when, you know, it pulled your dad away from doing stuff around the house. I remember one summer she tried to get us to host an artist's residency here with a painter she met at the diner."

"A regular Medici," Ollie said.

"Except, dear, it was our house she was offering up."

"That sounds amazing," Virginia said. "Petition to reinstate the artist's residency."

"I can show up to boost egos," Whit offered. "Like the idea that every Olympic event should have a regular person competing for comparison."

There was an artist's residency referenced in my dad's book, a summer when the Cahills decided to have a bunch of painters and actors come stay with them in Watch Hill. Amelia was the passionate art benefactor. Could that be based on my mother? I wondered again how much of the manuscript was real—was it historical fiction or nonfiction masked by history?

The lights in the kitchen had been turned low, and Virginia and I lit candles in an automated trance. Another task we were given growing up, once we were old enough to handle fire. Whit started setting the table; Ollie was already sitting down. A freckle-sized chin pimple stood out under the light from his phone. Mimi flung herself into the seat next to Ollie with a bottle of wine, the chilled chardonnay slick with condensation. Her face was in a knot, furrowed brow and lips squeezed together.

Then—a high-pitched crack.

The bottle of wine was on the floor in a reflective mess, green glass spread in a heap underneath Mimi's chair. She started mumbling a litany of apologies as Mira rushed to her feet with a dustpan she'd seemingly procured from under her sleeve. Whit was on his knees picking up the remains of the bottle. Mimi told him to stop, it was fine, she was so clumsy, it would all be okay. She was trying to tell us that she was in one piece as fractured glass surrounded her chair leg like a jagged wreath.

"Isn't this good luck?" Whit asked. "Breaking glass."

"If you're at a Jewish wedding, sure," Ollie said.

"Breaking the glass ceiling, then," Whit said. "A feminist mistake."

Ollie looked at Virginia, a split-second eye roll that no one else seemed to notice. I resented Ollie's dismissal—Whit's determination to make Mimi feel better about breaking the bottle was sweet, even if it came off as try-hard.

"And I'm only on my first glass of wine!" Mimi volunteered, apparently wiping the slate clean after sunset.

Dinner passed by politely. We talked about Rhode Island's governor, the volume of seaweed on the beach, the new HBO miniseries all over Twitter. The scallops were rubbery, a little overcooked, but the ratatouille tasted tangy and warm, and the wine covered my head in a pleasant screen that both reflected light and protected me from darker impulses. The best kind of tipsy.

Mimi drank seltzer and stayed mostly silent, asking clarifying questions without offering opinions or stories of her own. She brought out ice cream and Tate's chocolate chip cookies for dessert, holding a bouquet of spoons. The cookies made me remember a binge from earlier that week and feign fullness.

"Thanks, but I'm stuffed," Whit agreed. "Groom diet." He patted his stomach, a move that struck me as grotesque even though I wasn't bothered by imagining the acid and bile churning the scallops inside him, the kind of X-ray that would make most people lose their appetite.

"No one gives a shit about what the groom looks like," Virginia said, helping herself to a second scoop of vanilla. "No offense."

"Where will the ceremony be?" Ollie asked. His gaze was fixed on me from across the table, one eye on each side of a candlestick.

"At Watch Hill Chapel. It's really beautiful in there," Whit said.

Ollie's eyes locked on mine. "Didn't think you wanted a religious ceremony." He bit into a cookie and chewed slowly.

"I didn't know what I wanted."

He swallowed. "Didn't or don't?"

The room went still. I looked at the thick sage-colored curtains behind the table, trying to concentrate on a specific spot to stop my eyes from pricking with tears.

"We're all fucking winging it," Virginia said.

"Language," Mimi chimed in.

"People can change their minds," Ollie said. He'd finished his wine but still held the glass, moving his thumb and pointer finger up and down the stem. "But I will tell you right now that I would never get married with a church ceremony and a big party under a tent."

"Oh, but it would be so fabulous," Mimi gushed. "We could do an al fresco dinner party somewhere chic."

"Cart before the horse, I respect it," Whit said. "I have a buddy whose wife booked the venue like six months before they were engaged."

"Not sure I want to get on that particular horse," Ollie said. "Did you read that *Times* piece about why people marry the wrong person?"

"They also wrote about how anyone can fall in love after asking each other a bunch of dumb personal questions," Virginia said. "They're disqualified from giving out relationship advice."

"It's a dated institution, is all. Marriage. But I still appreciate an open bar."

Whit narrowed his eyes and turned toward Ollie. "So you never want to get married, or you just haven't found someone who will marry you?"

It could've come off as a joke, but Whit's body language—

elbows on the table, chin jutting forward—made it look like he was being held back by an invisible leash.

"No issues in that department," Ollie said, making me want to punch him, too. "What do you all think? Makes total sense to be with a single person for the rest of your life?"

"Well, not a single person," Virginia interjected. "The whole point is that they're not single anymore."

Ollie gave her a mock laugh, a *ha-ha* to both acknowledge and belittle her juvenile teasing.

"The point of the Alain de Botton article," Ollie continued, pausing on the writer's name and making it clear he was proud of himself for remembering it, "is that we're working out issues we have with our parents in our relationships. This line got me: 'We marry the wrong people because we don't associate being loved with feeling happy.'"

"Oh, that's a bit harsh," Mimi chided. She hadn't finished chewing her cookie and talked with her hand over her mouth, which she only resorted to with urgent messages. "You all had happy childhoods."

By "you all," she meant the childhoods that were under her charge: Virginia's and Ollie's. Whit's relationship with his family was strained at best, and I barely spoke to my one living parent. The childhood math did not come out with a positive number for our pairing.

But a few beats after her statement, Mimi looked at Ollie—not me or Whit—with remorse, her face twisting from accusatory to apologetic. "Oh, I'm sorry, honey. Your mom would be so proud of you."

"And Callie's dad, too," Ollie added. "Losing a parent—it's not the best blueprint for healthy relationships."

"Well, of course. We're always remembering Teddy," Mimi said. "And Lisa." She added Ollie's mom as a hasty afterthought, even though she was the reason we were talking about dead people at the dinner table.

"I wish I could have met him," Whit said. "Mr. Holt."

"He'd make you call him Teddy," Mimi replied.

Virginia was picking at her split ends, the long strands fissuring like small veins in the candlelight. "He was the best. Remember our trips to Newport?"

We slipped into an easy memory swap, the light back-and-forth free from weightier subtext and making it feel like he was still alive.

"God, timing," Whit said. "I was looking into this the other day for some work research. Revlimid—the drug that treats multiple myeloma—was approved soon after he passed away."

"Do you need to make this about work?" I asked.

Ollie smiled from across the table. "The pharma bro," he said. "Who read about *that* guy?"

And we were off on another cultural dick-measuring contest, competing for who could spew details from articles (Ollie) and statistics about an industry (Whit). Thank god for Virginia, who poked holes in both of their comments with sarcastic asides as she continued to pick at her split ends.

Before bed, as Whit washed his face with the fast, brute forcefulness only men applied to skin-care routines, I reread my last text to Ollie. **See u this weekend?** He'd liked the text, not even bothering with a real response. Whit's snores rippled the top sheet as I picked up my computer, its glow a nightlight in the dark room, and started typing.

Amelia's left hand trembled on the banister. She considered the children that did not slide down the wooden slope, the small boot prints that had not marred the expensive runner she'd installed without Fred's blessing. She descended the stairs to look for Sterling, her new *North Star* [TOO CLICHÉ? BETTER METAPHOR TK]. From the kitchen, voices bubbled.

"Amelia, dear!" Dorothea exclaimed. "We've arrived!"

Dorothea and Fred stood at the counter next to a pale Sterling, who sat over an untouched pastry. He looked like he'd seen a ghost, or become the ghost himself.

"Hello, love," Fred said, pecking her on the cheek. "Dreadful few days we've had, missing you."

"We made it just in time for this sunshine," Dorothea enthused.

"How did you get here?" Amelia was at a loss for words, grasping at logistics to anchor herself in reality.

"What a queer question," Fred said. "In the carriage, like I'd always planned." Fred began pacing the room. He raised his chin as if he were inspecting comrades to ensure their uniforms were satisfactory. "Has Candace been round?" he asked, referencing the maid who came weekly.

"It was a hurricane," Amelia said. "She was stuck just like you two."

"I can tell." He picked up two empty wineglasses on the side table by the couch. Red wine sediment had pooled and crusted like the remnants of a gash. "It looks like you've been having a gay time."

"We've just been wailing about how much we missed you," Sterling said. Amelia knew he was trying to paper over the tension, but it still stung. He kissed Dorothea on the lips, and Amelia turned to look out the window like she'd witnessed a union as unsavory as the one she'd dreamed about for days.

"I have some news," Dorothea said. She wore a smug expression knitted into her too-serious face. She was too somber and reticent for Sterling. "I was going to wait

*until we were in private, but oh, darling, I cannot bear
another moment between now and the rest of our lives."
She paused with a dramatic flourish. "I am carrying a
child."*

"Go to bed, babe," Whit slurred. He'd rolled toward me
with his eyes still closed.

I shut the computer, my head full of an imaginary fetus
floating underneath petticoats and skin.

> **meet.virginia** good one, W ✺
>
> **mimimurph** STUNNING
>
> **calliememaybe** so i'm marrying a professional
> photographer

22 September

Two weeks later, I sat on the closed toilet seat as Virginia showered. We were in the apartment getting ready for Mimi and Walter's thirtieth anniversary party at Doubles, the private supper club in the Sherry-Netherland.

"What's she wearing?" I asked.

"Something white. She ordered four options and only returned two."

I couldn't see Virginia's face through the fogged glass but knew it was pinched in a grimace—an expression of disdain for capitalist consumption and other alliterative evils. Fast fashion. Millennial malaise. Gas guzzling. Virginia had her hypocrisies, but she mostly shopped vintage and never learned to drive well.

Her arms rose to massage her scalp, creating a blurred diamond around her matted hair. The shape of her naked body was familiar enough that its effect had been defused with time, those small breasts and tapered waist taking on inanimate, flat qualities like striking paintings that eventually cease to make their owner pause.

She stepped out of the shower and wrapped a towel around

herself, tucking the edges in with tight fluidity. Her long hair was a brown spill down her back. She wiped condensation from the vanity and pulled at the skin on her cheeks, looking for blackheads.

"Does it make you excited?" she said, meeting my eye from the mirror. Was she referencing her body? Before I could answer, she continued. "This could be you someday, hosting an anniversary party."

"How aspirational."

"I wish the idea didn't terrify me so much. Forever." She drew out the word, her mouth an O in the glass.

"This is just my first wedding."

"You'll do well with forever. Better than I could." She brushed her hair with a tortoiseshell comb that left clean lines in its wake.

"Has there been anyone recently?" I mumbled, half swallowing the question.

"What?"

"Never mind."

"No, what did you say? My hearing's getting worse."

"Any new *friends* in your life lately?" I used Mimi's euphemism for *significant other,* hoping she'd laugh in recognition.

"Don't ask me if I'm more into men or women."

"Fine, you caught me. I'm the heteronormative bore who just wants to know which you prefer."

"It's not like that. I'm figuring it out. I could fall for either or both."

"At the same time?"

"Polyamory is pretty common now."

"I listen to Esther Perel, I know."

"I don't need *someone special* in my life at the moment. I already have Georgie."

"Who's that?"

She riffled underneath the vanity and pulled an object from a pink silk pouch. It was a rubber beetle, light blue and the size of a set of car keys, with two winged flaps on either side. It took me a second to identify the object.

"A vibrator. How is he?"

She raised one eyebrow and crossed her arms, daring me to challenge her. "How do you know it's a he?"

"Sorry—is *she* any good?"

"*They* are excellent. You should try them out."

I asked her about its settings and variabilities (light touch, medium, full frontal; with or without a partner; in or out of the bath) and how she'd picked this particular model (an ad on her feed). Virginia showed me the "sexual health" company's social accounts with a gleeful flick on her screen. A wryness in her face made me think she was testing me. I said I wanted to order one.

"Whit would flip," she said.

"I think he'd have fun with it."

"He's competitive. Some men can't handle the idea that a piece of rubber beats them at their own game."

"Seems crazy that this tiny thing could actually be better than a human."

"A human or your husband?"

"Fine. Better than Whit. Whit's good in bed. I didn't want to say his name because I hate when couples act all smug about their sex life."

"You just hadn't mentioned it to me. Whether it was good or not." Virginia was looking at the phone, eyes in an unfocused glaze.

"You hadn't asked. It's good. It's really good. I mean, I haven't had sex with that many people, but it's up there for me."

"I figured." Her thumbs flew across her phone, texting

someone, as she walked from the bathroom to the closet. I followed her. "Which one?" she said, placing a silk dress and a dark jumpsuit on the bed side by side like deflated lovers.

I was having trouble focusing on the two options she'd pulled. Did she assume our sex life was good because she couldn't imagine my being with Whit for any other reason? "You never know what happens behind closed doors" was just an implicit disapproval of someone's partner choice. *Maybe they come to life at night,* the personality version of the *Nutcracker* toys. *Maybe they're amazing at giving head.*

"Try them on, but I think the silk. More elegant," I said.

She put on the midnight-blue silk slip dress, platform heels, and the turquoise earrings Mimi gave her when we moved in. Her collarbones were a ledge under her neck. Mine were still hidden, even though I'd barely eaten the week before the party in hopes that my bones would start showing through the surface of my skin, too, like messages under a scratch-off.

I browsed the clothes hanging in my closet and put on a black wrap dress. We stood side by side in the full-length mirror as I curled my hair and she applied red lipstick.

"Have you lost weight?" she asked.

"Doesn't feel like it."

"Just making sure you're okay." She made eye contact with me through the mirror again, and I had the strange sensation we were FaceTiming while in the same room, making a mediated connection.

"Everyone loses weight before their wedding. Gray lost half a person."

"Yeah, but, you know. College," she said.

"That was a long time ago."

When Virginia came back from Paris at the beginning of our senior year, she caught me once. I was kneeled over a trash can in my dorm room when she walked in holding a bottle of Yellow Tail and a tower of plastic cups, an offering to absolve her year away. She asked me what I was doing like I'd been painting my nails a strange color or cutting my hair. There was no shock, only curiosity. I bet she thought I should've been skinnier for turning myself inside out. I'm sure she couldn't believe someone who looked like me could try this hard—make myself sick, force myself to the ground—to look more like her.

I told her I had food poisoning, but she'd seen my finger down my throat—the fleshy gun that left little room for alternate explanations. The more I insisted, the more she pushed. I finally admitted that fine, sometimes I made myself vomit. It wasn't a big deal. So many of our peers threw up after a night of drinking anyways. Princess Diana did it. Katie Amato down the hall did it, too. "You're bulimic," she said, the term sounding dirty and dire, a much starker diagnosis than an upset stomach or food poisoning or too many glasses of punch at the frat party.

I agreed to see a therapist, a woman named Pam whose office smelled like mayonnaise and desperation. I told lies about my psyche to shock her: bestiality fantasies, murder scenarios, dreams about skinny models covered in blood. I was high on the idea of my own infallibility, the delusion that my eating disorder was just a phase or an experiment. If I'd known about my future relapse, I might've actually sat down and told the truth. *I'm scared I'm unlovable.* So cheesy it ironically makes me want to vomit. But rebranded, don't the lower end of human emotions circle the same dark drain? The fear that we are ultimately all we have. The realization that the confines of one body and mind will never be enough.

My wrap dress looked frumpy in the mirror next to Virginia's sleek slip. I'd chosen it for its forgiving silhouette, tight on the chest and loose on the stomach.

"This dress is ugly," I said.

Virginia laughed. "It's—"

"Don't you fucking dare say flattering."

"Cute. It's cute. Want to borrow something to make it better?"

Offerings to share her wardrobe gave me an anxious combination of fear and gratitude. I was always excited by the intimacy, especially because she never let Gray touch her clothes, but I also worried about navigating a swarm of jackets and sweaters that looked malleable but had the potential to detonate if I couldn't pull them across my back. Dresses and pants were off-limits, no matter how many times she tried to push some flouncy size 2 maxi on me, insisting it stretched.

She picked out an oversized velvet blazer like the one she'd worn to Gray's engagement party and a pair of vintage dangly earrings that fell nearly to my shoulders, making it look like my lobes had grown beautiful, jewel-encrusted branches. I looked good. I looked more like Virginia.

"These are incredible on you." She brushed a piece of lint off the sleeve and buttoned one of the closures in the middle. "Here, this will look good, too," she said, handing me the tube of red lipstick, a black plastic bullet with a gold seal in the shape of a pout.

"You really think I can use this thing? I'll look like a clown."

She put her hand on my shoulder and asked me to open my mouth. Pressing down, she brushed easy strokes over my top and bottom lip.

"Voilà," she said, a distinctly Mimi expression. "Your new look."

"I look different. Good different."

"You look hot."

I tried to take this as a compliment instead of a nod to all the ways I'd looked un-hot before. The bright slash turned my lips into the type of filtered pillow morphing faces all over my feed. My @bridalbodyyy account attempted to illuminate our chaotic, shared interiors, the parts whose gleam inspired disgust versus glowing accolades. No amount of money or taste could change the placement of one's colon, the texture of a kidney. Stripped of the accoutrements, the Murphys and I had always been made of the same stuff.

But money and taste, those slippery tricks, did have the power to alter the exterior. Side by side in the mirror, my mouth and Virginia's were nearly identical. If they'd been lined up like mug shots, a discerning detective might not know the difference.

At the party, I went from buoyant to dizzy somewhere around the fifth margarita. One minute, I'd been laughing with Virginia, dancing to the Jackson 5 and wondering out loud if we were still allowed, deciding together *yes*, because it was before Michael grew up and became a predator. The next minute, I was stalking toward the ladies' room, convinced that if I could sit down in a stall, the grounded porcelain might sober me up. The toilet seat was cool on my skin, and I touched my goose bumps, imagining them multiplying like crop circles. I got up, glanced at myself in the mirror. The lights should have been more forgiving, given that the age of the Doubles clientele bottomed out around fifty-eight. Virginia, Gray, Tommy, Ollie, Whit, and I were the only "young people" here tonight. Mimi still called us "the kids" even though we were over or pushing thirty.

The bathroom door swung closed behind me, and I walked out to Ollie standing in the hallway wearing a skinny tie. His arms were crossed in front of his jacket, wrinkling the shirt underneath.

"Hey," he said.

"Hey."

We paused there, standing awkwardly far apart like two kids at a middle school dance.

"We'd be miserable on the apps," I observed.

"The appetizers? They're good tonight."

"The dating apps. Apparently some people on there never make plans and just say 'hey' back and forth until they die."

"Hey," he said.

"Hey."

We laughed, though it wasn't very funny.

"Are you on them?" I asked.

"Here and there. I've been on a few dates, but everyone's either miserable or an influencer."

"Or a miserable influencer."

"The Holy Grail."

"Is sending nudes still a thing?"

"No nudes. Just wedding dress pictures."

We'd moved closer, and I slapped him playfully. "Only from the ones good enough to marry."

"Good enough to marry, bad enough to text someone who is not her fiancé."

I had no retort; phrases flipped through my head with infuriating futility, none of them matching his flirty edge. "I'm going to get another drink," I said, starting toward the main ballroom.

"Wait," he said. He pulled on my hand, and I felt a tiny pop in my shoulder. "Can I have a last dance?"

"I'm getting married, not dying."

"What's the big date again?"

"February seventeenth."

"Good. You photograph nicely in the winter."

"Do I?"

Ollie turned his phone toward me and toggled to his "favorites" folder, flicking backward with ease.

"I thought you deleted everything from your phone," I said.

"Only what's disposable. Look."

He'd pulled up the image of me on the snowy beach in Watch Hill, the picture where he instructed me to look serious. It looked like a still from a black-and-white film, and I passed as a leading lady: regal, pensive, hopelessly in love and trying to remain calm. I spent so much time that year worrying about my weight, angling and sucking in my cheeks and stomach, willing my body's infrastructure to peek through. This photograph was proof that my efforts were misguided: through Ollie's lens, I was a beautiful part of the scenery, not a body to be scrutinized. I couldn't believe he'd kept the picture for so long and referenced it spontaneously.

"Anyways," he continued, slipping his phone and my face back into his pocket, "I asked for a last dance because I'm leaving."

"Before the toasts? Mimi hired a speech coach, I think you need to stay to see that."

"*Moving* leaving," he said. "Going to the West Coast. L.A."

I couldn't believe this was the first I was hearing of this, but I shouldn't have been shocked. Ollie operated according to his whims. This time, though, I'd believed, like a brainwashed cult follower, that the narrative would end differently, that we could find our way back to each other—never mind that I was about to walk toward forever with someone else.

"Original," I said. "Why?"

"The family. New York. Too many people I've known for too long. It's getting a little suffocating."

"A lot of people move to be closer to their families, but okay."

"You seem pissed."

"I'm not surprised. You're always running away somewhere."

"Those were all temporary." He looked toward the dance floor full of his friends and relatives, dozens of faces spinning and shouting over the music. "I want to really start a life somewhere new."

"And what do you have here—a half-life?"

"An old life."

"Which you've outgrown."

"Something like that. I'll come back and visit all the time, though. I'm sure I'll miss everyone too much. I'll miss you." He looked away, his face visibly softening. This was the Ollie that kept me coming back, the snatches of vulnerability reaching through the hardened facade. "Let's just dance, okay?"

The idea of Ollie moving both saddened and calmed me. If he was out of sight, maybe the real estate he took up in my head would get transferred to Whit, its rightful owner. I could spend time with the Murphys without the tension of seeing Ollie. I could live the life he wanted to leave behind.

An unexpected perk of having secret, sporadic hookups with your best friend's relative: you can dance with him in front of people you've known your entire life without any questions. The ring on my finger further inoculated me. If it had been another ex, it would've looked suspicious and prompted dozens of questions: *How is he? Is he still in love with you? Are you still in love with him?* Now, we were just two bodies on a floor, family and friends of the Murphys spinning around clumsily to "Brown Eyed Girl," the song we all know was just written to make women with the least appealing and most common eye color feel better about themselves. I didn't have a complicated relationship with my brown eyes, but I was attracted to people with notably colorful eyes: Virginia's beer bottle green, Ollie's dark blue, Whit's hazel. Their irises like mood rings, changing slightly based on the color of their clothes or the lighting in the room. Mine were immutable, always the color of dirt. They matched the place I'd eventually return if Composure had its way with me.

My head was directly in line with Ollie's shoulder. His tweed blazer covered his skin, the humeral handle I wanted to roll around in my hand, feel the hard bone. Grind him down between my fingers, between my legs. We seesawed back and forth to the music, the *sha-la-la-la*s giving us an excuse to move our hips in tandem. I let him guide me through the days when the rains came. We were down in the hollow playing a new game when he dipped me, and I realized he hadn't mentioned I was a brown-eyed girl. I took in his lips (full, fuller than Whit's), small nose, and dark blue eyes.

"It's my song," I said.

"I didn't know you were into him." He looked over my shoulder.

I stared at him, trying to maneuver his eyes toward mine. "'Brown Eyed Girl.'"

"Not his best. I'd vote 'Into the Mystic.'"

"My eyes are brown."

I was begging a man to notice my shit-colored eyes.

"Oh yeah." He pulled back to look at me. "You probably think this song is about you."

"Okay, Carly."

We kept swing dancing. He did an elaborate derivative of the pretzel, and I let my body get flung through his. We swayed for a brief moment, and I felt him harden against me. It looked innocent. We could've been relatives, but we weren't, not even close, and even *thinking* about what we'd done together felt delicious inside the gilded pretension of Doubles.

Looking over Ollie's shoulder, I caught Whit's eye. He waved—*waved!*—and pointed at my eyes, smiling. He loved my eyes, or so he said, and played this song in the apartment. I should go to him, my handsome fiancé who noticed my eyes, but I didn't want to move. *Want* was a perverse verb, a fickle and stubborn hitch in a smooth expanse of needs and haves. Why couldn't I want what wanted me?

Van faded into Bruce, and Ollie pulled away.

"Thanks for the last dance," I said.

"Who says it has to be the last?" He let go of my hand and walked toward the bar. I thought he was about to look back over his shoulder, but he didn't, which was just as well—I could imagine the expression on his face, the underground smile only I'd notice.

I joined Whit and Mimi by the bar. They'd been talking for a while, and I wasn't sure whom I was saving from the interaction.

"This sounds like a big deal," Mimi was saying.

"It's huge. The drug will make it so millions of people don't have to suffer from this condition anymore. Your husband—a legend, I don't need to mention—is a real inspiration to me, career-wise."

Whit had been working on a new deal for a drug that would treat psoriasis, the skin condition made famous by Kim Kardashian and characterized by bumpy red patches that turned epidermis into cracked earth. He'd ushered in the deal, and his company had bet big on taking it to the clinical trial phase. Now it was a waiting game to see whether it worked.

"So this *psoriasis*—is it quite unsightly?" She pronounced the name of the condition like it was an exotic designer.

"Unsightly and uncomfortable, yes. It's basically a buildup of skin cells that forms angry red rashes."

Well, now I knew whom I was saving from the conversation. "We don't need to talk about this here, do we?" I tried.

"Oh, I love skin," Mimi said, sounding like a porn addict. "It's fascinating. I could've been a dermatologist in another life. Do you remember Gray's acne battle? God, you would've thought I was gearing up for war, I bought so many creams and ointments for her."

"There's actually another interesting Accutane-like drug we're looking into."

"Have you gotten into the injectables market?" she said in a stage whisper. She looked at me. "This is morbid, but when you were telling us about embalming fluid the other week—the way it makes the corpses look more lifelike—I thought, well . . ." Here, she paused and straightened, the way she preened before a punch line. "That sounds like it could put Botox out of business."

We laughed and looked at her glassy forehead.

"When I got married, we had none of this stuff your generation has. It was pink lipstick and concealer and a blow dryer and voilà—down the aisle!"

"Sounds nice," I said.

"It was horrid. I look better now than I did on my wedding day."

"What was yours like?" Whit asked. "Where did you do it?"

She described the church in New Canaan—where she *never* thought she'd move, but such is life—and the yacht club reception, the dry chicken and the cheap band, and the lack of photo booth or after-party because those things just weren't *done* then. Mimi's voice got louder as she rambled about the reception. Her pupils were dilated, and an arc of sweat dampened her hairline. As she kept talking, her tone took on a manic edge and her cheeks reddened. She was overexcited, even for her.

"Your parents weren't there," she said. "We became friends a bit later, since you and Virg were born so close together. It's just as well they didn't come."

"Why's that?" Whit asked.

"Oh, her dad hated weddings. The pomp and circumstance, you know."

Sterling Barnett also disliked superficial social rites—and he'd used this same terminology. My dad had written that "Sterling recoiled from the pomp and circumstance of their social stratosphere—the debutante balls that became weddings that became afternoon teas and children's birthdays. Small talk constricted his spirit, squeezed humanity into a corset."

Mimi took a long sip of her champagne, draining the glass. "Refill, anyone?" She threw her champagne flute in the air and caught it like it was nothing but a tennis ball. Her odd behavior was making me uneasy.

"How can you hate weddings?" Whit asked.

"He liked making fun of everyone's dance moves," I said.

"Let's have a bad dance in his honor." Whit offered me his hand, and I loved him more than I had in weeks, maybe months.

We danced to Marvin Gaye, Walk the Moon, Aretha. Billy Joel, Whitney Houston, Beyoncé. I was flailing my arms, jumping up and down, deliriously drunk after a refill and endless spinning. Whit was doing his towel-on-torso moves, plus some literal interpretations of pop classics. *I wanna feel the heat with somebody* made his hand into a fan, *only the good die young* got an invisible dagger to the stomach. Mimi danced without moving her legs. She pointed her fingers upward and in front of her like the world's happiest air traffic controller.

"Do you think Mimi was acting strange?" I asked him, trying not to shout over the music.

"Nothing too out of the ordinary for her," Whit said, smiling.

At some point, Virginia and her dad joined us.

"My favorites," Virginia said, looking at me and her parents. Whit didn't notice the slight; he was too busy taking care of TCB.

Virginia was wasted, too. She rarely showed affection while sober, and especially not toward her parents. She closed her eyes and swayed to the music, in her personal trance. Walter was the most awkward dancer I'd ever seen and one of my dad's many reasons for abstaining when he was around. "Do you want me to look like that?" he'd ask, pointing at Walter's orthopedic sneakers and goofy smile. I thought it was cute, in the condescending way everyone called old people cute. Walter was usually so stiff, and on the dance floor he let himself loosen a little, enough to move his hips and mouth some lyrics.

"His memory!" Mimi screamed over the music and looked at Walter confidently mouthing a verse of "Respect." "He knows more songs than I do!"

This particular song was coded into the memory of every human alive during the last quarter of the twentieth century, but I didn't need to mention that.

"Sweeter than honey," he said. *"And guess what? So is my money!"*

As if I'd conjured him, Ollie walked up to our dysfunctional little circle, slapped Walter on the back, and whispered in Virginia's ear. "Born to Run" came on. I stared at Mimi's wide eyes, the black pupils that had expanded like planets through a telescope, the sweat appearing not just on her forehead but also on her diamond-ringed neck and tanned forearms. We all started jumping, and my discomfort morphed into sentimentality. Emotions shape-shifted quickly when mixed with margaritas. All these bodies I knew so well—from either touching naked, sleeping next to in matching pajamas, crying on through the night, getting cried on through the night—flailing and trying and moving despite it all. I knew their *despite it all* was less dire than for people who faced real issues, but still—being alive was hard. Having a body was strange, and having decades-long relationships with other bodies was even stranger, and didn't our shared presence count for something, all of us in the same space, uncensored and cheesy with our shared joy?

Then Mimi fell, and the harsh overhead lights in the room went up, and we didn't dance together with abandon for a long time.

belindapbergin sending love and hope 🙏

bexjones 🖤🖤🖤🖤

23 September

Mimi had multiple seizures on her way to the hospital and went into a medically induced coma. The doctors were running tests, trying to figure out what happened. The immediate family had gone with her; Ollie, Whit, Bex, and I were back at the apartment, waiting.

"I just don't get it," Whit said. We were all in shock, mostly silent, but Whit had been trying to get to the bottom of the diagnosis and play armchair MD. "Was she on any medications?"

"Antidepressants," Ollie replied. "I think Zoloft for a long time, and she might've tried out some others, too."

I remembered the orange bottles I'd found during that autumn Watch Hill trip in college. I hadn't taken those meds seriously, failing to check the dosages or investigate the specific drugs. Half of my class at Brown was on antidepressants.

"But she was so happy!" Bex said. We all looked at her, waiting for the flawed logic to dawn. "Sorry, that was dumb."

"We were just *talking* to her," Whit said. "Right before." He shook his head, incredulous that the human condition, the line between alive and dead, could change so rapidly despite evidence that it could and did—all the time. Car crashes. Heart attacks. Cancer diagnoses. We aren't wired for change or calamity, even though they're the source of so many headlines and therapy sessions.

We talked about Mimi's demeanor in the hours and days leading up to the fall, the grimmest kind of gossip. Did she seem different? Was she stressed about the party? Ollie got quiet as we teased out the possibilities. He was picking at a cuticle, a habit of mine that he'd disliked.

I mentioned my conversation with Mimi and Whit, the suspicion that she was acting manic. Whit countered that it seemed like she was having fun, maybe *too* much fun.

Her breakdown in the bridal salon was another clue, one I didn't want to share with the room out of an instinct to protect her or desire to hoard the information for myself.

Now, it was a waiting game. Mimi was unconscious, and it was a matter of when or whether she stabilized. I put *when* at the front of my mind, trying to will her recovery with optimism. *Manifesting,* her astrologist would call it. I turned my headspace into a vision board, a Pinterest of inspirational quotes and platitudes. *Where there's a will, there's a wake.* As in *waking up,* not a funeral wake. Not a casket or a Composure vessel, Mimi's thin frame and chunky gold jewelry comatose like a WASPy Cleopatra.

Whit turned on the local news to give us a target to focus on outside our email and text boxes, the jittery refresh that made us all look like drug addicts hunched over a hit.

There was a shooting in Queens, a climate change protest in the East Village, a man paying it forward with random acts of kindness on the Upper West Side. If Mimi died, it would outweigh these headlines on the news scale. The *NYT:* "Mimi Murphy, Philanthropist and Wife of Walter Murphy, Dies at Age 56." The *Post:* "Pharma Wife Takes a Dose of Her Own Medicine." If she survived, it would be covered up, fixed by therapy or rehab, turned into a self-deprecating anecdote she referenced at cocktail parties. They'd put a cursor on the story, delete and reframe the events to fit a particular narrative.

I was focusing on the external reactions to her potential death instead of looking at the unseeable: Virginia couldn't lose her. *I* couldn't lose her. I'd taken Mimi for granted—her generosity, her de facto wedding planning, the easy way she let us all laugh at her—and assumed that she'd always be there, my satellite mother.

We went to bed without news from the hospital. Bex had gone home, wondering with performative nervousness whether this crisis should make her postpone her Mexico wedding in six weeks. She wouldn't—she'd been obsessing over #bexico nonstop for a year and Mimi wasn't her mom—but she needed us to know that she took the situation seriously. If I'd been less numb, I might've told her that this wasn't about her at all; she could do, hashtag, repost, and marry whomever the hell she wanted.

Whit and I were in my room, and Ollie passed out in Virginia's, saying he didn't want to be alone. Whit had fallen into a deep sleep: chest rising and falling, face smashed into a pillow, snores piling up with an almost physical weight. I couldn't nod off. I kept thinking of Mimi's prostrate body on the slick wood floor. Her tea-length dress had bunched up to reveal light varicose veins on her calves. She looked peaceful: eyes closed, mouth set. She was usually in frenzied motion, and suddenly she seemed at rest. The EKG monitor hadn't flatlined, but it had settled. Settling. What we were all supposed to do eventually. But settling like a stomach is different from settling like a marriage, and settling into death is its own dark weight.

I got up from the bed and walked to the kitchen. On the banquette table across from the bright white cupboards, I started sketching Mimi. I dashed off her legs in four horizontal lines that disappeared under her dress. I took my time with the plantaris tendon and soleus muscle, making them denser and more pronounced than the latticed blue trails I'd seen on her calves. Her organs were a geometric swarm. I started to draw them with my usual accuracy, but then they became warped like a Picasso, crowded by a nest of ink.

"Can't sleep?"

Ollie stood in the kitchen entryway wearing nothing but a pair of Walter's old Princeton sweatpants. He looked even thinner than usual; I could almost make out the notches of his sternum.

"Sleepytime can't even help me."

"You need new tricks. What's this?" he asked, looking at the notebook as he sat down in the chair next to me.

"Oh. It's nothing. It's embarrassing, really. I've been fucking around with this side project."

I started explaining, and it instantly sounded like the dumbest idea for a social media account—sillier than the handle that matched Meryl Streep's outfits with different food items or the one that exclusively featured fat animals sitting on ottomans. I tried to talk about it using the external versus internal. The external pressures of weddings eclipse internal desires, the idea that we're looking for "soulmates" when we're just cages of skin filled with identical beating parts. I wanted to show him that we were the same—he had no reason to hide our past and turn away from my larger frame, favoring women whose exteriors matched the exalted images fed to us in fashion spreads. Thigh gaps and faces that turned a profit had no bearing on whose interiors could revolt, make them fall, turn their organs into spoiled meat.

I turned the @bridalbodyyy page to him so he could see the explanation in action.

"Twisted," he said, scrolling through the images. "These are raw."

"I think, maybe, that's part of the point. It's all the stuff we don't want to look at."

"Like the power cords running from the TV screwing up the feng shui of the room."

"Our anatomical real estate doesn't exactly look like Zillow."

Ollie started explaining a Damien Hirst body sculpture that had shown at the Tate Modern, and I was grateful that I could align my instincts with those of a real artist.

"You know the dinosaurs at the Museum of Natural History?" he asked. "It's like that, except for a human. One side's stripped down and the other's all fleshy, but it puts out the idea that our bodies are worth magnifying. And examining."

"I'm trying to draw Mimi right now. I couldn't get the image out of my head. How did you know she was on those meds?"

"Because I was on them first." He sighed, looking over my shoulder. He had trouble making eye contact while discussing weighty topics. "When I came to live with the Murphys, I was a mess. This doctor in Connecticut put me on a whole cocktail of stuff that I was probably too young for."

"And Mimi went on them, too?"

"Soon after, yeah. It was right around when your dad died and I left for college. I remember her asking me about my meds and the doctor, whether I liked him or not. I forget how, but I knew she started seeing him, too. He was barred from practicing a few years later. Overprescribing."

"Jesus."

"I found another psychiatrist at Brown and don't see

anyone consistently anymore. But I can't help but think, if I'd never come and lived with them . . . maybe she wouldn't have gone to that doctor. Maybe she would've figured out a different way, or gone to a psychiatrist who could have put her on the right meds, and we wouldn't be here now."

"We don't even know if her meds have anything to do with the seizures."

"What else could it have been?"

"I don't know. There are a lot of different reasons someone's body turns against them."

"A therapist would say I'm just trying to assign blame. Which is futile, I know, especially when we're not sure what happened. I just wish I could go back and tell her not to see that doc. Let her know how much we all loved her. She shines so fucking bright, I forget to worry about what it's covering up."

I hadn't known Ollie was capable of regret. His confidence, forward momentum, and bad memory made me believe, wrongly, that the past couldn't drag him down.

"You could go down those paths all night and it would change nothing," I said. "You were a kid. And medication *works*—when it's prescribed and taken correctly."

"Still. Fuck."

He stood up and walked to the pantry. I had a sudden, strange appreciation for his mobility in light of Mimi's comatose state.

"I'm craving mac and cheese," he said, riffling through the cupboard. "Want some?"

"Sure."

He made Annie's with a gourmet twist, Parmesan shards and hot sauce swirled into the pale yellow mash. We ate silently and slowly next to each other. It was delicious, and so much pleasure felt sinful with Mimi still out of commission, still in limbo.

Our phones lit up at the same time.
Virginia had emailed from the hospital.

> **freddiesmith3** whoa, nice one

> **samanthaqt** ur organs are showing 😏

> **cassiefrassxo** want to make money from your living room? Link in bio for FAST cash!

> **olliemmphoto** 👀

24 October

The diagnosis: Mimi had been knocked unconscious by too much happiness.

Serotonin syndrome, the life-threatening condition caused by an excess of serotonin, had made her body go into overdrive: "neuromuscular excitability" and an "altered mental state" were the two main symptoms. Ollie was right—the antidepressants were partially to blame. She'd mixed her usual Zoloft with a more experimental, natural mood booster called St. John's wort, triggering a rush of chemicals too much for one nervous system to bear.

"I knew that homeopath was full of shit," Virginia said, referring to the witch doctor who'd told Mimi to try out the remedy.

Mimi was still in a coma, and the doctors' prognosis varied on a daily basis. Information came to us on a single email thread refreshed by Virginia or Gray. I tried to focus on work, but the very existence of Composure, the possibility of Mimi's body becoming dirt, triggered dark daymares. I spent

216

more time rewriting my dad's manuscript, escaping through fiction.

In a perverse parallel, Amelia's face fell as Sterling's rose.

"A child!" he exclaimed.

"A son," Dorothea said.

"I'll get the champagne," Fred offered, patting Amelia's back on his way to the wet bar with nothing more than conciliatory swiftness.

Amelia imagined Dorothea's stomach stretching to contain this child, the offspring of the man Amelia feared she loved. The small limbs would pinwheel inside that ethereal sac, liminal liquid holding life in a hidden chamber. They'd all wait, trimesters extending to labor, labor reaching out its gruesome hand to deliver Sterling his progeny. Amelia wanted Dorothea's very self to puncture with the child, explode like a bubble carried away by shifting winds. Amelia had stepped into Sterling's sun; she didn't want to be relegated to her familiar shade.

"How far along?" Amelia asked, staring at the unimpressive swell underneath Dorothea's dress.

"Eleven weeks," she said.

Further along than Amelia had been when she lost her children.

I thought of my mother's deflated stomach, stretch marks turning in on themselves with shame. She would've watched her friend grow with the natural ease Mimi attributed to her pregnancy with Gray—"my uncomplicated daughter," she always said, the one who conformed to expectations. My revisions to the manuscript proceeded with a nearly supernatural tug, an invisible rope tying me to the characters. Sterling, as an avatar for my father, made me ascribe attributes and plots to the other characters that mirrored our families. Was I rewriting my mom's loss by giving his wife a healthy pregnancy in this universe?

Virginia was spending more time away from the apartment, which was convenient for my compulsions. When I wasn't drawing skeletons or filling out fictional bodies with backstories and longings, I was eating and throwing up, rinse and repeat. I took down frozen lasagnas meant for entire families, nonperishable Hostess bombs purchased in case of apocalypse, clam chowder and chicken noodle soup scooped up with bags of Lay's, chocolate bars, cheese wedges, saltine sleeves. Nothing was safe from my mouth.

When I pulled the rip cord, I keened toward the black hole of the toilet bowl—a sacrifice, an undoing. I'd rise lightheaded, shaking, delirious with an emptiness that belied the truth: I couldn't rid myself of it all, my terrifying table of human contents.

In the week since Mimi's fall, I'd seen Virginia twice: once when she came to the apartment to pack a bag, and another time when I went to the hospital. I'd gone alone, knowing that Virginia wouldn't want Whit there in such a raw moment.

She and Gray were in a fight when I arrived. Gray had emailed the thread of thirty people asking for pictures of their good times with Mimi to put together a scrapbook for "when she woke up." She'd been posting a series of pictures of Mimi, too, with premature tribute captions. Virginia was worried all of this would jinx the recovery. "It's like she's preparing a fucking vigil," she said, looking straight ahead while sitting on the sofa of a special waiting room/atrium for the families of long-term—and, I suspected, wealthy—patients. A Caesar salad sat untouched on the coffee table.

I asked Virginia if she'd eaten and she said yes, of course. There was nothing else to do in this godforsaken, depressing place. She was defensive enough that I knew she was lying.

I went to the Wendy's across the street and got five spicy chicken sandwiches, thinking it was better to have too many versus too few. Walter had been working in the far corner of the atrium, rising only to use the bathroom or receive updates from the doctors. Virginia thought it was ridiculous, but she also didn't want him hovering over her. "It's better this way," she said.

I scooped a handful of ketchup packets into the greasy bag, then two more. A bunch of barbecue sauce and enough mustard to smother a cow. When I binged on the preparation aspect of food, I often resisted overindulging; home-cooked meals rarely provoked an episode.

Walter barely looked up when I passed him a sandwich. "Thanks, Cal," he said, raising one arm from his keyboard for the handoff. His bald head was especially reflective, nearly wet with light, under the harsh overheads of the atrium.

Gray ate half of the spicy chicken and some fries. Virginia took one bite and said she'd had a big lunch, claimed she'd finish it later.

"You need to eat," I said.

"I'm just on a different schedule."

"Food will help."

"Will it?"

I couldn't handle her calling me out for my bulimia—not that word, not in front of her family. I took an audible breath and regretted it on the intake. She'd be able to sense my fear.

"You know I've been through this, the hospital waiting," I tried. "Having regular meals was the only way I stayed sort of sane."

"But you knew there was no hope." She looked at me head-on for the first time since I arrived. "He was terminal. And you had time to say goodbye."

Why had this turned into a battle over sob stories? She'd witnessed the way my dad's death had crushed me. His absence had congealed my identity into an unexpected form: a death-based job and a disorder that sought both heady abandon and tightly wound control. With each passing year, I was embarrassed that it was my *trauma*. It seemed somehow not enough, too juvenile to qualify, and her insinuation hit on this insecurity.

"I can't pretend to know exactly how you're feeling right now," I said. "Just saying I might have some idea. I'm here for you."

"I'm being a dick. Sorry. This is just . . ." She looked away again, toward her dad's hunched figure underneath a fake palm tree. ". . . a lot."

I rubbed her back lightly, the way her mom used to when we had sleepovers at Idyll Wind from age seven to around thirteen, until we thought we were too grown-up. It was the only ritual that could make us stop talking about My Little Ponies and Polly Pockets, the precursor to late nights spent dissecting Josh Hartnett and Nick Carter.

"It's going to be okay," I said.

"How do you know?"

"I just *know things*," I said with the same tone and emphasis that Mimi used to discuss her astrologist.

Virginia's usual subdued laugh built into a freer outpouring. I joined in, our laughs chasing each other until we weren't responding to the joke; we were just letting ourselves go, an ineffable abandon.

Walter looked up at us, alarmed, and Gray took out the headphones she'd been using to stream Netflix.

"What the fuck?" she asked. "What could possibly be so funny?"

Neither of us responded and instead let the laughs taper out. Virginia had happy tears in her eyes.

"Well, at least you're finally crying," Gray continued.

She'd been worried that Virginia wasn't emoting enough, that she'd been repressing her feelings—the stage of sadness that registers as emptiness instead of saturation. This, at least, I could do: laugh with her. I felt more accomplished than I had in weeks.

When I got back to the apartment, I didn't binge for three whole days.

belindapbergin sending love and light ✨

nancywallace12 Oh no, I just heard the news. We are all praying for a speedy recovery! Love, Nancy, Ted, Louisa, and Conor

bexjones ♥♥♥♥♥ we love you, Mimi

25 November

After Bex's wedding reception, we went swimming. From the beach in the dark, the Mexico ocean could have been a mirage—a shimmering, distant turf. But when I ran into the expanse, it became a pure, cold fact. I dove into the first large wave and plunged my hands in front of me like I was touching another person.

And then I did.

It was a man's leg, and there were only two men with me: Whit and Ollie. I thought it was the latter but, jolting up into the night, I realized it was the former. My fiancé. My *same penis forever*.

Ollie was floating in front of us with his hands behind his head, looking up at the sky. Drunk and blissful in his own pocket of the night. Two of the other bridesmaids, Bex's co-workers, splashed near him, doing handstands in the water like ten-year-olds at the local pool. It seemed like they were in a staring contest over who could stay up later and take Ollie back to her hotel room.

I was surprised that any of us were even there. Virginia had begged Bex to go ahead with the wedding and insisted that we should go represent her on the big night. I felt guilty until

I stepped off the plane into the warm Tulum air and experienced a distinct loosening of muscles that had been tense for weeks. We'd be gone for only three days; she didn't want us buzzing around her at the hospital anyways. Still, we'd been checking our phones after every long margarita sip or hors d'oeuvre bite. The split-second hangover of a visceral pleasure made it impossible to forget who was missing and why.

"What do you see up there?" Whit shouted at Ollie.

He didn't answer. His ears were underwater, or he didn't want Whit's voice to puncture his bubble. The stars looked like a screensaver. I wished I could map them, point them out like my dad used to. He gave everything a name, something I could call the world. A solid surface for me to project my life onto. He would show me the stars—half covered by clouds—while sitting out on the back porch, the two of us transfixed like the manifestation of a dumb country song. "The crab," he'd say. "The old man with his fishing rod. The female lover scorned." He made most of them up, telling fantastical stories and resurrecting instincts that lay dormant in the drafts on his ThinkPad. Sterling would also romanticize this sky, compare its vastness to his newly tapped well of feeling for his friend's wife.

Whit pulled me in for a kiss. His lips were salty and surprisingly tasty, like the plump flesh of shellfish, but I couldn't help but feel self-conscious in front of Ollie and these girls.

They weren't looking at us at all.

"I now pronounce you merman and wife," Whit said. He squeezed my hips, kissed my forehead, and wiped a strand of wet hair from my face. I almost let myself surrender to how nice the warm water felt on his hands. But then I remembered: *Mimi*. This was followed by a different reminder: *Me, me*. As in *my body*. Whit's hands on my extra hip flesh pulled me into a dark corner of wedding internet that urged brides to "look like the best version of yourself."

This was a euphemism for the skinniest version of your-self, which I was not. Our wedding was in two months, and I'd gained weight. Of course I'd gained weight. I'd been taking down thousands of calories at a time and attempting to hit rewind without my old extra credit tricks (fasting, two hard workouts for each binge, no sugar, no gluten, no-no-no diets that never stuck for long). I didn't have energy for long-term penance anymore, just the immediate physical release.

Ollie had one of the girls on his shoulders while the other one splashed them, a Canadian doubles chicken fight. Whit urged me to get on his shoulders, too. I couldn't bear the thought of anyone, especially Ollie, watching me sway on top of Whit's frame, my subcutaneous fat jiggling and vis-ceral fat packed around my organs like they were breakable objects inside me.

I said I felt too nauseated. I'd been using the sick excuse a lot, and Whit had made an appointment for me with a GI doctor, which I knew I'd have to repeatedly reschedule to avoid. I couldn't let a doctor inspect the damage I'd been doing to my body.

The girl on Ollie's shoulders had on a high-waisted bikini that didn't give her a muffin top, probably because she didn't eat muffins. I took down a Starbucks blueberry last week and it came up tie-dye in the toilet bowl, swirls of dark blue against the porcelain.

Whit shouted that we were going to bed, and Muffin Top-less waved her hands excitedly, probably happy that two more obstacles had removed themselves from Mission Ollie. She was biding her time like I'd done at Gray's wedding—a night that felt like years, not months, in the past. Ever since Mimi's coma and our moment in the kitchen, Ollie had been going silent on me. He said he was working on a new project with Virginia and didn't want to break his creative flow. After losing his contracts at *Nat Geo* and Condé—which I still only knew about secondhand, from Virginia—a new project was a big deal. It was strange that he could focus in these circumstances, but it was also typical for him, the single-minded submerging. I was jealous. I'd been slacking on both the Composure and @bridalbodyyy fronts. Every time I started to get in a rhythm, I'd check my email for the update thread or text Virginia. Whit would rub my shoulders and mutter well-meaning assurances that made me snap at him. Like Virginia, I didn't want to jinx Mimi's recovery. I thought that if I imitated her superstitious nature, she might decide to wake up and give us a reward for playing by her unwritten rules.

I couldn't sleep. I was facing away from Whit, looking at the beige-painted wall. Bex was probably still awake, too, editing pictures and packing for her mini-moon the next day. Her reception was beautiful. I looked through my feed at the pictures she'd managed to post so far from her already-updated handle.

The first look, the scoop back of her dress highlighting the dip above her hips.

The wedding party, all of us on the beach in white-and-blue floral dresses and linen suits.

The seafood tower, shrimp like toes curled in orgasm.

Outside, Ollie was at the pool. Alone.

This setting was better than the apartment kitchen, riper for an encounter. Was it significant that we kept finding each other at night? I stopped on the path, my body blocked by the palm trees and hedges lining the walkway. I wanted to see what he did when he thought no one was looking.

He sat there, staring out at the water. Glanced at his phone, but not for long enough to register anything besides the time. His skin was like a projector screen for the turquoise. Wavy lines of light moved across his face. He closed his eyes and scratched the space above his hip, and I thought that he was going to masturbate in plain sight. I was horrified, even though I'd once made him masturbate in front of me when he didn't finish. "Please do it for me," I'd said, egged on by the myth of blue balls.

I walked softly down the walkway and shouted, "Boo!"

"Jesus," Ollie whisper-screamed, sitting up in the folding beach chair. "What the fuck are you doing?"

"Just prowling," I said. "Looking for stragglers."

"You might find Greg's best man puking in the bushes."

"Love a guy who can get vulnerable."

I sat in the chair next to him. His calves and feet were much bigger than mine, and it made my body feel small next to his.

I turned to him. "What are you doing out here?"

"Thinking."

"Sick of the chicken fight?"

"I couldn't sleep."

"Me neither."

He stared out past the pool and toward the ocean. "Just working something out in my head."

"It wasn't your fault she was on those meds."

"I was thinking about sharks. How they don't sleep." He looked at me, finally, those deep blue eyes reading as black in the dark.

"Nice to have company. Remember, the spot pattern on every whale shark is as unique as a fingerprint." I smiled and he smiled back, our faces mirroring each other and our minds overlaying with the same memory. We'd watched Shark Week together in his off-campus room over Indian food and IPAs. This fact must have remained bright in his head, too. But then his smile curdled from recognition to confusion.

"Where did you hear that? I'm not sure that's true."

"When we watched Shark Week—it was in one of the first shots, with the whale sharks in Australia."

"God, you have a good memory."

"It reminds me of a fact I just learned. Did you know that when a body decomposes, fingerprints are one of the last parts to break down? They're stubborn."

"When you turn the bodies into dirt or whatever?"

"Whatever." I laughed. "Ollie Moskowitz-Murphy, blasé even in the face of death."

I could tell he liked the sound of his full name in the night, attached to definitive characteristics like a famous person. His name followed by a colon of his accomplishments, his multihyphenate justification for living.

"I think about it all the time," he said. "Death."

"Imagining all the praise you'll get at the funeral?"

"People praising God for taking me, maybe. Or certain people. Exes."

His tone indicated that he wasn't talking about me, that he didn't think of me as an ex, especially one who would want to kill him.

"What happened with that?"

"It wasn't it."

"Eloquent."

"She couldn't go there with me. She's a great girl," he said, making it sound like a bad consolation prize, "but she wasn't my girl. Like talk about death? Wouldn't go over well. She just kept moving, day in and day out. She didn't question much."

"Is that a bad thing?"

"For someone else, no. For someone else, it would be the greatest thing in the world."

"Do you ever wonder whether all that questioning . . . is super privileged?" He swiveled his head toward me. "I do it, too, all the time. Am I doing it right? Did I order the wrong thing? Am I in the right career, right city? Will this deodorant give me cancer? You have the time and luxury and, you know, safety net to ask these questions. Maybe she just kept moving because she had a kid to feed and a job to do."

"I don't think analysis and struggle are mutually exclusive," he said. "It's kind of demeaning to assume that people with fewer means aren't capable of self-reflection."

"That's not what I meant."

"What you said isn't what I meant, either."

We stopped talking for a minute or two and stared out at the pool. Our feet were side by side against the backdrop of neon blue.

"She wanted me to adopt her kid. She didn't say it outright, but I knew."

"And you weren't ready for that."

"I don't think I'll ever be ready for that."

"There's a diagnosis for your disease, you know."

"Commitment-phobia?"

"Peter Pan syndrome. Side effects include flying to India and Fiji to take pictures."

"You get it, though."

"What?"

"Wanting to be multiple places or people at once."

"Wanting to eat the world."

"Sucks that we only have one body." He smiled his half-curved smile that communicated wistfulness, not happiness, and looked out, probably thinking of how he wanted to fly over the ocean and inhale or fuck it all. I shared his insatiability, and my bottomless desires were part of the reason I worried about long-term commitment. I craved an expansiveness I feared was in opposition to marriage.

"Do you think photography helps you achieve that?" I asked. "Capturing other lives through your camera. I don't know, it must feel kind of like possessing a place or a person, re-creating it."

"Definitely," he affirmed. He looked at me head-on, and I was reminded of the connection I'd felt with him years ago. In college, I hadn't yet abandoned my hope of melding my right- and left-brain interests. His creative drive fueled my latent artistic talent.

"I'm starting to think that writing can accomplish that, too," I said. "Living multiple lives." Before I could question it, I started telling him about my dad's book and the revisions I'd been making. I was talking far too quickly, as if running from some essential truth in my words.

"So, you're reimagining his story," Ollie said. "That's what art's all about—taking a concept and applying your own unique filter."

"Exactly. It's more than straightforward revision. It's like I'm summoning him while also making it my own."

"All of our ideas come from somewhere. Proximity to your source material, achieving more distance, is where art occurs."

"So, art is manipulation."

He paused. "That's one way of looking at it. I prefer to think of it as interpretation."

He was talking to me as if I were a creative, a peer. His bouts of mansplaining were neutered by the equality intimated in his tone.

"What makes someone an artist?" I asked. "I sound like Randall."

"Not a degree," he said. "No offense to Virg. It's something like the right mix of delusion and obsession."

His dismissal of Virginia's grad student status perversely thrilled me. I could've never afforded Columbia and hadn't even let myself consider an art degree, let alone an advanced one. Ollie's definition of an artist colored in a hollow of my identity. My fixation on @bridalbodyyy and my dad's manuscript, the rushes of confidence followed by sobering comparisons to "real" artists. My intention to major in art overshadowed by premed and then communications. The slow replacing of my far-reaching desires with easily grasped realities. My lack of delusion had declawed my obsessions. Only recently had I let those forces back into my private life, allowed myself to be swept up in the illogical rush.

Out on the water, waves crested and fell. The eternal push and pull of the tide—the back and forth that orients the moon, our moods, and the rhythm of plants breaking through dirt—comforted me. It was indifferent to our anxieties and regrets. Ollie's eyes hitched on mine for an extra second. Through this conversation, Mimi, Virginia, and Whit had been sitting silently in the space between us. I willed them away for a moment. *This is private,* I wanted to say. *Look at me, only me.*

I moved to the end of his beach chair. Before I could over-analyze it, I was tracing the hair on his calves, running my fingers lightly toward his kneecap, the place that (along with sneezing) middle schoolers claimed equaled an eighth of an orgasm when stimulated. He closed his eyes, and I continued moving upward, toward the band of his boxer shorts, until—

"Bad idea." He sat up in the chair and retracted his legs.

"But you're single."

"And you're about to get married. We can't keep doing this."

"But what if *this* is right."

"It would've happened already."

"Things don't just happen. You make them happen. We can make something happen."

I avoided concrete statements, abstract pronouns standing in for the weight of what I was scared to voice: *We can belong to each other. Ease our isolation. Elope and screw the tented circus.*

"We've been over this," he said. "I don't want to ruin anything between all of us."

If our relationship could be described in artistic terms, Ollie and I were interpreting the piece differently. I was ready to ask a basic question that I'd always avoided in fear of the answer: "If you wanted to be with me, wouldn't you find a way to just . . . be with me?"

He didn't respond right away. My pale thigh spread against the latticed beach chair, fat poking out each woven hole. Of course he didn't want to be with me—there was too much of me.

During the semester of our affair—could you call it an affair if neither party was married?—I ran into Ollie at an off-campus Mexican restaurant a few weeks after our trip to Watch Hill. I noticed the girl across from him first. She was a sophomore named Maya who'd been on the Juicy Campus lists of "Hottest Girls at Brown" (which Virginia was still a stalwart on, even though she was in Paris). Unlike the other list-makers, Maya wasn't in a sorority. I'd looked her up on Facebook and discovered she was a film major who shot artsy black-and-white shorts featuring the trees on campus, ghostly amateur efforts that hinted at nascent talent. She was thin. Really, really thin. I'd put her at 123 max, and she was pushing six feet tall. She had long, dark hair and large, wide-set eyes that seemed too sophisticated and worldly for college.

They ordered another round of margaritas. I realized it

was Ollie when he turned to the waiter and I spotted his nose, that perfect slope I'd watched in the dark seventy-two hours ago. That night, we'd gone to bed at ten—which I took as a sign we were easing into coupledom—after he watched an episode on his laptop while I finished his physics homework and wrote a detailed outline for his English paper.

I walked the long way to the bathroom, avoiding their table. I'd been having dinner with Bex and some other girls in my pledge class, housing chip after chip in oblivious bliss, thinking I might even mention Ollie to them now that I was *playing it cool, calling the shots,* and sending us closer to the precipice of togetherness.

In the stall, I stuck my fingers deep into my throat, clawing at what I could not see.

"You know it's not that easy," he said, knees drawn up to his chin on the beach chair. "Especially now, with Mimi."

"Would it be that hard, though? *We're* not related. There's no law against us being together."

"You're the one who's engaged."

"I'm telling you," I said. "I'm trying to tell you. I don't need to be."

"This is too much. I don't want you blowing up your life for me."

I wish this ended with me getting up and walking away, back to my hotel room and fiancé. Painting over the disaster, finishing off the scene with dignified calm. But Ollie left first. He patted my shoulder on his way out, a pat like you'd give a poorly behaved kid in a moment of pity. A gesture that said—loud and clear, even though it was a light touch—*I'm sorry you're like this.*

Alone at the pool, I traced my hips and squeezed the fat

bulging from my midsection. I started to touch myself, but it was no use. I was numb.

graymbosker QUEEN B! Congrats my loves 🫶👑

lbmofficial best night, best love!! 🫶

madisonsully omfg I'm dead 💀 Mexico + your wedding = heaven

calliememaybe ily, best weekend!!

dorman_liz oh my guaccc, this is perfection. CONGRATS

26 November

meet.virginia talking body ♥

When she woke up from her two-month nap, Mimi's first word was *macaron*. She'd evidently been deep-sea dreaming about Ladurée.

"I'm buying her enough of those to fill a bathtub," Virginia said. "I'm just so, so relieved."

Gray was sobbing. In between gasps and tissue grabs, she managed to divulge that she'd really believed her mom was gone and even told her therapist that she'd braced for the worst-case scenario. Of course Gray acted as her own therapist and used professionals as a backboard.

Mimi wasted no time becoming best friends with her nurses and learning all their kids' names and birthdays, making astrological predictions about small humans she'd never met. Everyone encouraged this return to normalcy, her quick arc from close to dead to very much alive. We weren't supposed to press her on what happened, not yet. The doctors said it might take a while for basic motor functions and memory to return to 100 percent, so it was best to keep things light. She'd start physical therapy and therapy-therapy within a week. We'd get answers and treatment plans soon enough.

In the wake of Mimi's waking up, the hospital transformed from a sterile purgatory into minimalist serenity. The fluorescent bulbs were luminous instead of harsh, the bouquets on her bedside went from wilting to upright. It was incredible how much context could affect surroundings. Our collective mood uplifted a drab space into a bearable waiting room, even an oasis.

She transferred to outpatient, and we all headed back to our usual corners of the city: me, Virginia, and Whit to the apartment; Ollie back downtown. After two days of commuting in from Connecticut for appointments, Walter decided that Mimi should stay with us in the apartment for a few weeks. Mimi quickly got to work sprucing up the place and reacquainting herself with the neighbors, while I dreaded having a real adult around. How would I binge and purge and enact other strange late-night rituals (drawing bodies, examining bodies in the dermatology book, revising the manuscript) with a parent on duty? But it soon became clear that her focus wasn't on me. She zoomed in on her actual daughter.

"Does she seem a little manic to you?" Mimi whispered to me in the kitchen one day while Virginia was working away in the office. She'd been focused on a new project with Ollie—they said they wanted to surprise us at a gallery show.

"I think she's just really excited about the show."

"I wish she put half this effort into dating."

I longed to challenge Mimi on the reasons this was problematic—no one would say or even think this about a man prioritizing work—but the doctor's instructions came back to me, the ticker tape running underneath all our recent interactions: "Don't push her."

She went to bed early and got tired easily. But otherwise, she seemed normal, or at least normal for her. She was back to telling stories about everything from her college days to a prosciutto sandwich she'd once eaten in Florence to a man wearing assless chaps on Fifty-Seventh Street. The apartment went back to its pre-Mimi rhythm, with Virginia and Ollie in the office prepping for the show, Whit at work on his psoriasis drug, and me on the couch emailing journalists and Maxine. Mimi was a flurry of purpose, too: physical therapy in the morning, lunch with friends, cognitive behavioral therapy in the afternoon, followed by chair reupholstery and curtain redesign meetings. She'd decided the apartment needed a face-lift and appointed herself plastic surgeon.

The art show was on a snowy Friday night, and my nipples poked through my black silk top.

I taped them down and adjusted the straps, looked in the mirror at my all-black ensemble (slimming) and decided it was the best I could do at the moment, when most of my pants didn't fit and my stomach fat hung over the waistband of any rise that didn't stretch far past my belly button. Dresses were out of the question, as every one I owned was either too summery for December or too tight for my current shape.

Mimi, Whit, and I Ubered downtown together. Mimi was in a bright mood, telling us about the fabric she'd picked out for a living room ottoman.

"It's fabulous. We sourced it from India, it has this buttery, cinnamon feel. It looks so lush I almost want to eat it."

She asked us about our wedding after-party; she was thinking we should do a small tent outside with a DJ—"What about a silent disco?"—and I was amazed that she was plotting this far ahead when I hadn't thought about our wedding in days. Then I realized this wasn't micromanaging on her part; it was procrastination on mine. The Big Day was in two months, and I hadn't even considered my vows or picked out a rehearsal dinner outfit.

We speculated on the art show, making bets about the content Virginia and Ollie insisted on keeping a surprise.

"I think it involves technology," Whit guessed. "Or it's a commentary on social media."

"Not Virginia's style," I said. "She hated all the Richard Prince stuff."

"It will be moody, I can tell you that much," Mimi offered. "Brooding. Those two have always been my dark ones."

Snow came down in steady pulses outside the car window, turning the city into a pointillist painting. We pulled up to the show as Mimi was on the phone with Walter discussing quotes to renovate the apartment bathroom. She pinched her cheeks and slapped her face lightly three times "to make it rosy." Since moving into the apartment, I'd noticed that Mimi did this every time she left the house.

A stack of brochures sat in the entryway to the gallery. I picked one up:

HUMAN CONTENT: Interior Design for Flesh Houses
  by Oliver Moskowitz-Murphy and Virginia Murphy

A small brain was sketched underneath the show title, a knot of curved lines. Contained yet menacing, like a piece of shit.

"Interior design, how timely," Mimi said. "Do we think they did this for *moi?*"

"It's some sort of metaphor," Whit observed. "I'm curious."

I walked into the gallery clutching the brochure. I squeezed it so hard that it turned into trash in my fist. It took my eyes a few seconds to adjust to the pieces on the walls, like I'd emerged from a movie theater. I wondered later if this was my brain cushioning the shock, giving me a moment to process.

The pictures were mine in every way that mattered.

Ollie had taken photographs of people and exposed the images to an X-ray effect so that you could see through their skin. Virginia had added paint and objects to the interiors: floral upholstery on a liver, a lamp for a brain. Some of them were starker, her paint highlighting the organs in their unadorned state. The bodies were creative dissections, exactly like my @bridalbodyyy feed.

I got closer to a picture Ollie had taken at Leila's wedding in Watch Hill. It was the same pose that I'd sketched for my account. Ollie and Virginia had labeled the exposed body parts with descriptions that were intentionally ripped from real estate listings: *Spacious pancreas, heart with crown moldings, airy and light—full set of functioning lungs!*

For a few seconds, I thought that maybe we were all similar enough to come up with the same idea, that the concept had flown from me toward Ollie and Virginia like a fly caught in the apartment. Then I remembered: I'd shown Ollie @bridalbodyyy that night in the kitchen right after Mimi's hospitalization. I'd mentioned Zillow, made the connection between our selves and our homes. He'd sewn the thread tighter—but instead of pulling me close, he'd stolen from me and chosen Virginia as his accomplice.

I walked through the rest of the room in a near sleepwalk, isolating body parts as I passed them. The pelvis. The occipital lobe. Sternum, ear cartilage, tricuspid valve. The endless map that once comforted me was now a dead end, with the Murphy name printed on the blockade.

The gallery had filled up with art-world types: people whose unwashed hair and no-makeup makeup attempted to offset their $800 designer boots and hoodies that cost as much as wedding dresses. Virginia hugged me in a soft silk dress and curls that looked either expertly done or just-out-of-bed, the ideal line between effortful and effortless. She smelled like fucking gardenias.

"So, what do you think?"

I couldn't speak.

"Is everything okay? You look sort of sick."

"I—I'm fine. Whose idea was this?"

"Ollie's. He brought me in right away, though. I couldn't stop thinking about it once we laid out the theme. The body as a commodity, thinking our interiors are unique and giving ourselves traits like a Zillow listing, when our hardware's pretty much identical. Walking around with all of it covered up. Wild, right?"

Before I could respond, a stranger had two heavily tattooed arms around Virginia's neck and was going on about the dope exhibit and the impressive turnout and the reasons why this was major, sick, huge. I continued my isolated loop through the space, contemplating how I'd bring up the plagiarism to Virginia. She'd question why I told Ollie about @bridalbodyyy before her. She might even think I'd copied him, even though the time stamps were in my favor.

Ollie was talking to a man in a suit jacket and a striking, modelesque woman wearing a sweatshirt three sizes too big for her. The audacity of the stolen idea built like bile in my throat. He could've asked my permission or credited me, at least. He could've worked with me instead of leeching off me like a parasite.

Ollie was still talking with the model, but suit man had been replaced by Mikey, the gallery owner who counted Scarlett Johansson as an ex and had tattoos of his own veins up his arms and neck. Ollie was laughing, smiling, basking. He was the command center of this gallery's diseased body. The *brains* behind the operation. I overheard an old dude with a goatee talking about how this was a commentary on human trafficking, and his companion in a flowy skirt insisted that no, it was simply about the body as currency.

Either way, the idea was mine. Virginia and Ollie were together now, getting their picture taken with Mikey. Virginia couldn't have known about the idea's source—she would've objected on the spot—but it pained me to watch her get the credit. She had so much already: a bloated bank account, non-bloated figure, symmetrical face, artistic talent. Did she also need to monopolize my hidden corner? I felt the piercing regret of holding an idea during a meeting and listening to someone else voice a similar opinion and get praised for it.

As Virginia gestured to Mikey with one hand and held a glass of whiskey in the other, the gap between us hit me, much wider than her thigh gap I'd obsessed over for years. She knew nothing about the jealousies and double crosses flickering in me. My alleged best friend, and I'd kept so much from her.

I almost told her about Ollie once.

He'd started publicly dating that artsy girl, Maya, the one I'd seen him with at the Mexican restaurant. Privately, he was still BBMing me to hang out, messages I scratched with rabid embarrassment. I went over to his off-campus place once a week, sometimes two, and came in the back door, sliding myself around a set of golf clubs and boxes of old textbooks that blocked the staircase.

He told me he and Maya weren't really together, just working with each other on a project for a visual arts class. I convinced myself to believe the story because I wanted him near me. The longer our secret relationship went on, the harder it became to tell anyone. Because I'd have to explain that he didn't want to be associated with me. Because I was fat. Because I wasn't pretty or smart enough, even though he seemed to enjoy both my body (in bed, on the desk chair, in the shower) and my brain (on his papers, his problem sets, and the DNA of his stories). I'd learned to mimic his handwriting for homework, which wasn't hard—boy letters usually just meant a loosening of the wrist, a carelessness bleeding into the transcription.

Our final creative writing class assignment was a twenty-five-page short story. He gave me a page-long outline, and I stayed up until five a.m. in the library, turning his bullet points about a small-town bakery into a yeasty family epic involving a miscarriage, sibling rivalries, and the taste of tears mixed with sourdough. I'd already finished my own story, which I'd dashed off in an afternoon. His took more time. I wanted Ollie's praise. I wanted the made-up words to prove I was real-deal special.

I told myself that it was good practice for finishing my dad's novel—this was back when I was still actively looking for the lost manuscript—and I had fun with the characters, letting people dictate the plot instead of vice versa. To make sure Randall didn't notice my ghostwriting, I made our voices different, putting Ollie's reticence and mystery on his pages while infusing mine with a nervous buzz.

After Ollie read the story, he kissed me on the forehead for the first time.

"This is so great. Wasn't the bakery a good idea?"

He didn't say thank you. But damn, that forehead kiss. It was soft and full, and I told myself it communicated what he didn't express with words: *Thank you, genius with a dewy forehead. I love you more than that film bitch.*

He was wearing a goofy T-shirt. ONE RING TO RULE THEM ALL, it read over a cartoon of an onion ring. He massaged my shoulders for a minute and told me he had to run but would see me in class. I think I let him get away with this meager payment because of the shirt (endearing) or because I still wanted to take it off (unfortunate).

A week later, Randall read an excerpt of Ollie's story out loud in class, praising his subtle use of metaphor. He got an A; I got a B+, the little cross weaponized in red ink. After class, I had an email waiting from my academic adviser with the subject line **checking in**. She was concerned about my grades. I'd received my first B– on an organic chemistry test after staying up late to finish Ollie's take-home physics midterm. My neurology and English grades, usually strong, were slipping, too: 3.8 slid into 3.6 dipped down to 3.2, and my academic scholarship hung in the balance.

I should've fought my way back and told Ollie that I couldn't help him anymore. But my priorities had shifted like cranial bones moving imperceptibly to create a skull misalignment. Making him need me was more important than my own needs.

I finished his last assignment for the semester on a Thursday, while he was lounging before an off-campus party. His body lying in bed—laptop on his stomach and headphones in his ears, a mangled power cord snaking over his chest and a plugged-in phone lit up on the covers—made him look like a patient in a hospital. My patient.

On the phone, I told Virginia that I had to switch out of premed to preserve my scholarship. She couldn't understand what happened ("You've always been such a nerd," she said), and I wanted to spill everything: the first time in the photo lab, the snowy trip to Watch Hill, the help that turned into ghostwriting. The date sighting and the secret-keeping, the betrayal (and semen) I'd swallowed. How he reminded me of her in his best moments, their confident mischief and lanky glamour and ability to make me laugh so hard I howled in pajamas in a childhood twin bed or naked in a college full. Their pulling away and rationing of affection, a coldness that came without warning and made me hold out for remembered warmth.

Virginia said something in French to a guy in her apartment, which she'd started calling her flat because her roommate was British. After a beat of muffled noises on her end of the phone, her voice was back in the receiver.

"*Qu'est-ce que c'est?*"

"What?"

"You were about to tell me something."

"Oh. It's nothing. Who's the guy?"

She started whispering about Edouard and the chicken paillard he cooked for her, and my moment was lost in the transatlantic gulf.

Outside the gallery, my breath came out in clouds.

I'd needed fresh air, but it was also claustrophobic in the cold. People smoked in small clusters, leaning toward each other as if their lit-up filters were bonfires. The bad pinot in my cup was almost gone. I zipped my puffer to my chin and walked back inside.

Ollie was talking to a new, but still impossibly chic, group of people underneath an X-ray of a chest cavity, with large letters and an arrow pointing toward the trachea: *Beautiful and welcoming entryway!* Next to the ventricles of the heart, the letters read *Generous foyer with four midcentury proportioned rooms.* I stepped into Ollie's circle. I saw him move to introduce me, but before he could—

I threw the red wine on his white sweater.

His fake friends gasped like I'd drawn blood.

I told them to check out my social account. See that his "one-of-a-kind" ideas were taken from me. They'd been lifted and reapplied, a botched organ transplant.

I spun away from him and did not look back at the thrum of people asking my name.

Except that didn't happen, not at all.

The images on loop in our heads are often so different, so much more, than the actions we actually execute.

Instead, I found Whit and told him we needed to leave.

In the Uber, I drafted a text to Ollie. Deleted it. Looked at his feed a couple hundred times and tried to figure out if he was seeing that model. Googled his name, hit the news tab, hoping to find a write-up in some art publication about his show. Could I post an anonymous comment outing him as a fraud? I wrote down my swirling thoughts in the Notes app.

He's a parasite on me. Take, take, take. Who are you, really, if all you do is capture the hidden parts of other people and bring them to light for yourself? It was all incoherent. Whit's profile was sharp against the black window and the glow in his palm. I didn't have the capacity to explain the situation to him yet. Why couldn't I share this with my future husband? Why was I busy fuming about a guy I'd loved years ago when I was about to walk down the aisle with someone stable, good, and bright? I was thinking about Whit like a piece of furniture. A flesh house.

Finally, I texted Ollie. I went with cryptic yet enraged, the staple combination for any woman who's been called a C-word (*crazy, cunty, conniving*).

Really? I wrote. **Taking from me again? Your brain has asbestos.**

The cab swallowed the streets as the city flashed by, dots of moving light speckling the view. Whit started talking about going to see his family over Christmas and mentioned an email his mom had sent him. I was half listening. I kept glancing at my phone to see if Ollie had responded. At first,

I did it nonchalantly ("Work," I said), but then I became increasingly paranoid that Whit would call me out. I could get away with a fair amount of distraction, since Whit stared at his screen for long stretches of the day, too. Relationships were often just tallies of how much time each person spent on their phone.

Email from Madewell about a 25 percent off holiday sale. Text from my mom about wedding flights. Tag from Bex (she was still posting bridal pictures at a steady IV drip). Email from Maxine about her interview on Kara Swisher's podcast. News alert about a hotel attack in Somalia.

Nothing from Ollie.

"Yeah, that makes sense," I said absentmindedly, responding to something Whit said that I didn't catch.

"Her maybe having dementia *makes sense*?"

"No!" I nearly shouted. "That's not what I meant. Sorry, I wasn't really listening. Has your mom's forgetting gotten worse?"

"Yeah, I could tell."

"I'm here." I slid my phone into my jacket, feeling a premature pang of separation anxiety. He started telling me, gingerly, about his mom's recent forgetfulness, how she kept sending him emails with subject lines that didn't match up to their bodies, texts that would cut off midsentence. Phone calls in which she called Whit her dead brother's name, conversations that went from an onslaught to simple breathing in the span of a few seconds.

I listened, I did. I asked questions. Touched his hand. I wanted to be there for him, but there was a pull inside my pocket. The possibility of Ollie's text gnawed at me as I tried to talk my fiancé through family trauma.

Back inside the apartment, Whit got right into bed. He said he felt emotionally drained, and I agreed without explaining.

On the feed, Virginia had put up the picture of herself, Ollie, and Mikey, plus stories of the art. The real estate tagline on a liver: *Open-plan living room, nontoxic!*

In the bathroom that Mimi wanted to gut, my skin looked wan and chapped. I imagined rashes blooming across my face, stains showing through my patched-up interior. I squeezed my pores, the little pricks. The openings that made me receptive to dirt and grime and the nicer stimuli, too: oxygen, sun, and the serums I patted on my skin like fertilizer. They were tiny, aerated clues to what lay below, black holes revealing how little light I let in.

bexjoneswilliams GO O&V! Amazing

mimimurph so proud of you

graymbosker talent runs in the fam

charliexo fuck ur COOL

27 December

Camera Roll
A sheaf of paper in a drawer

The merry-go-round was dusted with snow, the metal ponies ice-slick and gleaming.

"Unicorns," Whit said as we passed them in the car. "Like Composure, once you're done with it, babe."

We'd come to Watch Hill for twenty-four hours of on-the-ground wedding planning. Mimi and Virginia were joining us—they'd arrived earlier for spa appointments at a new hotel in town. Our itinerary read like a bride's fever dream: florist at eleven, wedding planner at noon, caterer at one, hair and makeup trial at three. The bridal blogs described this point in the process as a culmination of stress, with a side of giddy impatience. I should be buzzing with anticipation. Instead I was buzzing with a darker fuel, a force focused on the past more than the future: rage.

In the days since the art show, I'd swallowed my anger and let it simmer. Rage wasn't calcified under the skin but rather a mobile agent released into one's bloodstream. I thrummed with indignation, the betrayal traveling through my body and twisting my expressions into fake, frozen forms.

"What are you thinking about?" Whit had asked me multiple times since the show. "You look so far away."

I'd decided not to tell him about the stolen idea. He wouldn't understand the @bridalbodyyy account—he called the art show "weird as hell" with a dismissive flick of his perfect chin that didn't manage to disturb his gelled hair—and the admission would open up a flood of information that traced back to my relationship with Ollie.

At the house, Mimi greeted us with a stack of terry cloth.

"Robes!" she screamed as if she'd spotted a whale. "Monogrammed and everything. Doesn't this make it feel so real!?"

Mine read MRS. HARRIS in coral script. I thought of Whit's mom and her frumpy reticence. *She might have dementia,* I reminded myself, *be nice.* Either way, I didn't like the idea of sharing a moniker with her, or a future where people addressed me in a formal tone that marked me as an appendage of my husband and invoked a woman I didn't particularly like. No one had asked me if I was changing my name.

I put on the robe anyways. It was high quality, a plush hug on my skin, which had prickled with goose bumps in the thirty-five-degree December chill. *Callie Harris, Callie Harris,* I repeated to myself like a mantra. When Ollie and I had started hooking up in college, I'd written *Callie Murphy* over and over, embarrassing ink trails in my chemistry notebook when I should've been doing his homework or my own. He'd told me offhand, while discussing his hyphenated surname, that he'd want his future family to drop the Moskowitz. I didn't have a problem with an identity shift then; but perhaps I was more comfortable inhabiting a name I'd always aspired toward.

The florist arrived with a burst of growths I could not name. White and black blooms, the stems wild yet orderly.

"The anemones are divine," Mimi said. "And these white spray roses! Stunning, Martha, just wonderful."

Virginia, Whit, and Mimi gathered around the arrangements, picking out different flowers, smelling them, discussing their merits and drawbacks. The florist advocated for each one, nondiscriminatory with love for her "Earth babies," a term she spoke out loud without irony.

Flowers were on my dad's list of grievances. "You're buying an expensive death," he said. "They get you compliments for a few days or a week. Then boom! Dead." It was the same reason, with a slightly longer shelf life, he refused to get a dog.

In his book, my dad wrote about Sterling and Amelia watching the floral arrangements in the Cahills' Watch Hill mansion wilt each day, absent from sunlight and the housekeeper who normally tended to them.

The flowers—peonies, Amelia had informed him—had begun to droop like arms dangling to release heavy baggage. They told each other they should take care of the poor plants; no one else was here to preserve their integrity. However, a small thrill sparked in each of them with the casting off of responsibilities, the active ignoring of shoulds. The dishes piled in the sink, a precipitous tower of streaked porcelain. It was May, but they were off-season, carving out a space adjacent to, but entirely separate from, the expected procession of their lives. Sterling did not voice these minute rebellions out loud, but he knew Amelia shared his sentiment—they existed here outside time, though the flowers and the dishes were a reminder of its passing.

"Callie!" Virginia said. "We just asked you twice—what do you think?"

She gestured to an arrangement that looked like the others, but smaller. My bouquet: white roses and thistle, tied with a cream satin ribbon.

"It's great," I said. "Really pretty."

She gave me a pinched expression that telegraphed misunderstanding—she'd used it when I said I liked *NSYNC more than the Backstreet Boys in third grade and when I asked about her sexuality several months ago. A quick crowding of her features that seemed to say, *Wrong answer,* or *Wrong question,* while failing to illuminate the flaws in my words.

I showed up to dinner with a new face.

The makeup artist had taken too many liberties—airbrushing is all the rage, she'd told me—and turned my epidermis into a matte tarp. She assured me it was good for pictures. "But what about real life?" I'd asked. She laughed and said the pictures mattered more. They were the evidence I'd carry with me.

"Gorgeous," Mimi said. "You are a bride!"

"It's way too much."

"You can wipe some of it off," Virg said. "And honestly, it's good for—"

"Pictures, I know. I've heard."

"You look beautiful, love," Whit assured me. "I'm sure it feels like a lot now, but when you put the dress on, it will come together."

"How sweet," Mimi cooed. "I don't think Walter notices when I do a chemical peel on my face, let alone get my makeup done."

"I want to feel like myself, though," I said. "I'm worried I'll look like everyone else."

My concern was valid but empty. I didn't know what it was to "feel like myself." I'd spent years turning myself inside out to feel like someone else.

Mimi was off to Marcie Haffenraffer's house for a drink,

which meant a bottle. Marcie was in town redecorating, the only standard reason for being there in December.

"I'll just be an hour or two," Mimi said. "Preheat the oven in a bit, will you? I'm already starving, and you *know* Marcie won't put out anything besides her horseradish dip and gluten-free crackers."

I did not know, but I nodded along. Mimi pinched her cheeks forcefully, despite the fact that she was already wearing blush.

"Au revoir!" she shouted through the house.

"I need a nap," Virginia said, stretching her arms over her head.

"Me, too," Whit agreed.

I nodded, the day's stressful frivolity settling in.

While trying to nap, Whit's breathing provided a soundtrack to my growing list of questions. Inhale, what should I put in our welcome bags? Exhale, when will we find time to move in together? Inhale, can I live with a man? Exhale, can I live with *this* man?

I got up and wandered, trancelike, down the hallway toward Mimi and Walter's bedroom. An old curiosity unspooled as I approached the drawer I'd snooped through in college.

Their room was stunning. The term *master bedroom,* I'd been told, was being retired—but this space evoked *master* in the painting sense more than the problematic history sense. The room and its views would translate seamlessly to a canvas. Wooden carved headboard, cream sheets, powder-blue upholstered bench. A balcony that overlooked a rocky beach and the open ocean, an expanse whose contents shifted as its mass remained constant. A dark sheet of water containing hidden depths—clear skin pulled over an unsightly maze.

I slid open the bedside drawer and found the inside

unchanged. A folder of landscaping bills and HOA papers, ChapStick, an envelope of elementary school pictures, twenty- and one-dollar bills crumpled like afterthoughts.

Absentmindedly, I flipped through the folder of old bills and documents about speed bumps on sleepy streets that read like missives from the Department of Justice. I paused at a less cluttered page, clean lines of text with paragraph breaks.

It was an excerpt from "Off-Season."

I lowered myself to the bed and read, my stomach somewhere near my cranial cavity, my entire body tense. I hadn't seen this material before. I skimmed the first few sentences and realized it picked up at the abrupt and unfinished ending in the manuscript I'd found months earlier.

Sterling and Amelia watched the fire and the sky's simultaneous metamorphosis. The flames crackled as orange streaks engulfed the clouds that had afforded them their stormy reprieve. Their silence hummed with shared ease. Sterling was rarely silent with Dorothea, as their domestic logistics and planning provided necessary, unstimulating fodder. The clouds were a pink spill meandering across the gray sky in a line, hazy at the edges.

He turned to Amelia. "Isn't this nice?"

She was pinching her cheeks—to wake herself up or stimulate a sensation? Or perhaps it was because she wanted to look rosy for him. She considered him and her appearance in his eyes.

"You are beautiful," he said, three words sanctioned and repeated in art and marriage through the centuries, a benign romantic phrase turned forbidden on the tongue of a married man when directed at a woman who was not his wife.

*Her cheeks lit up like the sky or the hearth or one
thousand flaming hearts. "You are, too."*

*Sterling's words and Amelia's parroting of them
unlocked an unspoken truth: they'd found a latent
beauty in themselves through each other. Sterling had an
impulse to possess or become Amelia, a feeling so strong,
he reached out and broke the invisible barrier they'd
navigated for days.*

*Kissing her transcended the physical and sent Sterling
into a soft, ephemeral place. What should have been
tawdry was justified by the purity of his feelings. They
fell into a rhythmic dance, moving from the living room
to the bedroom, clothed to unclothed. There was nothing
more natural than an act society deemed unnatural.
When he entered her, Amelia let out a soft exhale, a
pressure valve releasing.*

"Voilà," she whispered. "Here you are, here."

*He laughed despite the seriousness of the moment.
Amelia was always peppering her speech with French,
borrowed from her time living abroad.*

I stopped reading. The cheek pinching, her marriage to
a friend, fucking *voilà*. My dad had taken pains to disguise
her identity, but this passage made it clear that Amelia was
based on Mimi. The direct passion of his prose, its lack of
self-consciousness, made me believe that the affair was real,
too. It would explain so much: my dad's slow retreat from
my mother, Mimi's depression in the months after his death,
even her overdose on the night of her anniversary party.
She'd stowed away the bulk of the manuscript and separated
these specific pages, suggesting she didn't want anyone to
make the connection between her and Amelia, but couldn't
bear to throw out the memory. I thought of how she brought

up my dad in conversation with excited frequency, as opposed to my mom's stoic silence. Mimi's tears at Kleinfeld weren't a generalized existential crisis—they were sadness that he wouldn't walk me down the aisle, that she wouldn't dance with him at the Ocean House.

Since I started revising the manuscript, I'd pushed aside thoughts of a real-life affair, but the suspicion now reared its head, nagging and impenetrable. Had it presented subconsciously in the way I made the Amelia character suffer, in the baby I gave Dorothea? I tried to rewrite history, reversing their roles and vindicating my mother's cast-off position in their twisted marital musical chairs.

I lifted the envelope from the drawer and held the elementary school pictures splayed like a deck of cards: Virginia, Gray, Virginia, Gray, Gray, me, me. Mimi. Virginia and I looked nothing alike, a sad reality, but Virginia and Gray also bore little resemblance to each other. They both had their mom's ski slope nose, the dainty swoop that Ollie had inherited as well. My eyes were the same shape as Gray's, smaller than Virg's blinking planets, and almond shaped. Short, dark lashes. Gray's face was heart-shaped while mine was oval, but our chins had a similarly pointed insistence—not a neat square like Whit's, more of an inverted peak as if our faces had been tied off at their ends. My dad had this same feature, and so did his fictional avatar. "Sterling's chin, a sharpened point." Plenty of people shared facial features without sharing genes, but overlaid with my suspicions about Mimi and my dad, this double take felt like more than a coincidence. On the back of the envelope, Mimi's Post-it remained, her indecipherable body parts list now illuminated. *Chin (GC),* it read. Gray and Callie. She'd also noticed our similarities, the indicting evidence of genetics.

I heard the front door open, followed by the distinctive suck and pull of the refrigerator. I shuffled out of the room, realizing too late that I'd taken the pages with me.

28 December

bridalbodyyy underneath your clothes, there's
an endless story 🎵🎵 #anatomy #shakira
#medicaldrawings

"I need another drink," Virginia said. "Want to open that Beaujolais?" Another task she liked to outsource, claiming ineptitude.

"Sure." We'd need wine for this conversation.

After a quick dinner in the spacious open kitchen, with a butcher block table described in my dad's book (unclear on whether he'd confirmed this was also a nineteenth-century decor trend or just copped the Murphys' look wholesale), Mimi and Whit were already upstairs. "Talking to Marcie is like running a verbal marathon, I tell you. The woman can gab!" Mimi had said, tucking herself in early. Whit had a call with Walter about his psoriasis drug on Monday and needed to research his talking points. Virginia was sprawled on the couch, her hair fanned over a tasseled pillow. I poured two glasses of the red she insisted on keeping chilled in the wine fridge. Virginia had made a public service side project out of telling people they were drinking their red wine too hot, a firm stance she'd taken up thanks to a friendship with an East Village sommelier. She twisted her hair into a topknot; there was still a splotch of blue crusted in those long strands from a painting session earlier in the day.

"You're already working on something new?" I asked.

"Just fucking around. I threw a ton of colors on the canvas, kind of like a rainbow orgy."

"Poor man's Jackson Pollock."

"Exactly." She smiled. I hated that this word, which some people tossed into conversation like salt, made me flush with self-confidence when Virginia said it.

"How are you feeling after the show?"

"Pretty amazing," she said, cradling the stemless wineglass in her hands like a bowl of soup. "The reception's been insane. *Vice* asked to do a profile; so did some Gen Z zine that's apparently cooler than *Vice*. I can't keep up."

"If you can't keep up, I'm basically dead."

"Ready to become one with the earth," she said, using Composure copy we'd made fun of together.

She sipped the wine and leaned her head back on the pillow. "God, that's good."

"Is it from Philip?" I asked, impressed that I remembered the name of the sommelier friend.

"Ollie. He bought me a bunch of bottles as a congratulations for the show."

I'd planned on warming up to this confrontation, but hearing his name in her mouth—vibrating through her uvula and slipping between the fingernail-thin gap next to her left incisor—pulled on an internal lever, made me bolder and less tactful.

"Who came up with the idea for the show again?"

"He did." No hesitation. "He came to me with the concept pretty early, though. I thought it was a little try-hard at first. Like no shit, people have organs, do we need to make some larger commentary about it? But he sold me once we came up with the Zillow stuff. God, I'm addicted to that website."

"You came up with it."

"We did."

I turned my phone to her, opened to the @bridalbodyyy feed. I tried to explain in succinct and cutting terms. This is my secret account. This was my idea first. Ollie stole from me. She was half listening, swiping her fingers across the screen and using her pointer and thumb to enlarge the images. She brought the phone close to her face and then moved it farther away again, as if it were a pointillist picture that emerged with distance, a chaotic coherence that accompanied a wider lens.

"Who drew these?" she asked.

"Me."

"I didn't know you drew. They're cool. Raw."

"That's the word he used, too."

"When did you start doing this?" So she hadn't been listening. Her topknot had fallen toward the right side of her head like an off-kilter punctuation mark.

"After Leila's wedding. So like six or seven months ago. I assume you didn't know he stole the idea from me?"

"Callie." She called me by my full first name only when she was angry, a maternal habit that didn't mesh with her otherwise childish impulses. "I don't know what you're talking about."

I stood up from the couch in an involuntary spring that positioned me above her. "What did he say to you?"

"That you've been kind of stalking him. I told him it was probably manic wedding stress, which reminder, you're getting married? You seem completely disinterested."

"I don't want to talk about my wedding right now."

"Clearly. You looked like you were in physical pain with the florist today."

"I want to talk about your cousin and how he's ruining my life."

"Well, that's dramatic."

"Did he tell you about college?"

"He didn't have to tell me. I guessed it years ago." Her bun shifted to the other side, a distracting pendulum, as she looked out the darkened window. "You kept acting strange around him and I thought it was just a crush. I asked him about it and he told me. He said not to talk about it, that it ended weirdly. I honestly just didn't want to think about it, so I sort of blocked it out."

"Why didn't you tell me you knew?"

"Why didn't you tell me it happened in the first place?"

Here was her trump card, the callout that made my accusations worthless. A creeping heat flooded my face, and my hands started gently shaking.

"He stole from me then, too. I used to do his science homework and write his papers for him."

"No offense, Cal, but he had like a 4.0. He's really smart. I don't think he needed help."

"Thanks to me. His grades. Those were mine, too."

"You're not really making sense. Sit down. Take some deep breaths."

"Don't tell me when to breathe."

She laughed. "I'm sorry. I know you're upset. I just— you're sounding a little like a *Real Housewives* transcript."

"I'm glad you find this funny."

"Look, even if he did know about your body drawings account—"

"He did."

"The show was different. Maybe he meant it as an homage to your idea. You know, like a riff on it."

"Plagiarism isn't appreciation. It's straight up theft."

"Do you remember that girl in my studio art class who painted the same French countryside scene as I did, with nearly identical colors?"

"You were annoyed."

"I got over it pretty quickly. Ideas don't belong to people like"—she looked at the ceiling as she racked her brain for a comparison—"pets. They're wilder than that."

"Birds," I tried.

"Yes! Like birds. Flitting between people and places."

"But birds can be captured."

"Who wants a hawk in a cage?" She was smiling, and I had a sense of vertigo that the conversation had been pulled out from under me.

"Ollie. He took my hawk and rubbed it all over a public art gallery."

"Ew," she said, the remnants of a sneer fracturing into a laugh. "That's disgusting."

We burst into laughter, an uncontrolled and disproportionate release like we'd had in the hospital. I didn't have time to analyze whether the build was unhinged, competitive, or both. I lost myself in a pocket of abandon that only Virginia and Ollie could provide. The sounds hit a peak and then went downhill, slowing to shallow breaths.

"I get that you're upset," she said. "I probably would be, too. But I really don't think he meant to steal or gaslight you. Have you talked to him?"

"He'll barely respond to me, remember? I'm a *stalker*."

She winced. "Sorry for saying that. You're a hot stalker. Anyone would be lucky for you to stalk them."

"That's like saying someone's a nice murderer."

"Aren't they all? Before they kill you."

Virginia poured us both another glass and started describing a true crime podcast about a missing teen model. For a minute or two, I lost track of my real reason for confronting her: the show was a skin-deep entry point to the question of our parents' affair. As the conversation moved on to harmless gossip about the overblown wedding of a college classmate,

I felt less inclined to bring up my suspicions. The suspicions themselves were cheapened in light of my quick one-eighty on the art show. Virginia had assuaged my anger with her defense that art doesn't have to be personal. Maybe Ollie didn't mean to steal from me and was instead inspired by my idea. Maybe my dad and Mimi didn't have an affair, and he was inspired by the idea of one. Maybe Virginia was right—ideas were ineffable and transferable, outside the bounds of reality and consequences.

The window in the living room opened onto the Murphys' lawn and the roiling ocean, motion still visible in the moonlight. We fell into a comfortable silence watching the waves.

"Feeling better?" she asked, as if my anger were an affliction.

"Can I ask you something crazy?"

"Always."

"Do you think our parents were having an affair?"

If she had taken a sip of wine, she would've spit it out. "Where'd you come up with that?"

"I found that novel my dad had been working on when he died." I rushed forward so she wouldn't ask how I found it. "There's an affair between two best couple friends. It's set in Watch Hill. It felt a little close to home."

"My dad wouldn't have the time, and my mom can't keep a secret to save her life. It's fiction, right?"

"A lot of fiction is based on real life."

"Or based on a possibility. A moment. A headline. There aren't hard-and-fast connections between art and reality. That's sort of the whole point of art—it's an *escape* from reality."

"Then maybe our parents were in love but never consummated it."

"Gross."

"I don't like thinking about it, either."

"So don't."

I'd done this with my eating disorder and my estrange-ment from my mom: pushed them aside and convinced myself that their causes were normal, easily explained. It was strangely intoxicating to ignore my instincts in favor of someone else's logic, and I counted this shift as a sign I was becoming practical and mature instead of repressed.

"Should I ask your mom about it?"

"About the affair you made up?" Virginia said, her face pinched with disapproval. "God, no. She's fragile right now."

"I just think if she can explain why she had my dad's man-uscript, if I can ask her about the book—it might help quiet these ideas."

"What do you mean, she had the manuscript?"

"Oh." I scrambled for an explanation. "I found it in the apartment." Admitting to also finding the sex scene in the drawer upstairs would sound too unhinged; I'd keep that part a secret for now.

"You were looking through her stuff."

"I wasn't, it was right there at the top of a box. I just, I tried to—"

"It's fine. *I* don't care. But she might be weirded out. She's really particular about her things. Just don't, Cal. She needs to gain strength."

Virginia swirled her red wine, remnants of the liquid clinging to the glass and beginning their slow crawl back to the basin. Sterling and Amelia, I remembered, had even-tually done those dishes in the newly discovered pages I'd continued reading back in the guest bedroom. They woke up tangled together to find that the storm had cleared. "Ev-erything," my dad had written, "circles a fixed drain, either succumbing to a gravitational pull or resisting at the edges. The soapy water trailed through the sink, a tiny ocean, as Amelia kept her head bent toward the plates, scrubbing each porcelain face with vigor. 'Look up,' Sterling said. He touched her chin, no longer able to resist tugging the line between them. And so they were taken, willingly and swiftly, down their own drain, whose dark bottom was not yet visible."

"I'm going to bed," Virginia said, finishing her last sip. "How are you not exhausted?"

"Bride batteries. We just keep going."

"Oh, I believe it." She stood and placed her hand on my shoulder, in an eerily similar gesture to the one Ollie had made when he left me on the beach chair in Mexico—an intended reassurance that came off as condescension.

She turned off the main overheads on her way up, leaving me with the weak light of a table lamp. I went back to my @bridalbodyyy page and then toggled to the images from the *Human Content* show, cataloging the projects' differences. I overlaid the Venn diagram of "Off-Season" and my dad's past with these art comparisons. Traits I once deemed too similar to be coincidental—Mimi and Amelia's cheek pinching, my dad and Sterling's love of the water—contracted and swelled, the truth as malleable as mixed paint. Discovering my dad's secrets had opened up a new drain in me. I couldn't decide if I was being pulled toward the wrong depth, or if I simply feared the dark infinity that waited once I allowed myself to go under.

zptheking who r u?

maddie666 sexy!

tinabsmith they look alike! #bodydouble

29 January

Sketches I drew during my one-month wedding countdown:

My simple, spaghetti-strapped wedding dress. Extension cord intestines curling from the bodice and running down the church aisle.

A stomach, huge and grotesque, with a stick-figure Ollie bobbing in the middle of the pouch. An arrow reading *You Are Here* pointing at him.

Whit's hands branching into thick fingers. A stretched-out version of me curving over his lifeline.

Sterling and Amelia, or my father and Mimi, sharing the same body—their legs and arms overlapping like conjoined twins with intersecting blood.

Virginia's pancreas. Virginia's liver. Virginia's deltoid muscles. I drew each part separately, making them hers through a chart only I could navigate. Her field hockey jersey number hidden in a ventricle. The plastic eye of Bowie, her childhood stuffed bear, pockmarked on an adrenal gland. There was something nauseating, serial killer–y, about this practice— leaving tokens of her through an anatomical maze. I didn't know it as my pencil-clutching hand flew over pages, but I was working out a theory in real time.

When I'd started this project, I was trying to illuminate the disconnect between our external fixation and internal naïveté. Our preoccupation with surface beauty juxtaposed with our less-than-beautiful anatomies. The equalizing power of the body, its indifference to money and external status. I thought we were all the same inside—a chest of drawers stuffed with similar, unwieldy products. But bodies are also a ledger, an accumulation of nicks and cigarettes and seventh cocktails. Colonics and babies, or lack thereof. Because Virginia's history had closely mirrored my own, I was able to imagine the melon-split of cutting her open, the seeds you'd see in the spill. These thoughts I could not say out loud. They made me sound creepy and obsessed with her, when I was really searching for scraps of myself.

Those elementary school pictures I'd found and the physical traits Mimi had listed on a Post-it kept me up at night. Had she been trying to figure out whether I was related to them? Was my dad Virginia's or Gray's dad, too? *You're not on the* Maury *show,* I told myself. But still, the possibility gnawed at me. I'd been striving to make them my real family for years, not knowing that my claim could be genetic and undeniable.

    roslyn_fx instant $6,000 for the first 7 lucky people to message me. Stay blessed, y'all!

    parkersmith15 funkyyyy

    body.bysabrina 🤭

30 January

Camera Roll
A view of Battery Park from a floor-to-ceiling
window

The day we started looking at apartments, the forecast did a deepfake. A cold, high sun gave way to clouds crowding lanes of slate-gray sky.

It was January. Three weeks from the wedding, the most miserable month in the city, and the time when Whit decided we had to begin the hunt for an apartment. We were getting married, after all; we should have our own, proper place. The new year brought the promise of a clear-visioned start.

The week before, I'd been offered a promotion at Composure to VP of communications. The catch? I'd have to move to Seattle. After long discussions and pro-con lists that Whit detailed on a legal pad, I decided to sacrifice the raise and title jump to stay in the city and move in with him. Whit's career was on the upswing, and he convinced me that it would be catastrophic for him—for us—to relocate. My sacrifice made Whit even more eager to move in together and solidify ourselves as a unit.

"This is the best month to get a deal," Mimi said. She was coming with us to look at apartments because her best friend's sister's former nanny was a top broker and Mimi just had to introduce us. I followed Virginia's advice and didn't bring up my dad's book, not wanting to destabilize our relationship a month before the wedding Mimi was partially paying for. Every day eased the gut punch of the discovery, sanded down the certainty of my suspicions. It was fiction, I reminded myself. My dad was even more creative and reality-bending than the Zillow listings applying *spacious* and *airy* to a five-hundred-square-foot studio with a dusty window AC unit and view of a concrete wall.

We walked into a Battery Park high-rise that had a waterfall and a doorman who looked eighteen in the lobby. Mimi waved at him like she did with Marcus at 1100 Park, but thankfully didn't break out in a British accent.

"Octavia is *the* expert on Manhattan real estate," Mimi assured us. "She won't lead us astray."

We opened the door to a six-foot woman in a pantsuit, elegant and as thin as Virginia. I was already triggered, and I hadn't even been asked to pay a broker's fee yet.

"This is a stunning building," Octavia said. "All about the amenities." A far cry from invoking the "charm" or "coziness" that was endemic to co-ops and West Village walk-ups. She talked about the marble island (new) and the living room (functional), while gesturing to the natural light, which was negated by construction cranes (temporary). The sleek metal accents and polished nickel reminded me of the Composure warehouse. The one-bedroom was impersonal and small, and asking for $4,900 a month.

"How's the gym?" Whit asked.

"State of the art. There's a pool and yoga studio, too."

When Mimi and Octavia started lightly gossiping about a mutual friend, I pulled Whit aside, though there wasn't much open space to pull him toward. "It's pretty small. And we can't afford it."

"I'm probably getting promoted at the end of the year."

This stung. I had a sudden vision of an apartment in Seattle, walking distance to my office with windows where I could watch the city's signature rain trickle and merge on the glass like capillaries.

"We'll want to save money, though, right?" I ventured.

"I think it's important that we live somewhere we really love."

"But I don't love it."

"I do."

"We should keep looking."

"We're not going to find one-bedrooms for much less in doorman buildings. This is within our budget."

"Do we need a doorman?"

"I do."

"You're saying *I* a lot."

"Sorry, we do. Think about packages. And it's safer."

He skimmed the *New York Post* "for the ridiculous puns," but I knew that the hyperbolic crime warnings had seeped into his psyche, too.

"You sound like Walter," I said.

He smiled. "Compliment taken."

The broker talked about how she had two other clients preparing materials, so we'd have to act fast. Whit said he'd send over the forms that afternoon.

"I want to keep looking," I said.

A crane rotated outside the window, its sharp-angled split a robotic joint.

"But, honey, I thought you both loved it," Mimi said.

"He loves it. I'm not ready."

"Lots of other fish in the sea!" She waved her hand cheerily to indicate all those other spaces we could inhabit.

"Not really," Octavia said. "This is the only one-bedroom in this neighborhood that's asking under five thousand."

"It's maybe the most expensive neighborhood in the city," I said. "We don't need to live here."

"It's a five-minute walk to my office," Whit argued. "And it's so clean. Target and Whole Foods are like right next door! We won't get that anywhere else."

"It's not close to my office."

"You work remotely, babe."

"So I want to live somewhere I love."

He was mad. I could tell because he fake-smiled when he was angry, like a disgruntled retro housewife wielding a tin of muffins. He wrung his hands; the thick fingers that had fascinated me on the F train platform when we'd met now looked eerily unlined and pampered. He wouldn't know how to fix a toilet or an existential crisis. I was potentially on the verge of one, and his presence was exacerbating instead of minimizing the build.

He talked about how it was in our best interest to get this apartment, saying we'd miss out if we didn't jump on this deal. The more he persuaded, the more I glazed over and latched on to phrases he spouted. A reading nook under the window. Savings from no gym membership. Proximity to the Infatuation's top Italian restaurant in the city. If the apartment were a body, it would be sterile and faceless, a *Westworld* robot with shiny skin and appliances. With all the wedding decisions piling up, I was tired of choosing and suddenly found a release valve in letting Whit's preferences eclipse mine. Maybe it really was a deal, like the broker said, and as far as Manhattan spaces go, it wasn't so bad. Its lack of character became its character—and what if that character was simply a vessel, the opportunity to reflect ourselves onto its glossy surfaces?

"Let's do it," I said. "You're right."

Mimi and Octavia clapped and exclaimed that we had to pop champagne. Octavia and Whit discussed logistics and timeline for getting our materials together, and Whit pecked me on the cheek, saying he'd kick the application into "overdrive," which made me think of my dad's stick shift lessons. *You have to keep going,* he'd say. *You can't let the car stall.* Idleness leads to danger and so does disembarking from a vehicle in motion. Bodies in mirror are less willful than they appear.

Whit and I walked out of the apartment arm in arm. Our new block was full of strollers, putty-faced newborns and toddlers pushed by nannies with pinched expressions. The street was clean, save for an empty green juice jar that had spilled out of a recycling bin and a tiny, muddy sneaker at the edge of an elementary school's chain-link fence. Target, with its neon-red typeface, manspread half a block, with the Freedom Tower looming southward and stories above. Battery Park wasn't quite a gateway drug for the suburbs like the Upper East Side, but it was still a haven for gentrified hangers-on, rich families who didn't want to bend to the siren call of a real backyard, their stubbornness threatening to crack when their babies had poo explosions in packed elevators and crosswalks.

On the other side of the street, in front of the Barnes and Noble, a lanky man talked to a redheaded model. She was one of those women in the wild whose career could never be questioned: rail-thin, unusually tall, high cheekbones. The man appeared good-looking from behind, with a confident lean, oversized puffer, and fitted jeans. Sneakers that could've been $10 or $1,000. I recognized his posture.

It was Ollie.

As we got closer, I tried to steer Whit across the street, but the subway entrance was steps ahead and my divergence made no sense. Whit course corrected, using his big, gloved hand—those leather catcher's mitts I'd splurged on as a gift because he was always burrowing his freezing fingers in his jacket pockets—to steer me right into the man I'd cheated on him with.

"Sorry, Ollie. Hi," I said.

He turned around. It wasn't Ollie.

This was arguably a more attractive specimen: bearded, chiseled face and green eyes, same build as Ollie but with a universally more appealing profile. Like Redhead, he was also an obvious model. I apologized for mistaking him for "a friend"—ha!—and walked into the subway bowels with Whit.

"That guy looked nothing like Ollie," Whit said. "Do you need an eye exam?"

"They were the same build."

"That dude was definitely taller."

As the 1 train pulled up and strangers all around us shifted their bodies like flowers toward a grimy sun, I almost told him everything: the art show, the stealing, my college secret, my eating disorder, Dad's manuscript. I imagined it would come out of me like a purge, swift and sacrificial. I could offer him my fucked-up past in exchange for absolution in our marriage.

Before I could start in, saving the hardest parts for when we were in private again, Whit let out a celebratory yelp.

He was staring at his phone. "The drug is a go," he said. "The psoriasis drug. The results from the toxicity test came back and it works. Thank god, it works. Let's go out tonight!"

I asked him questions to explain. While the drug didn't work to treat psoriasis, it helped lower the toxicity of a cancer drug that Murphy had to pull years ago when its trial results were too harmful to participants. But when combined, Whit's drug and Walter's drug created a kind of superdrug, a discovery leading both men to the bank.

I congratulated him. The subway stops flashed through the windows, topped with ads for DTC brands that sold optimized versions of shit that didn't need optimizing. I thought of our meet-cute—a less crowded train, a more optimistic morning—and how our presence in the same subway car had set the rest of my life in motion. The randomness flooded me with something sharp and conflicted, a pang of wonder tinged with regret.

31 February

bexjoneswilliams Oh, it's a marvelous night for a moondance. My best friend married her best friend and we are over the ● ✨

The band sang about the night's magic, how it seemed to whisper and hush. Whit held my hips lightly, barely gripping them like they might shatter under his palms.

Faces crowded the outskirts of the dance floor. Dozens of screens pointed toward us, capturing this first dance that must have looked like so many other first dances: flailing and earnest, clumsy with sporadic moments of smoothness. Unchoreographed but not unconsidered. We'd planned the unfurling and the snap at *my love,* the cha-cha-cha at *seems to shine, in your blush.* The crowd went wild at these lukewarm moments of coordination, making me feel like we were professional dancers and not just twenty-four-hour celebrities. It was our night to be on the receiving end of congratulatory bullshit, and I knew that I should be enjoying it more.

Mimi and Walter swayed together as she snapped pictures on her iPad because "the camera is better," though the device was three years old and clunky as hell. Virginia stood near her table, not wanting to gawk and knowing, rightly, that the photographer and videographer her mother overpaid would capture these moments better than any of our spiderweb-cracked iPhones. I didn't end up having bridesmaids—the social politics stressed me out—but Virginia's black silk dress, patterned with off-white flowers, made her look involved somehow, bride-adjacent.

The string lights in the Ocean House's ballroom threw bright dots onto the surface of Whit's glasses, which he'd insisted on wearing to make his "two left feet a little less left-leaning."

I gazed into his eyes, because that's what you were supposed to do when you were in love. I didn't like that they were separated from me by a partition. The other eyes on us must have made me consider his eyes, the ways they were mitigated and held back from me. They could never fully merge with my own. But wasn't that the joy of having a partner, going through life with a separate set of eyes? My impulse to possess another body, make it part of my own, scared me. It was untenable, it was messed up—yet I wanted it all the same.

"I love you," he whispered. "Can you believe it?"

"I can't," I said. I knew his question was about this night and its beauty, and I made him believe my answer was as well, when really, I was stuck on the impossibility of his first statement. *I love you.*

Off the dance floor, I found my personal waiter, the woman assigned to make sure I didn't pass out. She had the whole assortment of hors d'oeuvres, the tuna tacos and shrimp skewers and cheese puffs, the mini tomato soup shot with a pinkie-finger-sized grilled cheese—the one-two punch that was more unusual and elegant than sliders, the wedding planner had gushed. I ate one of each selection, ravenous after depriving myself in the days leading up to the wedding.

Bex had told me, with the gravity of delivering earnest

marriage advice, that I had to frontload socialization so I could get properly drunk for the dance floor portion of the night. I could obey this instruction. I made the rounds with a light touch, commenting on the mini-moon (the Bahamas), the decor (stunning, I cannot take credit), and the food (amazing, ditto).

My mom was talking to her sister's husband, an alt-right conspiracy theorist who collected model trains. She'd come into the hotel suite to see me before I went down the aisle, but I'd wanted to walk alone. It was too painful to have her as a stand-in, since we'd drifted far apart.

"Mom," I said, cutting in on her conversation with a hug. "How's your night going?"

"This is something else," she said, gesturing to the tent. "Mimi outdid herself."

Compared with most of the weddings I'd attended, it was understated. String lights and minimal florals, assigned tables but not assigned seats. Chicken or fish option instead of a surf-and-turf combination on every plate, a band that took a break instead of being paid to play through. Though Mimi and Walter covered half the cost, we'd still had a clear budget—a word that didn't mix with a real Murphy wedding. My mom's quaint overhype made me embarrassed for her in a complicated way, since I was also embarrassed for myself in deeming my wedding not *that* nice.

My mom asked questions about the mini-moon and Whit's parents, whom she was meeting for the first time at the wedding. Her tone revealed that she thought this was strange. But wasn't it stranger that my mom had barely been in my call log during seven months of planning?

"They're really nice," I said.

"A euphemism for boring."

I laughed. "Not necessarily Dad's cup of tea."

The "boring" line was my dad's, and I used to agree with

him. But after six years in the city, I'd changed my tune: *nice* was notable in its own right.

"Are they like Whit?" my mom said.

"Like what?"

"Whit. Your husband."

"They're . . . no. Not really. He's more ambitious and outgoing than they are."

"Good to know. I barely know him!" my mom said. She quickly realized that negativity had edged into her voice and squeezed my arm as if to physically reroute this line of thinking. "He is wonderful."

"Well, it was fast."

"When you know, you know."

People kept saying this to me—it was one of those clichés whose ubiquity hadn't ebbed its overuse. Each dispenser thought he or she was imparting real wisdom. I started ignoring Bex's advice and drinking with increasing frequency, each champagne flute and Whit's End signature whiskey cocktail softening and numbing my interactions. Multiple targets stood around the bar, guests I'd need to talk to before my BAC climbed too high. Whit stood with Walter, and I approached them with trepidation.

"Cal," Walter said, giving me an enveloping hug, "you look stunning. What a couple!" He held each of our shoulders and beamed.

"I caught a good one," Whit said.

"I'd say she did pretty well for herself, too," Walter said in the deep, stiff tone I bet he used in board meetings. His robotic nature was buoyed by confidence that marked his speech as important, not stale. "Did your *husband*"—he paused at the word—"tell you about what he pulled off at work?"

"The drug combo," I said. "Exciting."

"I'd call it inspired," Walter continued. Whit was borderline blushing. "He took this no-name psoriasis drug and used his network of scientists and doctors to bring it back from clinical death."

"And now you're teaming up!" I tried to sound genuinely thrilled. "I heard."

"I hadn't thought of Nobutrin since it was killed in phase three," he said. "It was this gangbusters drug"—Walter loved a Mafia reference—"that we were expecting to bring in fifty mil in its first year on the market. Had to pull the plug. But now, thanks to your husband's ingenuity, it's back in the game."

"What kind of cancer does it treat again?" I asked, trying to seem interested.

"Blood cancers, mostly."

"Like multiple myeloma?"

"That's one of the big ones."

I paused, working something out in my head. "What year did you say it was pulled?"

"2006, if I remember correctly." Walter looked at Whit, who nodded in encouragement.

2006—the year *The Devil Wears Prada* movie came out, Beyoncé sang, *To the left, to the left,* and my dad's survival odds went from hopeful to grim. I remember cultural happenings from that year because I'd watch E! News to numb out. Pop-Tarts and Maria Menounos lulled me into a sugar-laced, middle-of-the-night sleep for weeks.

"I'll let you two keep making the rounds," Walter said, using the elegant conversational exit we all leaned on.

As Whit watched Walter walk away, his face creased with the private glee usually reserved for an impending meal or sexual encounter. He smothered me in a hug. "I love you so fucking much."

"You just love that I brought you closer to your boyfriend," I said teasingly.

"Manfriend. Walter is the man."

Walter was a lot of things: a patriarch, the person who essentially paid my rent, a character in the twenty-first century who would be at home in the century of my dad's novel. His blunt drive was a foil to my dad's mysterious creativity, that well he'd drawn from to create worlds and provide warmth to others, while Walter only provided the good primarily associated with providing. Walter's money, and Whit's role in multiplying it, suddenly struck me as a farce, more detached from reality than even my father's fiction. Dumb luck in the birth lottery had propelled Walter to a position in which he could decide who to save. If that cancer drug had been green-lit slightly earlier, my dad might have walked me down the aisle tonight, or given me the confidence not to rush, flailing, into forever.

It was an unfortunate coincidence that the timing of Walter pulling the drug lined up with my dad's cancer getting worse. Despite a flicker of initial paranoia, I knew Walter didn't squash the drug because he thought my dad was sleeping with his wife—Walter cared about his business's bottom line above all else and couldn't pull off something that Machiavellian—but the resurfacing of my dad's death and the interconnectedness of our families brought up my questions around a real-life affair.

I started drinking red wine, the heavy pours filling me in a drowsy haze.

Ollie stood holding a negroni next to his table, which had been cleared of everything except wineglasses and abandoned pieces of cake.

I'd been avoiding him all night, my view of his curls from the altar the only time I'd let my mind settle on his face. We hugged because that was the polite thing to do, but I pulled away as if his suit were burning.

"I recognize this dress," he said, the corner of his mouth twitching into a half smile.

"Thanks so much for coming." My autopilot response to every single person I'd seen that night.

"Wouldn't miss it."

"Back to the city tomorrow?"

"I need to pack. I move in three weeks."

"California, here you come."

"So this is our last opportunity to kiss and make up," he said. He was smiling as if our history were a big joke.

"Excuse me?"

"It's your night. I just thought you'd want to apologize for the way you overreacted."

"You copied me," I said, a juvenile response that sounded like I was chiding a school friend on the playground for buying the same sneakers.

"Have you heard of Louise Lawler?" Before I could respond no, he barreled on with his pretentious soliloquy. I tried to keep my face placid, but my body was humming with anger and wine. "She's a famous artist from the eighties who took photographs of other artists' pieces on display in museums. By reframing their creativity, she challenged the concept of who owns art. Her photo *Does Andy Warhol Make You Cry?* was revolutionary."

"Did you rip that from an *Artforum* article?"

"Ideas aren't copyrighted. They're open to new interpretations from different artists. Weren't you revising your dad's novel?"

"That's different."

He raised his eyebrows, pleased for trapping me in his self-serving logic. "How so?"

"Well, my dad asked me to, first off. Also, he isn't here to do it himself."

"Ah, but I'm sure he wouldn't agree with all your choices.

Your creation, with his work as a jumping-off point, becomes an entirely different animal."

While I had tried to tilt history to my mother's advantage and declaw the scratching persistence of a relationship between Mimi and my dad, I was still the author's daughter, revising with his blessing.

"I was honoring him," I said, "not stealing from him."

"What if I was honoring you?"

"Bullshit. You've been sucking me dry for years."

"You really want to go there on your wedding night?"

The smirk on his face and the way he twisted my accusation into sexual innuendo unknotted a deep, tangled mass I'd tried to bury.

I thrust my glass of wine onto Ollie. The red mark exploded on his white shirt and left a splattered mess trickling down to his pants, as if I'd cut him open with a too-dull object. I turned around and realized half the room was staring. Virginia rushed toward Ollie with a bottle of seltzer, looking at me with disdain and a hint of fear.

My peripheral vision had weakened during the fight, and now people around me emerged again as if I'd turned the focus dial on a telescope. Whit had been right behind me; his face told me he'd overheard the entire interaction.

He pulled me outside, walking quickly with infuriated purpose. I almost resisted following him, because I wanted to bask in my attack. For the first time all night, I was powerful and at peace.

"What the hell was that?"

The black outlines of the ocean wavered above the shoreline before exploding onto the sand in a haunting, airy rhythm. It was too cold for us to be standing outside.

"You know Ollie and Virginia's photography exhibit? He stole my idea. I had to put him in his place."

"What are you talking about?"

I tried to explain—my secret account, the work I'd done for Ollie in college, the way he'd claimed my ideas without wanting to claim me—and Whit's angry, puffed-up posture deflated in withdrawn confusion.

"When was the last time you slept with him?"

I paused.

"Callie."

"In Italy. At Gray's wedding."

"That was right before we got engaged."

"Everything's been fucked."

"Including you."

His raised voice went on about monogamy as a nonnegotiable, like this was a contract he was signing in a boardroom. "How could you?" he kept saying. "I don't understand. Why would you?" Stock phrases of incredulity.

"I'm sorry," I said.

Whit undid his bow tie, the two sides bookending the buttons I should have wanted to undo; the body I should've wanted to spill into my own.

I tried to tell him it was a mistake, saying I was confused and could put it in the past now. He made it clear that I wasn't saying the right things, if the right things existed.

I attempted a defense. "You haven't exactly been there for me in all of this. This goes both ways."

Whit started crying and curved his head into his hands. I put my arms around his convulsing form, rubbing his back and moving my hands over his white button-down. His muscles felt tight with emotion, but my hug was hollow. I couldn't mirror his outpouring. I wasn't even crying. I knew then, with the brick-from-the-sky clarity that I'd never found in a relationship, that I didn't love him enough for forever. I couldn't empathize with his pain like a psychosomatic twin, and wasn't that, ultimately, the meaning of love: finding someone who made you experience life twofold, who eased the isolation of having only one body?

Whit faced the ocean as I looked up toward land, staring at the cocktail tent floating above the water, a giant paper lantern. It was an illuminated beast, wedged into this slice of lawn by the force of money and Mimi and the wedding planner who insisted on sea bass over cod even though it was twice as expensive and I liked it half as much. This night was our first invention as a couple, the kickoff for a long list of expected creations: the miracle of life, the birth of home renovation, the development of traditions and shared language and nicknames, our private lexicon that would distinguish our family as happy and unique. This should have felt like sliding into place, a cozy ease that would let me grow while staying put. Instead, it felt like a sentence (death, prison) or the end of a sentence—a period that weighed me down, a mark that wouldn't let me continue a thought. *Let me have more clauses,* I wanted to say. *Let me run on and on, becoming more incorrect and messy and true.*

"Let's go back up," I said, removing my hand from his back.

"We're not going anywhere."

I paused; we looked at each other, his face wet and without glasses. It was the first true statement he'd said all night.

Back in the ballroom, I found Virginia at the dessert table, stacking mini cookies and lemon tarts into a tower that wouldn't take up residence on her body. When she saw me, she swallowed a pistachio macaron, seemingly whole, and set down the plate.

"What happened earlier? That was insane."

"I was drunk," I said, because it was an easy excuse.

"We're all drunk."

"You know what? I was pissed. Ollie was being smug and trying to mansplain the limits of, like, intellectual property theft, and I just couldn't. Fucking. Take it. I'm tired of not saying what I think around you people."

"You people?"

"The Murphys! My bill payers! The beautiful and the damned!"

Her eyes widened as she laughed awkwardly. "Tell me how you really feel."

"Oh, that might take a while."

"It was just an expression, but sure," she said. "Go for it."

"I feel like something's being kept from me. Something is going on and no one will be up-front about it."

"You're still not saying anything."

"I learned from the best! I ask about your love life, and you say nothing except make me feel like a total square for wanting to know if you prefer guys or girls."

"Because I know the answer won't satisfy you."

"Maybe I am no longer okay with half-truths."

"Is this about us or about you and Whit?"

"What does that mean?"

"I just . . . I saw your face at the altar, I've been watching your disinterest through this whole process. I can't believe I'm saying this on your wedding night: you don't have to get married."

"Too late."

"I mean, you don't have to stay married."

"I already blew it up anyways."

"Because you threw wine all over Ollie?"

"Something like that."

Across the room, Mimi was dancing with my uncle Jeb,

a handsome and recently divorced furniture designer ten years younger than her. He threw his non-balding head back at something she said, as her green silk dress fanned behind her like a wake.

"I need to go talk to your mom," I said, planning on tapping her shoulder before she made another hapless man fall in love with her.

"No, no, no." Virginia held my wrist. "You are not bringing up all that shit to her now."

"I only want her reassurance that there wasn't an affair. That's it! Just a simple yes or no."

"She's doing so well. I don't want her to spiral over something in your head."

"Why would she spiral if it's not true?"

Virginia paused just long enough that I knew she was unconvinced. "It will throw her off completely, being accused of a decades-old affair with the bride's dad. She needs peace right now, not drama."

It was that word, *drama,* that set me stalking toward Mimi. I was sick of Virginia inadvertently calling me too much—too sensitive to the perceived art theft, too obsessed with her cousin, too far-fetched in my affair theory. *Drama* was simply exposing my internal hurt, an emotional sort of surgery.

"Stop!" she shouted after me with uncharacteristically manic desperation.

Before I could follow her instructions like I always had, my hand was tapping Mimi's shoulder.

"BRIDE!" Mimi screamed. "Woman of the hour, woman of the night!"

The band was playing "Walk the Moon"—ironic timing, because I would not be shutting up or dancing.

"Can we talk?" I asked.

"Did Cynthia screw up the icing? I told her *no* confection-ary flowers."

"It's not about the wedding."

We moved to the edge of the tent, and before I could speak, she hugged me with force, more of a smother than an embrace. "Such a gorgeous night. I wish your dad could be here to see you."

I pulled away. "I read his book."

"Oh?"

"'Off-Season.'"

She paused, lacking words for once. Her recovery was quick. "It's fabulous, right? How did you find it?"

"That's the thing. You knew I was looking for it. Why didn't you tell me you had it?"

"I don't remember you looking for it."

"Better question—*why* did you have the book?"

"I have so much junk in these houses, I don't know what's where and what's what! That reminds me, I need to tell Norma to clean out that closet."

"So, you read it. What did you think?"

"I've always loved Wharton, and I thought your dad did a wonderful job in invoking that time period. Sterling was quite richly drawn. But it's been so long; I don't remember the specifics."

"Do feelings that strong ever really fade with time, though?"

"Yes," she said too quickly. "And no. Emotions and books move through me like powerful currents, but then they're washed away. I guess they leave a mark, like—oh! The water outline on the beach." She was delighted by her metaphor, but when met with my unamused stare, she deflected. "I've had too many signature cocktails. I'm at my Whit's End! Let's dance!" she shouted, and laughed at her joke, as Fleetwood Mac exploded from the stage. She floated back onto the floor, leaving me with more questions, but also more certainty, than I'd had before.

My mother was alone at a table near the bar. She'd been alone for far too long.

I sat with her and answered her questions about the Ocean House's wedding planner and the cost of winter versus summer. She squeezed my hand while stifling a yawn.

"You should go to bed," I said. "It's late."

"If the bride says so. Thank you—I've been sleepwalking for fifteen minutes."

The idea of her staying up for me, pushing herself beyond her physical limits to be present, touched me more than the gesture warranted.

"I love you, you know," I said. "And not as the mother of the bride. As my mom."

"That's sweet," she said hazily. "But what do you mean?"

I didn't have the energy to explain that I was referencing the early failure of my marriage. She was the mother of an *expired* bride, a distinction I had no problem breaking to her given her ambivalence about the relationship and marriage in general. But it could all wait until she'd slept, until I'd shared a bed with my husband for the first and last time.

belindapbergin CONGRATS!!! @calliememaybe @whitty_

elizasamuels woooo stunning 😍 😍 😍

katerightwood_ omg wow, so much love

32 Now

Notification: Low Battery

I put down the phone.

The empty pizza box is still at my feet, greasy shadows reminding me that I consumed a meal meant for a family and then spent hours on my phone gobbling my own history.

I wonder if I'll always imagine my life with Whit like an alternate reality running underneath my real life, whatever that may hold. I will be on a beach in Thailand, watching sails cut through the horizon, and see a flicker of the other me, making an omelet while the morning shows play and Whit wrangles a toddler into overalls. I will be on a first date, sipping a sugary drink and making tentative conversation about my family, and picture myself drinking good wine with Whit on a velvet couch we bought with his money. I will be alone in a shitty apartment with a wheezing radiator and picture myself with a baby, her little arms out against the backdrop of a backyard, throwing her up, up, up, the only kind of throw-up that can cleanse me.

But no—I can't picture married life like a positive process of elimination, whittling down life to its essential parts. Soiled diapers, I remind myself. Half orgasms from a man who'd rather be glued to a spreadsheet. Falling in love with someone else, having an affair, burying an explosive that will detonate years later.

I may never have tangible, unassailable proof, but I believe my dad and Mimi were in love. The emotion on the page is enough. In a twisted sense, I wish my dad could have lived longer—that Walter had greenlit that drug—for more time with me *and* Mimi.

The hot cheese churns in my stomach, but the impulse to redo the past and thrust my mess into a deep hole is gone. I can't change what's already happened; I can only move forward, acknowledging the memories in my body and on my feed, while refusing to be pulled back by their immovable weight.

A new text box pops up on my phone; it must be from a random relative with insomnia, congratulating me on a *beautiful night,* or Maxine, forgetting that this week is a no-email zone.

The second I realize it's another text from Virginia, my screen turns black.

At first I think the sudden death is from a mass power outage, ignoring Occam's razor—the blankness is my inability to remember that technology relies on external power sources and our phones aren't just extensions of our hands. I didn't feed the device, so it's dead. Ready to be turned into soil for trees or thrown deep into the ocean.

What did Virginia say, and where is my charger? In the black screen, my makeup is smudged, the bruised-looking shadows under my eyes from mascara or from staring at a three-by-six-inch hellhole for hours.

My charger is buried somewhere in my mini-moon bag, the trip to the Bahamas that we'll never take. Whit still wants to go, or he did when he fell asleep one hundred years ago. He thinks it might help us "strategize," like our failed marriage is a revenue target we missed in Q1. I take Whit's charger from his bedside and plug in my phone, waiting for the message from Virginia to load.

I walk toward the curtains, the gauzy columns that made me predictably think of ghosts when I first saw them. Now, nothing in the room looks like something else. It all looks like what it is: dark.

Outside, the waves are splintering. A streetlight on the edge of the sand illuminates the foamy tips on the water. I put on clothes, stuff my wedding dress into a tote bag embroidered with c & w, and grab my barely charged phone.

I go to the beach.

Digging my fingernails into the sand, I carve out a heavy palmful. I continue grasping, moving sand from below to above, until I have a sizable hole to bury my dress. When my dad was lowered into the ground, I'd covered my eyes to avoid seeing him as a husk that would rot underground. But I keep my eyes open with the Composure demonstrations, watching strangers fold back into the earth.

Once my dress is stuffed inside the hole, I read the text message from Virginia.

I believe you, it says. **Call me.**

She picks up on the first ring.

"Cal," she says, exhaling.

"I know I was being crazy. I'm sorry." I'd told myself I wouldn't apologize, but her voice on the phone makes me ache for her presence.

"I'm the one who should apologize. I wasn't there for you tonight."

"Have you ever thought—"

I almost ask her the questions I cannot answer—about

Gray's paternity, her sexuality, and the secrets we've kept from each other. But I want to stay in this pocket of innocence for a bit longer, revisit our childhood before we blow it away like the sand sculptures we used to make on this beach.

"I believe you," she says. "Whatever it is. We will figure it out."

"Well, I might be losing my mind. I just shoved my wedding dress into a hole I dug on the beach."

Virginia laughs and I start to explain, but she interrupts with a welcome request.

"Can we not talk for a little while?"

The silence is eerie. I breathe into the phone and she breathes back, until I can't tell the difference between her inhales and my exhales, until the input and output of our bodies are entwined.

This goes on for a minute or two, and then there's a cawing sound, a bird. At first I think it's coming from her, but then I realize I'm the one outside at the beach. It's my end.

I listen to our joint breathing like a goddamn yogi, push against my chest like I'm trying to dig for those pulpy fists underneath. No matter how hard I try to map what's inside me, there are so many parts—memories, excretions, switchbacks of the veins—that I will never see or understand.

The call clicks off to complete silence. She hung up on me. Seconds later, a hand on my shoulder:

"You crazy motherfucker." Virginia's wearing a pair of Paul Frank pajamas she's had since we were teenagers, cartoon monkeys open-mouthed in the moonlight. She lowers herself to me, staring at the dress in the hole. "I didn't like it anyways," she says.

I laugh, my usual offense at her bluntness washed away. "I didn't either, really. But I didn't hate it."

"Didn't love it, didn't hate it. Etch it onto our gravestones."

She puts her arm around me, and I rest my head on her shoulder. More words will come, we will always have words— the captions, comments, and messages, truths and fictions to shape our recollections. Right now, I just want to sit body to body, unmediated by screens or language.

I place my phone on the sand and go back to listening to her breath in my ear or mine in hers, looking at the waves replacing and replicating what came before them.

Acknowledgments

Writing a book is solitary; publishing a book is anything but. I'm incredibly grateful to the wonderful—or as Mimi would say, fabulous—team in my corner. Voilà, we did it!

Thank you to my agent, Allison Hunter, for taking a chance on me and always responding with an exclamation point or three. Your enthusiasm is contagious and your savvy is unparalleled. And Natalie Edwards, thank you for being a brilliant reader and welcoming me so warmly into the Trellis family.

I'm so grateful to my editor, Molly Gendell, for believing in *Social Engagement*, coming up with the perfect title in a day after months of my agonizing, and understanding exactly what the story needed from our first call. Your wisdom and sharp eye consistently impress me, and I'm the luckiest to work with you and Mariner. And thanks to everyone else on the Mariner team who brought this book to life: Kate Nintzel, Maureen Cole, Jes Lyons, Allison Carney, Eliza Rosenberry, Tavia Kowalchuk, Lisa Glover, Yeon Kim, and Renata DiBiase.

Liz Riggs: I wouldn't have finished this book without you.

Your texts crack me up, our retreats and trackers keep the momentum alive, and your first reads are spot on. I love your writing almost as much as I love our friendship. Heather Karpas: I wouldn't have started this book without you. Always decisive and always right, I rely on your gut checks and expertise to keep me sane. Cheers to more conversations that become books.

Carola Lovering, thank you for paving the way and turning from an acquaintance who was living my dream into a generous friend who helped me live it, too. Colleen McKeegan, thank you for your shrewd advice, heart-to-hearts at Athena, and getting the Unyoung band together.

My NYU MFA advisors—John Freeman, Katie Kitamura, Hari Kunzru, and Helen Schulman—were an invaluable part of this journey. Paris was a dream; packet deadlines brought me back down to earth. Thank you for making me a better writer. Thanks also to Deborah Landau and Lisa Gerard for running a program that exceeded my wildest expectations.

I'm very grateful to Emily Barasch and Alex Willkie for reading a full, early draft of this book and providing smart, discerning feedback while also convincing me I shouldn't throw the whole thing out.

Carly Zakin and Danielle Weisberg, thank you for your support and advice from the days when my novel writing ambitions were confined to the Notes app.

To the writers who've been there in workshop and beyond, both to commiserate and keep the hope alive: Sheila Yasmin Marikar, Lina Patton, Brittany Kerfoot, Erin Connal, Jenni Zellner, Ellen Wright, Hayley Phelan, Andrew Porter, CC Bernstein, and Kate Vos.

Thank you to my parents, Leigh and Ben Carpenter, to whom this book is dedicated. You gave me the mix of passion and grit (and a healthy dose of confident delusion) to become a writer. Anything I accomplish in this life started with you two. Kendall and Cameron—how lucky am I to have brilliant sisters who are also voracious readers? Whether we're workshopping titles or discussing structure, you're my go-tos for both hype and hard truths.

And finally, Al: spending the last decade with you gave me the determination to keep going. No one works harder or loves better. Thank you for taking care of our real life while I floated into a fictional life. To Campbell, who will be five months old when this is published: I wrote this book while dreaming of you and revised it while growing you. I can't wait to meet you and someday, inevitably, embarrass you with my bound stories.